MISKATONIC UNIVERSITY

Broken Eye Books is an independent press, here to bring you the odd, strange, and offbeat side of speculative fiction. Our stories tend to blend genres, highlighting the weird and blurring its boundaries with horror, sci-fi, and fantasy.

Support weird. Support indie.

brokeneyebooks.com

twitter.com/brokeneyebooks
facebook.com/brokeneyebooks

Welcome to Miskatonic University

WELCOME TO MISKATONIC UNIVERSITY:
FANTASTICALLY WEIRD TALES OF CAMPUS LIFE
Published by
Broken Eye Books
www.brokeneyebooks.com

Cover illustration by Michael Bukowski
Cover design by Jeremy Zerfoss
Interior illustration by Michael Bukowski,
Yves Tourigny, and Jeremy Zerfoss
Interior design by Scott Gable
Editing by Scott Gable and C. Dombrowski
Illustrated headshot likenesses modeled after
authors and patrons by permission.

Tremendous thanks to the support of our Kickstarter backers
for making this possible. You're all wonderful!

978-1-940372-23-5 (trade paperback)
978-1-940372-24-2 (hardcover)
978-1-940372-41-9 (ebook)

Welcome to Miskatonic University

Edited by Scott Gable and C. Dombrowski

Table of Contents

Introduction

Scott Gable

MISKATONIC UNIVERSITY.

These storied halls. And unending possibilities. This is a place of both proven tradition and wide-eyed speculation. This is a place where one's intention and perseverance blossom in the face of collaboration and control, where inspiration and discovery are honed by the deliberation of peers, where students devour knowledge and barter in experience, all to shape a new tomorrow. This hallowed institution stands as a bulwark against the darkness of ignorance and the tyranny of fear, individuals collected together with minds wide open to the unknown, safeguarding against that which would harm while accommodating that which enriches.

Nestled in the beautiful Arkham Valley (and scattered around the world in satellite campuses and isolated research stations), Miskatonic University presents truly unique learning opportunities. Every year, the university attracts students hailing from all over the globe, seeking to avail themselves of our cutting-edge research driven by professors and graduate students at the top of their fields.

Good old Miskatonic—ol' Misk, MU, "that place." Few institutions have adapted quite so well. But then, when you're a magnet for the weird, you won't last long if you can't adapt. In the face of its many and varied challenges, this place has grown into a strange brew of both deep-seated tradition and progressive attitudes.

These are tales of Miskatonic University today. What might Miskatonic look like if it existed right now? What might student life be like? These tales combine college life with the strange, mixing the thrill of the unknown with the titillation of the occult. Of course, there's beer, sex, and parties; study groups and all-night cramming; campus activism and impassioned discourse; vital research and faculty struggling for tenure. But also, you know, magic and monsters and psychedelic oddities.

What avenues of study might such a university sanction, either publicly or privately? Where are they getting so much funding? This university's been around the block—seen a thing or two!—and they're at the bleeding edge in certain realms of research. Occult studies have seeped, seemingly innocuously, into various branches of nearly all academic departments and inform everything from quantum physics to computer science, sociology to modern American literature. Its library studies program is simply hands down the best, most advanced in the world, likely one of the most well-funded of sectors at the institution with ever-evolving safeguards and best practices.

But there's bound to be lingering effects from all the occult activity. People disappear all the time; sometimes they even come back. Entire wings are off limits to humans indefinitely. As a whole, this anthology is about the angst and drama of college life, the promise of big occult ideas, and the dread (and the hopeful, headfirst exploration) of the unknown, of the forbidden. And some well-placed dark humor.

These are stories with modern sensibilities. We're presenting a living, breathing MU. Sure, people die, just as new faculty are hired and new students fill empty seats. Buildings crumble or disappear into wormholes, but there is always new construction. Monsters come and go, sometimes with fanfare and sometimes not; some even stick around as lab specimens, secret pets, or disguised as faculty.

But above all, the university persists.

Some Muses Are Not Gentle

Brandon O'Brien

When, long ago, the Goddesses carved Earth,
In complex forms, they shaped out Man at birth,
And beings of ev'ry part were then designed;
Yet lower down, a space left undefined,
A gap still hollow, underneath the plan
that our fair Mothers filled—with lesser man!
They made a child, then turned Hatred's spigot
O'er its lips, and called its drinker "Bigot".

—Anonymous, graffiti on office door
in Miskatonic Literature Dept., 2011

Darryl straightened up, lifting his head off the floor of his apartment and holding his temples. Aside from the headache, he felt a pain in his thigh. He squinted in the dark to find the source and saw not much of anything. By his hands on the floor, he felt sheets of paper rustle and shift, dozens of them dragging against their own faces. The sound of his phone vibrating was what woke him. He felt the reverb of it against the ground beneath him. When he passed his hands over the floor, all he found were more sheets. More and more until his eyes finally grew accustomed, and he could see it trembling against the floor. He brought it to his ear with a yawn.

"Hello?"

"Darryl, where are you?"

He cleared his throat. "Noelle?"

"Yeah. Noelle. The same Noelle you promised to go on a double-date with this evening? What happened?"

He sighed. "Shit. I was . . . I still have this manuscript for Poetry, and I thought I'd crack out something that came to mind before I left, and the next thing I kn—"

"Goddammit, Darryl. You mean to say you couldn't stop being such a pained artist for one night?"

"But Noe, I swear, I just needed to—"

"Wait." In the beat before Noelle continued, Darryl could sense their frustration. "I asked you to stop calling me that."

"Sorry . . . I—" Darryl shifted, and only then did he notice the searing pain in his thigh. He placed his palm against his leg, and the pain grew as his fingertips found it. A whole wooden pencil. Piercing his skin all the way through. He didn't even know that he had a pencil this long—maybe nine inches, in one portion of muscle and out the other end, just under the bone. Hell, he didn't even write with these. His preferred weapon was still on his bed: a point-three-millimeter drafting pencil with its clip glinting in the faint lights outside the window. He pulled the wooden one out of him, wincing into the phone.

"Darryl? Are you okay?"

After another few seconds of pain, he glanced at it, red glistening against the yellow and light brown. "Yeah, I'm good." He took a breath. This was new. The blackouts he could deal with since the dream—he figured it was overwork, a kind of thing he'd eventually recover from. But . . . the more he thought about it . . . the nearest wooden pencil was unsharpened in a box on the other end of the room.

"You sure? Because if you're okay, I'm fucking mad at you." Noelle chuckled.

"I meant to come, Noelle. I'll make it up to you and Colleen and Will soon. I promise. How are they though?"

"They're good. Colleen says she misses you during their D&D sessions. Also I brought back some pineapple chicken, okay?"

"You ain't—" He caught the creole before the sentence finished. "You don't have to do all that."

"I figured, since you insist on working so hard and never eating if I don't make you anyway, I might as well."

"Thank you."

"I'll talk to you later, okay? Love you."

"I love you too, Noelle."

The phone let out the faintest of beeps to signal the end of the call, and he tossed it behind him onto his bed. He put the pencil down against the small puddle of papers, and his eyes caught the first words of a sheet beneath his hand. He snatched it up by the corner and brought it to his face to get a better look.

everything is marble
inside here,
each mold glares at me
like they expect me to rob them,
lift them at the waist,
leave with them over my shoulders.
they think I came for them,
to study their every joint
and mock their masters.
but they're barely infants.
they don't know what these hands
have made.
they still can't find their own
throats, they just linger,
scarecrows for imagination,
trying to cast off pests
like me.
they can't catch me.
didn't their fathers think
I'd notice? how I
grew up in a garden that moves, dances with the breeze,
talks for itself?
my obsidian brings music with it
and will dance ahead of
any legacy behind it, will
duck blades, will step handsome,
will not let you lock its feet.

He read it once and again, making sure of each line, studying it as if it were a reading from class. And was it? It was in his hand, written in pencil rough and panicked like so many others. But . . .

"When did I write this?" he muttered.

He reached back for the bloody pencil and squinted at the poem again for a few more moments before making a scribble in the bottom of the page: *following the theme of decentering Masters-Witt's style and tone from her racist and homophobic undertones, this piece exists as almost a public challenge to the poet, a callout after works such as "Columbia Lost" and "Noble Men Drowning in the Street"* . . .

He took a handful of photos of it, and two others, and sent them to Elaine from his Creative Writing class with the caption *tell me what u think about these?* He got a reply almost instantly: *sure thing, man. you've been going crazy with the words lately.* He put the paper and the pencil down and sighed at the sight of the rest of the sheets.

"In the morning," he muttered, crawling up into bed with a painful grimace.

In the morning, there was no more wound in his left leg. He almost didn't notice until he went to take a shower. He wasn't sure if it was one of those dreams again, under the glooming shape of Heaven, staring up at the approving gods as they spared a muse for him.

Eleanora Lily Masters-Witt. Of course. The white woman with the darkest heart that the early 1900s had ever known. What other poet to supervise the work of an Afro-Trini college student in the States?

He placed his hand on the space where the wound would have been, sliding his fingertips over the skin of it. Nothing. No lingering sensation of pain, not even a tenderness.

He still stared at it when Noelle entered the room. They were still putting away papers strewn across the bedroom. "Hey, babe," they whispered, "how you feeling?"

Darryl frowned. Drowsiness opened the door for some of his island voice to slip through for one moment. "Okay? I ain't know I shoulda be feeling some other type o' way."

Noelle shrugged in reply. "I swear, you sounded like you were in pain last night. But anyway." They fell onto the bed with a pleasant sigh, grinning at him. "You wanna go out today?"

"Hmm?"

"Neither of us have class right away. And I haven't seen you in how many days? I wanted to go out and spend some time with you. Please?"

"Yeah. I can do that. Where do you wanna go? There was this really nice bistro you mentioned before . . . Baroque, you said the name was?"

Noelle nodded. "Yep. I promise you'll love it."

"It's easy for me to love someplace—they just need to have good cake."

Noelle drove, grinning the whole way. They had been talking about the place since forever and talking about going out more often since the days before Darryl's project consumed his attention. They'd go on about the flakiness of the pastries and the sweet softness of the cakes. Darryl replied with a chuckle. "You don't have to sell me on it, hon. I'm looking forward to it already."

Noelle made all the orders: cheesecake and grilled sandwiches and chocolate raspberry–flavored coffee, still raving about each plate and cup. They smirked, watching Darryl enjoy each single morsel in silence, and then they thought to ask a question: "You mind if I hear one of the pieces you're working on?"

" . . . hear?"

"Yeah? I mean, I know published poetry is a completely different atmosphere from spoken word, but I figured it'd still be better to hear it the way you want it read, y'know?"

"Um . . ." Darryl fidgeted. "Well, I didn't bring any of it with me, so—"

They reached into their purse for several stacks of folded binder sheets, each one scribbled almost all over. "I'm sorry, I just figured—"

"No!"

They rolled their eyes. "I asked you not to call me that."

"I mean *no*, the negative particle. Why did you—" He reached forward to grab them, but Noelle leaned back, frowning as they pulled their arms away. "Why did you bring those with you? And without my permission?"

"I'm sorry! I just . . . your writing is always . . . even when it goes over my head, it always sounds so grand and compelling and lovely. So I wanted to see what you were working on, but you've been so secretive about these . . ."

"Because . . . they're not done yet. They're all rough drafts."

"*Dozens* of rough drafts? I must've picked up eighty pages off the floor!" They took a slow breath before handing the sheets over to him. "Okay. I really shouldn't have. I'm sorry."

He took them back with a slow sigh, folding them away in the pocket of his jeans. "I don't feel good about sharing work until I know it's absolutely ready, and none of this is. I . . . don't feel like I got its intention right. For any of them."

"And what's the intention?"

He pursed his lips. "So I had, like, this idea? To try to channel the voice of Masters-Witt's work while also writing poetry that deliberately challenges . . . everything else about her. She's . . . quite a shit person, in her work and outside it. An N-word every other poem, no lie. So it's about rejecting those parts of her politics while still being obviously after her."

"Ohhhh. So like, *after* as in following and then *after* as in—"

"—yep. Work that comes for her. Corrects her. Takes her to task."

"Oh, okay. And I take it you don't think you've gotten there?"

Darryl shook his head, looking down. "I will. I'm close."

Noelle smiled. "And I look forward to seeing you get there."

Darryl beamed, lifting his head from the slice of cake before him—

Ahead of him, on the other side of the table, was no longer his lover but was replaced with the visage of a woman he had seen dozens of times on the dust jackets of the best lyrics with the worst themes. The woman glowered at him with a special cruelty, squinting at him and scowling like he were a stain.

When the woman opened her lips, no words came out, just a kind of unearthly screeching like in the other world where he dreamed her up. He could read her lips in the moments before it all became black: *you damned monkey, you think you can wield a pencil and stab me with it, but you can barely scratch a whole sente—*

On a white sandy beach, Darryl woke and found the heads of the great and terrible things of his dreams above him, gazing off into the dark of eternity. He felt the touch of fine dust beneath his fingers. It was dark, but it didn't feel like the dark of the earth. It felt bright, amaranthine and august and lacking any delicacy. The gods were like moons; they drew his body up to them, torn between the three and four and five of them as they continued with their own cosmic business.

And then Darryl noticed the shadow approaching him from the other end of the beach. It stepped toward where he lay, drifting to its right and stumbling awkwardly into the edge of the still sea. The night was somehow bright enough for him to make out the details of anything else around him, if there were much of anything. And yet, he couldn't tell anything of its body or its face or its clothes.

The shadow was feet away from his body, still straightening up against the sand. It seemed to want to say something, and he desperately wanted to hear what. Was this where he would get something new? Would it wash ashore for him, a brand new work from the gods themselves?

Or would it draw something long and dark and blurry from behind its back, continuing to make a drunken lurch toward him?

Darryl awoke with a start, gasping for breath. He thought he was holding his hands over his head, but really, he was pushing himself out of his bed with such force and swiftness that he almost propelled all the way backward, flipping a little out of the bedsheets, landing headfirst against the floor, his legs still dangling over the mattress. Noelle shrieked, running into the room, a slick kitchen knife in their right hand. "Oh my God, are you okay?"

"Yeah, it was just a . . ." He paused, trying to put together the events of the day. "What time is it?"

"It's, like, past two."

"Past two?" Darryl tried to straighten up but mostly ended up crawling away from the bed. "What happened to breakfast?"

Noelle's eyes widened. "What, you don't remember?"

"I remember going out. But I don't remember eating anything."

"That's because you didn't!" They put the knife down on a dresser far from the bed, staring at him with an intense worry. "I was gonna take you to the hospital, and then you started . . . talking."

"Talking?"

They nodded. "Yeah. In a language I don't know—as in, one I've never even heard before. After you had a nosebleed and blacked out. I mean, I checked your pulse even—you didn't have one. But you were talking. Like, *to someone.* Asking questions, giving answers . . . getting upset . . . getting scared . . . and then you stopped."

Darryl leaned up against the nearby wall, scratching his head. "So you saw I had no pulse and decided to take me home? It sounds like you're describing a seizure—"

"But it wasn't! And I didn't know what to do. How do you explain that to an EMT? So I took you home. I know it wasn't the best idea, but I didn't have any ideas. I was freaking out, Dee. And then . . ."

" . . . then what?"

Noelle sighed before opening a drawer at Darryl's usual writing desk to reveal a fresh stack of paper. Not all binder sheets—some were printer pages, torn strips of napkin or fabric—but they all bore scribbles in his handwriting in blue and black from pens he could see in the tin waste bin on the other corner of the room, spent completely of their ink.

"Wait . . . those are new?"

"What the hell is happening, Darryl? Is this some kind of . . . guerrilla performance art piece about inspiration or some shit because, if it is, it isn't funny."

"No, Noe, it isn't—"

"Oh my God—"

"*Fuck*—Noelle, I ain't—I don't—" Darryl sighed. "I don't know what happened. I legit don't. Are you sure you checked my pulse properly? I mean, I'm here, and I'm fine, save for . . . that." He squinted at the sheets. More work. More to parse, to take apart, to polish until the collection came together. The gods smiled after all. But he tried to hide his delight under a thick mask of confusion and worry.

"Dee . . ." They took a ragged breath. "I am not exactly a person of faith. But this is fucking possession-type shit, and it isn't funny. I . . . don't get it. I've never seen anything like this from you. And I really don't think this is what being inspired is like. So you have to let me know. Is this a joke?"

"What? Why would I joke about something li—"

"Because if this isn't a joke, I'm worried about you."

Before Darryl could protest, Noelle was out the door. He brought his hands over his head and groaned, trying to piece together the description he had. Just like the other nights. But . . . the dream . . . the talking to himself . . . the dying? Those things were new.

He rushed to the desk and glanced at one of the poems. It was all still neat, still perfect—perhaps even more so than his writing would be when he was awake. He wrote fine against the lines of the page, so much so that Darryl had to squint at the words.

haunted by white stone,
patient hunters at the edge
of my history.
in my eye-whites
they write all the reasons
why I'll fade like crumbs of earth:
Your body pales to my body of work;
You are made of mud to my silver;
I've undone more than you can do,
Your mahogany is rotten, it
Creaks under brilliance—
it waits to press its alabaster ankles
against my neck in sleep.
a waxen shadow lurking in
the lines between justice and jealousy,
hands cold as piles of slush,
rushes at me, spits at my ink,
puts its fountain pen down my throat
to reach for youth.
it would tear me morpheme by morpheme
if it could. it tries anyway.
no matter how many majesties are
made from these fingers,
the snow will chase me to bite them off
and grin, polish its porcelain skin
with the remainders.

And in the margin, even finer, were words he actually didn't write at all. *I hope you're prepared to run forever then.*

He overheard it in class two days later. Elaine was in the hospital. Most people didn't seem to know what happened, but Darryl couldn't dare believe the story of the few people who claimed to. "Tried to kill herself," one classmate said. "Her boyfriend said she was talking to herself one night, saying something about how 'writing wasn't worth seeing this every day' and leapt from the roof of LaValle Hall. Call it luck, call it the devil, call it a cruel sense o' humor—she fell in the dumpster, which took most of the fall. Another inch off and it would've sheared her head clean off, but . . . at least she's still here, y'know?"

In his ear, Eleanora still whispered. *The dumpster! Where the dirty little chinky-chonky deserves to be. Would you like to make it easier and meet her there?* He wanted to turn and curse the sound, but he could already sense the eyes of his class on him. "I hear y'all were close," another classmate goes. "That you guys'd trade critiques and stuff. Did she ever . . . seem troubled to you?"

That afternoon, he returned home and took a long, warm shower, trying to wash off the sensation of his newfound muse. Did she do something to Elaine? Reach across the star-space just to find those poems he had written and tear her mind apart for being so unfortunately born a woman of color? Is that what this was? Not a musing but a haunting?

Eleanora Lily Masters-Witt would come to him again in the edges of the bathroom mirror as he stepped out of the shower. Sharp teeth muttering spites that he couldn't even clearly hear, a loud snow crash ringing throughout his skull. He tried to remain awake throughout it, watch her in defiance as she cursed him, cursed the island he was born on, cursed his voice, cursed his shade. But the sound grated, tore at his awareness. It wasn't long again until he crashed, watching drowsily as his head fell toward the kitchen sink—

He saw the home of the gods again, still careless and grand, hovering over the gold and purple heavens. He saw the shadow, but it was less than a shadow now—it was Eleanora, pale and cruel, a scepter of verdigris in her left hand, its head in the shape of a blazing sun with eight spikes jutting out of its edge. Her hands were covered in blood. And she would not stop staring at him.

They lingered in that stare forever. After a while, Darryl started asking himself about her, trying to recall some deep biography of her. How did she become so cruel in the first place? What had happened in her life to be so full of joy for nature, so plump with passion for romance and family, and yet, in the same breath, find it easy to write poetry about men like him being viciously destroyed by the same heavens he was in awe of now? Even as a specter hovering above his writing hand, could he even change her mind?

And then he blinked and was back in the bathroom, face down against the floor. When he gained focus, he noticed the blood. On his nose and lip and chin, streaks running along the tile. He straightened up in a panic, and it gained a wider context—he put them there. Each red line purposely built into letter-clays of word-bricks of stanza-walls as fine as a finger could afford; a simple sonnet curving from beneath the sink to the edge of the toilet.

I've laid foundations of ruddier
stories than your own.
In the sweet of their flesh I
found my reason, and I carried
on with their carrion, stored
warm on my tongue.
I painted murals of the forbidden
future with the lives of handsomer
mongrels than you; the lock
on Wisdom's gate was picked
with their dirty bones, and you
dared stalk me in,
facing the stars like you deserve them.
Play with the sandcastles you're left
with, hope to find a piece of glass
in the loam for now—or else, hide, rest
the darkness back upon your werewolf-bones;
I am not as gracious as the gods,
not as patient with desecrations
so deep as your dung-skin.
Put the symbols you have raided
back on their stools, show some scrap of sense
and dismember yourself on your own.
Know the things that owe you knowledge:
of stones, of monstrous mumbles,
anything below the sight-line of grace.
Don't lie at the altar of grandeur,
don't claim dogs can earn silver honors.

Give me back my rejoinders
and wait for my teeth.

His breath caught. He tried to calm himself, but his body wouldn't comply. It wasn't his voice. It was the other one's. Written to him, a threat from between two planes.

At this point, there was no doubt. Something more than just subtle inspiration was at work. Maybe those dream-gods, those visions he had of the world of creation, were real? *But that ain't makin' no sense,* he thought. *How I go get haunted so? Because of a poem?*

And besides, there was no time, right? He still had a critique session to prepare for. He'd have to sift through them all. Which was more important? Which would haunt him more terribly?

He straightened up and strutted to the bedroom, reaching for a pen and a steno pad from the bedside table, scribbling a note about *a poem that invades one's space and imposes upon the black reader.* He glared at the poem, slowly transcribing each letter of it, silently thanking the gods of the space beyond space that the thing stalking the corners of his mind still, in its own way, wanted him to at least pass his course.

"Noelle!"

Professor Price came huffing across the quad to meet them. A foot before them as they glanced at him in confusion, he doubled over to catch his breath. "Noelle? Where's . . . where's your boyfriend?"

Noelle's eyes widened. "He didn't come to class? I saw him on campus some hours ago, but I figured he was on his way—"

Professor Price slapped his thigh in frustration. "Talk to him, yeah? I get the whole, um, losing-a-classmate thing—I get that you gotta grieve—but grades aren't gonna put themselves on hold for that. We need to talk about his work."

Noelle frowned. "Is . . . something wrong with it?"

The professor straightened up and shook both of his hands in front of him. "What? No! They're brilliant even. Revolutionary. Viewing the legacy of one of our most beloved local poets through the lens of his own body, taking on this blood-curdling sense of language to embody the fear of being . . . you know, enveloped by a history that isn't yours. He could get published if he was patient enough to actually edit. That's what we need to talk about. To actually shop his work in class. This is supposed to be a building space, goddammit. I don't have time for students who want to play diva. Tell him I need to see him whenever he's ready. Okay?"

Noelle nodded meekly as the professor shuffled away, still mildly wheezing for a stray wind to fill his lungs. Noelle reached for their phone and immediately dialed Darryl's number. It rang out to voicemail. "Dee? Dee, what the hell is wrong with you this week? I've been trying to get your attention all day, and now you're ducking classes too? This stopped being funny a while ago . . ."

In the back of their mind—or the center of their heart—they imagined that Darryl wouldn't have gone a whole day ignoring their thirteenth, fourteenth, fifteenth call. They had no idea what to do next. Who to call, what to say. *I think my boyfriend is being too inspired for his own good . . .*

They sighed and put their phone away. Maybe they'd be lucky enough to find him in his apartment, working, being responsible, only so distracted by the reams of poems floating around in his mind . . .

Darryl hatched from the sky, red like clay. He felt himself careen downward, downward, to the beach of his dimmest dreams and most honeyed nightmares. He looked up as he fell, up at the heaven of the terrible angels of every other dream, ignoring him, not even noticing his descent.

It is still sand against his back, but he struck the ground like falling onto a mattress. He straightened up almost immediately, the sand gentle and warm between his fingers. He gazed out to the water, dark and unreflective and forever into the horizon.

Darryl made to scream. The wind would not let him; the sound rang dull in his ears, as if he pressed his hands tightly against them and merely whispered the scream to himself.

He could hear another voice though. Clearly, even harshly, like a sharp scratch against the walls of thought. "You don't even know how to speak English. But you want to write. Your mother should have spared you the embarrassment of life—but then again, she's probably as feeble-minded as you."

He turned and saw her. A gown glowing as if stitched with light, feeling warm against his cheeks even though she stood too far away to touch. Despite the acrimony in her voice, she came to Darryl like a saint, even like a mother, smiling warmly at him, her movements gentle. This scared him even more, raised the panic through his bones in a strong current. And yet, he couldn't find the will to move. He found himself deferring, in fact. Eleanora beckoned him, and even in his horror, he rose and approached. He closed his lips, swallowed, reverently nodded. Eleanora nodded in reply, wrapping her fingers softly around his throat.

"Who told you that you deserved this?" she whispered.

When she drowned him, she did it with his eyes to the dark and daunting heavens, watching the gnarled god-planets in apathetic orbit. One of them, it seemed, met his gaze, watched him panic and gargle. Even it wouldn't remain long enough to notice the life escape him.

And then Darryl hatched from the sky once again, descending in the same fear as before.

In it, he found dozens of poems. They hurried past him whole, like bricks of verse glancing him in the water. A fictional man died in each one, and each one resembled Darryl. They sounded handsome to Darryl, like something a publisher would print as a twelve-dollar chapbook. One of the men turned, facing Darryl's racing thoughts, as clear as if they drowned together. He asked, "Who the hell told you to put my whole business out here for the whole world to see? Huh?" Darryl couldn't hear his own answer, but it didn't matter. The man is an absent full stop in the last stanza of his own life before Darryl's first hollow word sounded.

And then Darryl hatched once more.

He ran, but Eleanora was always there. Never catching up with him so much as not letting him out of her sight. Her demeanor sank into clearer rage with each descent. "Why won't you fade away already, you broken little spade? Why do you keep staining this place?" she groaned near the ninth or the tenth or the eleventh time, grimacing to the night sky.

On his bed, still and dreaming it all, the two fresh puncture wounds in Darryl's arm made by his fountain pens bled onto the sheets. Adhering to the corners of torn pages scattered to his side, their words steeping in it.

The bedroom door shook with a violent knock. "Dee? Are you there?"

In the shimmering winds of his dreamworld, Darryl heard his lover perfectly, screaming to reach them. Still there was no sound.

"How many more poems do I have to write for you?!" Eleanora shrieked against the cold air, moments before the thirteenth or fourteenth time that Darryl died. And the next time he fell, he had an answer, however nervously he delivered it—this time in his own accent:

"You ain't write one scratch of my poems. I write each one o' them. They're just about you."

After the next death, a little braver, he adds: "And if I have t' dead here a t'ousan' times for each o' yuh nasty, faux-deep emo shit, then you better drown me facin' up—"

Despite herself, Eleanora never noticed in her rage that she obliged. She grimaced, disgusted by this black man's gall to give her an order. And yet, three more times Darryl struggled under the gods' feet and his lover's fading, distant voice.

"You think you're clever, boy?" Eleanora screamed. "Perhaps your fearlessness will end when you realize that you're here forever!"

His eyes widened in the water, and he grinned, just before that night's last breath. And Darryl hatched yet again, whispering just before his head hit the water.

"Yeah, but I's not the one *trapped* here."

For but one slow moment, Eleanora paused. Once-flooding anger briefly stilled before rushing through her spirit again. Another drowning, another descent.

When another poem asks Darryl in the water—"Why?"—he points with a tremble upward, past the dim water, past Eleanora's screaming face, past even the gods, to a world where even the poem knows how hard it is for men like them to live forever.

§

Brandon O'Brien is a performance poet and writer from Trinidad. His work has been shortlisted for the 2014 Alice Yard Prize for Art Writing and the 2014 and 2015 Small Axe Literary Competitions and is published in *Uncanny Magazine, Strange Horizons, Reckoning*, and *New Worlds, Old Ways: Speculative Tales from the Caribbean*, among others. He is also the poetry editor of *FIYAH Literary Magazine*. He is also creating content at www.patreon.com/therisingtithes.

Glory Night

Bennett North

When the scream shattered the mid-morning quiet, Beckah was in the middle of guiltily deleting six of her mother's emails from her work account, unread. It took her a moment to process. There was only one thing that kind of a scream could herald, and it was pretty late in the semester for it.

Beckah opened her office door at the same time as Professor Peters down the hall. A few architectural design students who had crammed themselves into a hallway niche were looking up from their drawing boards in mild interest.

"New guy?" said Professor Peters with a smirk. Beckah shrugged and strode to the interior balcony railing, looking down.

In the classroom below, Drawing 101 was doing a final critique. Thirty students sat in a half-circle, staring at a handful of charcoal drawings pinned to the particleboard wall. One was still settling on the floor.

The office door at the corner of the classroom slammed shut. The class burst out in nervous titters. Professor Peters leaned over the railing next to Beckah and *tsk*ed.

"Who did it?" Peters called down. Faces turned up to them, and Beckah picked out the culprit before the students even started to point. It was an older student with a particularly *local* look about him. The overhead lights glimmered off the faintly bulbous dome of his eyes and the iridescent skin under his jaw.

Professor Peters stalked to the stairs. She was in her element, playing the tough professor. Beckah followed the professor down the stairs and into the classroom.

"Show me," Professor Peters said. The student picked up the discarded drawing and pinned it back up on the wall. Beckah caught a glimpse of a writhing mass of unholy limbs, detailed in charcoal, before she skirted them both and headed for the closed door of the office.

No one answered her knock, but the door wasn't locked. Beckah pushed the door open as the critique resumed behind her. "Hello?"

A moan answered from behind the rolled steel desk. The office had a single window, covered in heavy mesh and a burgeoning curtain of ivy. It let in a yellow-green light, falling across the papers and laptop on the desk.

Beckah circled the desk. The professor, a thirty-ish man not long out of grad school, was sitting on the floor behind it, his knees wedged up against his chest, chewing on his thumbnail. His cheeks were bright pink and pinked up further when she came into view. He had dark circles under his eyes, badly hidden behind hipster glasses.

"Hey," Beckah said. "It's Robert, right? You okay?"

The professor made a vague hand gesture. Beckah leaned a hip on the desk.

"I'm Beckah," she said. "I work upstairs. I don't think we've met officially. This is your first semester here?"

Robert nodded slowly. "Yes," he rasped.

"What happened?" Beckah had a pretty good idea, but it helped to see if Robert knew.

"It was . . ." Robert said and knotted his knuckles together oddly. "It had . . . there were so many . . ."

"Mm-hm," Beckah said sympathetically. "I see. And that scared you?"

Robert straightened slightly, affronted, and looked at the door Beckah had closed. He shrank again.

"This is the first time you've seen that kind of thing this semester?" Beckah asked gently.

"I—" Robert said and pressed a hand against his mouth, swallowing whatever he'd been about to say.

"Don't feel bad. It happens," Beckah said. "Honestly, I'd take that as a compliment! You must have taught that student well if he was able to evoke that kind of eldritch majesty in his work. It usually happens to new arrivals at least once in their first semester." She decided to leave out the bit about the faculty betting pools.

"People try my apartment door handle at night," Robert whispered against his hand. "I'm afraid the lock won't hold them back."

"Well, it's May," Beckah said. "'Tis the season and all that."

"Sometimes I hear footsteps on the ceiling above me," he continued, his voice shaking. "*I live on the top floor.*"

Beckah kept her voice light. "Oh, are you renting an apartment in Phillips Corner? I used to rent there too before I had a falling out with the landlord. It's got great access to the downtown shops though. I miss that a little."

Robert closed his eyes and inhaled deeply through his nose. "It's not real," he whispered. "None of this is real."

"This part is," Beckah said, knocking on the desk with her knuckles. "I mean you did just run out of the classroom. That actually happened. But you're right, it was only a drawing. This is Miskatonic U. Creepy drawings are"—she stopped herself from saying *the least of your worries* and changed tack mid-sentence—"par for the course."

Robert opened his eyes again. His gaze wandered up to her. "Are they laughing at me?" he asked.

"Professor Peters won't let them," Beckah said. "She's taken over the crit. Honestly, don't worry about it. This sort of thing happens. It's . . . hard on people who weren't raised in the faith. We go through so many adjuncts."

"The faith?"

"MU is secular though. Don't get me wrong. There are a lot of employees here who don't celebrate at all, though it's so much a part of the culture that it's hard to avoid. I grew up in the Ebon Church of the Thousand Mouths, but I'm lapsed, so . . ." She laughed uneasily, thinking of her mother.

He was staring up at her, blinking slowly. She flushed a little.

"Would you like some tea? I have a kettle in my office," she offered.

"No, I'll have to—" Robert looked toward the door. "I'll have to walk past them all, won't I?"

"I can ask them to take the drawing down until you—"

"No, no, I can't just walk out of here." He shook out his shoulders and got to his feet, bracing himself heavily against the wall. He looked like he hadn't really eaten all semester. "My students deserve better than that."

"That's great," Beckah said approvingly. "Get right back in the saddle. The students will respect that."

Robert rubbed both his hands over his face and squared his shoulders. "Thanks for the talk, Beckah."

"You're welcome," Beckah said, her cheeks warming. She reached for the office door and saw him flinch, so she turned the move into an awkward stretch. "You, um, ready?"

"I can do this," he whispered, probably to himself. He nodded at her, and she opened the door for him. "This is going to be fine."

The bells of the interfaith campus church were chiming the hour as Beckah walked out to her car. After a rough winter, the spring air smelled so good, like sweet rot and growing things. The sun was still high enough in the sky to make her feel like she had a whole afternoon ahead of her, even though it was already five.

She rolled down the windows once she got in the car to let out the lingering afternoon heat. The parking attendant waved as she pulled out of the lot.

The road out of campus took her past the church, which was strung with bottle-green fishing floats and seaweed. Beckah caught a whiff of low tide and inhaled deeply. It tugged at something inside her, something that had enjoyed this time of year the most when she was a child, back before she'd ever thought critically about her family's beliefs.

Her upstairs neighbors were in the yard when Beckah pulled into the apartment building's driveway. Mr. Graham had hauled out the decorative lobster pots from the basement and was setting them up on the front stairs while Mrs. Graham meticulously arranged a well-worn fishing net over the bushes. Samantha was chasing her twin brother across the yard with a bucket, trying to splash him. Henry's back was already splattered red, proof that he wasn't running fast enough.

"Afternoon," Mr. Graham called to Beckah as she got out of her car and got her purse from the back seat. "We thought we'd get a head start on the decorating. Hope you don't mind!"

"No, no, that's fine." Beckah came around to the front steps. "Oh, those lobster pots look lovely."

Mrs. Graham stopped fiddling with the net and turned to Beckah. "I noticed you don't have any candles in your windows yet. I have a few spare if you need some. They flicker like real candles, but they're safe as houses."

Beckah ducked her head. "Thanks, but I'm not going to be around. I'm staying with some friends," she said, avoiding Mrs. Graham's gaze. It was silly to feel guilty about not wanting to celebrate, but she didn't want her neighbors to think less of her or, worse, pity her. "Don't worry about me."

"If you decide you need them, just let me know." Mrs. Graham grabbed the back of Samantha's shirt as she darted past. "Samantha Anne Graham, put that bucket down right now. You're going to be washing Henry's shirt tonight, and if there's even a hint of a blood stain, you're grounded, young lady."

Beckah took advantage of the distraction to slip inside the house and ascend to her apartment on the second floor. She had iced coffee waiting in the fridge and a box of Oreos with her name on it.

When she reached her apartment door though, it was propped open, and the sound of running water came from inside. Beckah stopped in the doorway.

Her mother was standing on a step stool and filling a bucket of sudsy water at the sink. The kitchen floor was already gleaming and smelled strongly of lemons.

Panic surging in her chest, Beckah backed slowly out of the doorway, stepping as lightly as she could. She reached the top of the stairs and eased down them.

"Beckah? Is that you?" her mother called.

Beckah's shoulders tightened. Footsteps crossed the kitchen, and she considered bolting, but instead she started back up the stairs.

"There you are." Her mother leaned out the doorway. "I thought I heard someone on the stairs."

"What are you doing here?" Beckah asked, reaching the top of the stairs again. "How did you get in?"

"I found your spare key." Her mother kissed her on the cheek and went back to the sink. "We've been having such trouble getting in touch recently that I thought I'd just come straight to the source." She hefted the bucket of soapy water up and started carrying it toward the hallway. "I'm glad I came. This place is a mess."

Beckah toed off her shoes in the doorway and tiptoed across the damp kitchen tiles. "Where's your car?"

"I parked around the block." Her mother hunched a little guiltily. "Now that I'm here, we can talk about your Glory Night plans." The bucket plonked down onto the bathroom floor, and her mother dunked her mop in it. "You'll be coming to ours, of course?"

"Mom—" Beckah sighed. She wanted to say, *I moved an hour away to avoid this kind of bullshit*, but that wasn't a thing she could say to her mother. "I have other plans. I'll be visiting a friend that day."

"Oh? Who?" Her mother straightened.

"You wouldn't know her. A work friend. She lives out on the cape."

"You'll be attending the service out there then?"

There was nothing Beckah wanted more than to say, "Of course," but she had never been able to lie to her mother. That was why she preferred tactical avoidance. "She's not, uh, of the faith. It's more of a cookout kind of thing."

Her mother leveled a stare at her. "Glory Night is a time for family and the gibbering god, not work friends and cookouts."

"I've spent the last thirty-two years celebrating Glory Night with my family!" Beckah exclaimed. "Can't I just take one off and do something else?" The argument over whether she actually ever intended to come back to the church could be saved for another day, preferably when her mother was an hour away from her.

Her mother looked down at the mop in her hands and leaned it against the wall. She turned fully to face Beckah. She was slightly shorter than Beckah, which somehow had always made her more intimidating. Beckah always felt like a gangly teenager.

"The fact that you're even asking makes me think you've forgotten the whole spirit of Glory Night," her mother said quietly. "Glory Night is about sacrifice and doing your duty to your god. It's not about indulging your own whims."

"Mom, I—" Beckah rubbed at her eyes, momentarily forgetting her eye makeup. "I know it's really important to you, but . . . I think I need some time to think about things."

"This is because of your job, isn't it," her mother said. "I told you that you should work for a religious college."

Beckah frowned at the eyeliner smeared on her fingers. "It's not my job. I've been having these feelings for a while. I just haven't been into it in the last few years. I think I should sit this time out."

"Do you think the Eyeless One ever takes a year off?" Her mother's gaze was intense. "Do you think the thousand crawling children would ever say 'that's fine, just worship us next year'? Do you know what happens to nonbelievers?"

"Haven't you ever questioned your faith?" Beckah asked desperately. "Even once?"

Her mother set her mouth into a line. "Once," she said. "There was one time before I met your father that I was seduced by a nonbeliever."

"Okay, wow, Mom, I didn't really need to—"

"I thank the drowned god every day that my parents kept me on the right path. If I had ever truly strayed . . ." Her mother's eyes unfocused for a second and sharpened again. "Well."

Beckah spread her hands, unable to come up with a rejoinder. She left the bathroom and flopped down on the couch, listening to her mother go back to mopping.

It wasn't that she was rebelling against her family or her upbringing. It physically hurt Beckah to lose this part of herself. Coming to the decision of leaving the faith had been like finally realizing a relationship had ended after a long period of drifting apart. Even though the split had been a long time coming, it was still a shock to find out how empty her life became after the official break. But at the same time, she couldn't force the spark back into the relationship.

How much did that matter though when it came to her family? She didn't want to celebrate Glory Night anymore, but insisting on that would hurt her mother more than it would hurt Beckah to go through the motions.

After a few minutes, her mother came into the room, drying her hands on a towel.

"There's a load of laundry in the washer, and I cleaned the inside of your fridge. Your father and I will both be here to pick you up the morning of Glory Night. If you don't come with us . . ." Her mother's wide face unexpectedly scrunched up into tears. She shook her head, sniffing, and said, "Please come with us, Beckah."

"I will," Beckah said, her chest suddenly tight. The sight of her mother in tears made her profoundly uncomfortable. "Don't worry, Mom. I'll be there."

Her mother nodded, dabbing at her eyes. Beckah got up and hugged her tight.

In the middle of finals week, Robert poked his head into Beckah's office and said, "Are you going to the president's party after work?"

Beckah looked up from her computer and blinked at him. "The president's party? Oh, his faculty holiday party. No, I'm staff. We used to have our own holiday party until the budget cuts."

Robert stepped further into her office. He looked a little better than when Beckah had last seen him but still underfed and a bit more hollow than he should be. He was smiling though, which was new. "If you're interested, I can smuggle you in. They're not going to kick you out. Plus, free booze."

Beckah laughed. "I've heard rumors of his chocolate fountains," she admitted.

"Come on. It'll be fun."

She glanced back at her computer and shrugged. She had nothing pressing. "Sure. Let's go."

The president's house was a grand manor house on the edge of campus, surrounded by willows. Green and gold balloons danced on strings tied to the iron fence out front. Glittering glass fishing weights were strung to the porch railings. The front door, propped open, had a wreath of bone-white coral.

The front room was full of professors taking a break from giving or grading finals. Waiters circled with platters of coconut shrimp and scallops wrapped in bacon. A string quartet sat by the empty fireplace, playing something cheery.

Robert beelined for the refreshment table where a waiter was pouring glasses of bubbly. Beckah followed and filled a paper plate with fruit. The center of the table held an ice sculpture of a man on his knees, his hands grasping his own hair, his face a twisted mask of madness.

Robert picked up two glasses but paused when he noticed the sculpture. Beckah gently took one of the glasses from him before his hand could go slack.

"The Awakened Nonbeliever," she said, gesturing with the glass toward the sculpture. "You'll see statues like that one all over town, along with the Devoted Follower and the Incomprehensible Divine. The house down the street from where I live has a big inflatable triptych on their lawn. It's so tacky."

"It's . . . lovely," Robert said, tearing his gaze away from the sculpture. "Anyway, here's to a nice empty campus." He tapped his glass against hers. "At least until summer session starts."

"To quiet days and a sharp decline in drunken vandalism," Beckah replied, taking a sip. "Are you teaching this summer?"

"Not here. I'm teaching two online courses, but I couldn't get one at MU. Hopefully they'll renew my contract for next semester, but they haven't told me yet, which is going to make this summer break nice and relaxing. Hashtag adjunct problems." He laughed in an embarrassed sort of way. "Do you get any time off?"

"Just for the holiday. I'm looking forward to a few days of sleeping in." She grinned at him.

He giggled a little hysterically. "I'm looking forward to being able to sleep through the night again. I've never had such vivid dreams before moving here."

"So you're not from around here originally then?" Beckah asked although the answer was fairly obvious.

Robert shook his head. "I'm originally from Texas, so all of this"—he waved a hand vaguely—"is a bit new. The snow, the trees actually changing color in the fall, the, uh, weird local obsession with tentacles . . . it's just different." He rubbed the back of his neck, and his gaze fixed over her shoulder. "Is that . . . blood?"

Beckah turned. At the front door, the president was laughing with the dean while he rolled up a sleeve. A servant was holding out a bowl of something red, and as she watched, the president dipped his hand in the bowl and raised it up again, his palm dripping. He pressed his hand against the front door to a polite smattering of applause. The handprint he left behind was a perfect imprint. The servant offered the bowl to the dean who did the same.

"Don't worry. That's as religious as this party is going to get," Beckah said, turning back. Robert's gaze shifted back to her, his face gone a bit tight, and she had an inkling of what this sort of ceremony looked like to an outsider. "It's probably not even real blood. That's unsanitary. Mostly they use paint now."

Robert swallowed hard and cleared his throat. As pale as he was, the circles under his eyes stood out.

"So, um." He blinked, and then looked down at his champagne class. "You're a believer in this . . . thing, right? This, uh, religion thing?"

"It's complicated," Beckah said, looking away as well.

"Could you maybe—" He cleared his throat again. "I just mean that since that class with the drawing, I can't stop thinking about . . . do you think you can direct me to a church? If it's not too much trouble? I'm just . . . curious."

Beckah opened her mouth to refuse and hesitated. She had purposely avoided getting involved with the local churches since she moved here and didn't have any to recommend, but since she was being forced to go to her mother's get together anyway . . .

"What are your plans for Glory Night?" she asked.

Beckah's parents lived out in the sticks, at the end of a cul-de-sac. It was the kind of tiny seaside village that was so threadbare it didn't even have summer tourists. Most of the houses on the street were decorated, from a few flickering candles in the windows up to the giant, well-rotted carcass of a swordfish hanging by its tail from a rope strung in a tree. Every single house had smeared rusty-brown handprints on their front doors, giving the impression that a murderer had run from door to door. In the lore, of course, it was the Awakened Nonbeliever who had done so, searching for other nonbelievers to save him from the seductive lure of the Incomprehensible Divine. The handprints signified that he hadn't found refuge there.

Her parents' house was at the tasteful end of the spectrum. The sun-seared lawn was trimmed, and the oyster-shell driveway was raked. The bladderwrack wreath on the front door was fresh and dripping. Her mother must have collected it this morning.

Robert pulled up in front of the house and stopped. Their cheerful conversation had slowly strangled as they neared their destination, and now they both stared at the house.

"So my mom is a little . . . enthusiastic," Beckah said, breaking the silence. "She'll probably assume you're my secret boyfriend, so be aware of that."

Robert choked out a laugh. "I'd expect nothing less," he said. He'd dressed in a gray suit and tie, which Beckah's mother would approve of. When she told them she was bringing a guest, Beckah's parents had given her a reprieve, and they'd let her travel with Robert in the early evening on Glory Night instead.

The front door burst open, and Beckah's mother came out, a grin splitting her face. For a moment, Beckah saw her as Robert must: short, squat, with a smile maybe too wide, and eyes maybe too big.

Beckah took a deep breath and opened the car door, sliding out. "Hey, mom," she said as her mother engulfed her in a hug.

"I'm so glad you came," her mother whispered, pressing a kiss to her cheek. She let go of Beckah and rounded the car. "You must be Robert! Beckah told us about you. It's so nice to meet you. You work at the school?"

To his credit, Robert answered politely and let her guide him into the house.

Beckah knew her mother could be a bit much—oh boy, did she know it—but Robert didn't seem to mind.

Dinner went as smoothly as could be expected as the sun set outside. The smells of dinner and the warm camaraderie were enough to make Beckah nostalgic for more innocent times, though the significant looks shared between her parents every time Robert spoke to Beckah soured that feeling. Once the plates were cleared, Beckah's mother lit candles and fixed everyone strong cups of sweet, black coffee. Across the table, Robert had become markedly more nervous, his gaze skittering over Beckah's family like he was afraid someone would catch it. Beckah sipped at her coffee and resigned herself to the evening.

By the time the sun was well down, there was movement in the street outside. They changed into their bathing suits—Beckah's father loaned Robert a pair of beach shoes—and lit an assortment of candles. When a heavy fist banged on the door, they were ready.

A path between two overgrown forsythia bushes led down the hill to the edge of the water. The sheltered harbor let in only the tiniest cat's tongue waves, licking the edge of the stone beach. There were others already down there, Beckah could tell from the candles. A fireworks barge was setting up out on the water.

"What are we doing down here?" Robert hissed to her. He was stumbling along next to her, a hand cupped over his candle flame to keep it from guttering.

"Bit of chanting and then a dark mass," Beckah said. "Then fireworks!"

"I can't swim."

"You don't have to go out far if you don't want. Just to your waist." They reached the beach and started picking through the rocks. Beckah heard her mother greet a neighbor.

Beckah stopped at the edge of the water, letting it lap over her toes. The sky was dark overhead but light around the edges from the neighboring towns. Out at sea, occasional lights glittered.

Robert stared out to sea, his jaw clenched. Beckah looked up at him. The candle painted the underside of his chin but left his eyes in shadow. Despite that, she thought she could see something desperate in them.

"You believe there's something out there?" he asked, his voice hoarse.

"I don't know what I believe anymore," Beckah admitted.

Robert fell silent, still staring out to sea. He was strained, almost gaunt with stress. Had he been this stressed all evening, or had the proximity of the ocean triggered it? Beckah studied the side of his face. Why had he wanted to accompany her really?

Behind them, back up the dark hill, voices started chanting. Beckah turned to see a string of lights coming down toward them. Two people in bathing suits guided a man with a dark hood tied over his head. His hands were tied in front of him, and he was wearing pajamas.

"Who's that?" Robert asked.

"That's this year's Awakened Nonbeliever," Beckah said with a shrug. "Not awakened yet, I don't think."

Robert made a small sound as if he didn't find that reassuring. The candle in his hand was shaking.

The neighbors around them picked up the chant, but Beckah felt weird about mouthing along to the words when she didn't even really feel it. The two people with their prisoner reached the beach. The prisoner was barefoot, and when they started across the rocks, he moved painfully slowly, picking his way among the flatter ones. One of his captors broke off chanting to apologize. They paused while someone else came over and gave the prisoner a pair of beach shoes and then started going again.

"What are they going to do to him?" Robert whispered. He took a step back, his foot splashing in the water.

"It's just a ceremony," Beckah said.

The threesome reached the water and started wading in; the chanting grew louder. Everyone around them took their cue and started in as well. Beckah stopped when she realized Robert was frozen.

"We're not going out far," she said. "You'll look weird standing out here on the beach when everyone's out there."

"Beckah," he said in an oddly strangled voice. "What is this?"

"It's a tradition," she said. "Don't worry about it. It'll take like five minutes."

"Are they going to sacrifice him?"

"Ceremonially, yeah. He'll be fine. They'll give him a shot of rum and a pat on the back afterward. Most of the nonbelievers in this town have been sacrificed at one point or another. If he's lucky, he won't even remember the shambolic truths of his awakening. It's hard to keep the unknowable in your head for long. Even the believers have trouble."

Robert's eyes were wide, his lips parted like he was going to speak but couldn't figure out what to say. A priest leaned in toward the prisoner, pulled off the hood, and whispered something in his ear. The prisoner's face twisted in horror, and he screamed. The two captors plunged him under the surface, his feet kicking. The chanting rose into a crescendo.

"Jesus," Robert swore and started splashing toward them.

Beckah grabbed his arm. "Don't make this weird," she pleaded.

"Beckah, they're drowning him," Robert said, wrenching his arm out of her grip. He tossed his candle into the water where it disappeared with a *plip*.

Beckah ran into the water after him, hissing at the icy shock of it. It was still so early in the season that the water was winter-cold.

Robert got out to his knees, struggling forward, and splashed down into the water, trying to doggy paddle. Beckah caught up to him easily.

At that moment, the chanting ended, and the captors lifted their prisoner out of the water again. The prisoner started coughing, and one of the captors patted him on the back. The prisoner looked dazed.

"See? He's fine," Beckah said. "Do you think anyone could sacrifice humans these days? The police would be on us in a second, even though they're all believers too. I mean, I'll admit that fake sacrifice isn't what our ancestors had in mind, but it's like near beer or vegetarian hot dogs. You take what you can get."

"The thing I saw," Robert whispered. "The thing my student drew . . . that's out there, isn't it?"

"If we knew for certain, there'd be no need for faith."

"I see it in my dreams," Robert said. "Every night, Beckah. Every night for three weeks. The sea and the salt and the blackness of the abyssal depths and the knowledge that it's down there, waiting, hungering—"

"Everyone experiences faith in their own way," Beckah said uneasily. Something in Robert's face was making her nervous.

"They slaughter the nonbelievers and feed them into the gaping maw of their eyeless god, and they chant its blasphemous name."

"They *used* to. Now it's more about spending time with family and eating too much food."

"It's calling me." He dropped to his knees, still in water so shallow that it only hit him mid-chest. "Make it stop. Oh god, it won't stop."

"Do you want me to get a priest?" Beckah asked, looking around at her neighbors splashing back to shore. "They probably could get you a shot of rum."

"Beckah." He lunged at her so suddenly that she shrieked, but all he did was grab her arms and stare up into her face, still on his knees. "*You don't understand what I've seen in my dreams.*"

Beckah looked down into his twisted, pale face. "I used to be that certain about it once," she said quietly.

A crack split the air, and the first five fireworks went shooting up from the barge, leaving white trails behind. On shore, people cheered. Beckah glanced over her shoulder. Her mother was spreading out a blanket, and her father was setting up chairs. They probably expected her to want some alone time with Robert.

"There's an apple crostata waiting," she said helplessly.

Robert let go of her. She turned back around to see him standing up, staring out to sea. The lights out there shimmered, and something far off splashed. The next set of rockets shot into the air.

"Is this what madness is like?" Robert said. He reached up to grasp at his hair. "There are truths in my head that are too big for my skull. Can you hear it? Can you hear the call?"

"The fireworks are pretty loud."

He looked over his shoulder at her, but his eyes were blind, unseeing. He turned away, and in one smooth, impossibly practiced move, dove under the water.

"Robert! You said you couldn't swim!" Beckah cried out, but he didn't surface. Beckah hesitated a moment and dove after him.

The cold was sudden, but it was better to go all at once than drag it out. The water was black until the fireworks exploded, and then it lit a watery red and white, enough for her to see the rocky bottom beneath her.

Beckah kicked, slicing forward through the water like a fish as the water went dark again. Every pull of her arms took her deeper, but it felt like she wasn't moving. She should have caught up, but he wasn't there. After a moment, she surfaced, taking in a deep breath and tasting salt.

"Robert!" she shouted.

A splash, further out than she'd expected. She turned, treading water, and saw his head part the surface. He gasped loudly for air and went under again.

She kicked under, heading for him. The harbor got deep quick out here, so the bigger freighter ships could make it through to the canal and the docks. When the next fireworks went off, the light wasn't enough to penetrate the water all the way to the bottom, but she saw Robert's kicking legs.

Beckah did ten laps in the university pool before work three times a week. She churned through the water, heading for him, but had to surface before he did. She went under again, waiting for a burst of fireworks, and this time she only saw a trail of white bubbles coming up from the shadows.

With three powerful kicks, she was down below where the light could go. Beyond this point, she couldn't see anymore. It was just blind faith that she would find him.

Overhead, the water lightened just marginally and then went black as pitch. Beckah cast her arms out wide, feeling for flesh. Her arm brushed something, but when she grabbed it, there was just a tangle of bladderwrack.

Her lungs hurt. She kicked up toward the surface again, breaking through the water with a powerful gasp.

"Robert!" she called. Nothing.

Under again. Down, down, down. She was panicking, and it was making her work through her air too quickly, but she kept pushing, even as the pressure started to hurt her ears.

A powerful firework, so loud that she could hear it through the water, went off, and for one fraction of a moment, she could see below herself.

Something in the back of her mind thought of that student's drawing, face down on the floor, and of Robert's tight, white lips whispering "*the gaping maw of their eyeless god.*"

Everything else in her mind lit up white with the need to get out of there *right now.*

Beckah didn't remember her panicked flight. All she knew was that she staggered ashore, shaking, while her mother rushed at her with a towel. The fireworks finale was already over, and people were packing up their beach chairs When her mother asked where Robert had gone, she found that all she could say, over and over again, was, "He woke up."

Her mother hugged her, and something far too understanding was in her eyes. "Sweetheart," she said. "Welcome back."

§

Bennett North lives near Providence, RI, and likes to take long walks near H.P. Lovecraft's grave. She currently works at a Miskatonic-esque university that inspired more than a little bit of her story. Everything she writes is true.

The Long Hour

Kristi DeMeester

SUBJECT: Formal 2005
FROM: Evangeline Murphy <evamurphy@mu.edu>
TO: zetaomicronzeta@yahoo.com
DATE: Sunday, April 10, 2005

Dearest Sisters,

Listen up, bitches. Last year's semi-formal with Omicron Chi sucked mega balls because you guys couldn't take three seconds to pull your shit together and wax your Neanderthal looking upper lips and do anything other than blather on and on about your classes or what professors you were thinking of taking next semester or what everyone thought about Dean Lockhart retiring. Seriously? Do you guys honestly think that's *compelling* conversation at a social event? Are you guys out of your bleached out minds? Zach emailed me last week to say they weren't planning any mixers with us for the rest of the year because you guys killed every boner in the room.

So this year, we're changing shit up. If you don't follow every. single. one. of these instructions, I'll put you on social probation faster than panties drop during Spring Break.

Don't ask questions, and if you think any of this is weird, shut the ever-loving fuck up.

1. You WILL read the packet I passed out at chapter. It took me three

hours in the library to photo copy it. Three. Hours. Read it front to back. Memorize it. You'll need to know every bit of info.

2. Your dress (and it must be a *dress*, no pants, we aren't a *progressive* sorority) should be white. No sequins. No beading. You aren't fucking Jon Benet Ramsey, and this isn't a beauty pageant. Keep it simple, and elegant, and make sure it actually *fits*. If it doesn't, stop shoving your fat face with subs.

3. No jewelry. Not even your pin. Don't question me on this.

4. Your hair should be clean and brushed but absolutely no hair spray or styling products or any kind of heat applied at all. No curling irons. No flat irons. No bobby pins. None of those dumb ass butterfly clips. None. Period.

5. No food, no drinks, no water starting at midnight the night before. That means no pre-gaming of any kind. I swear, if I find out you've had even a drop of alcohol, I'll rip your eyelashes out by the roots.

6. No makeup. Not even powder or lip balm.

7. At formal, you are permitted to discuss the following: the contents of the packet I provided. That's it. That's all. If it's not in the packet, don't open your mouth to say it. Our guests don't want to hear you blabber. They have bigger things to worry about than whether or not you might look weird with bangs (Caroline H.). Personally, I'd rather fellate a hot curling iron than hear you tell that story again.

I've spent a lot of time on this, ladies. Formal is in two weeks. Don't fuck this up.

Yours in Sisterhood,

Evangeline Murphy
President, Zeta Omicron Zeta
Beta Phi Chapter

SUBJECT: FW: Formal 2005
FROM: Lily Adams <liladams@mu.edu>
TO: Allison Pattson <allipattson@mu.edu>
DATE: Sunday, April 10, 2005

Have you gone through this packet thing yet? It's fucking . . . weird. Like, half of it, I can't even read. There's an entire section where it looks like a kindergartner scrawled all over the pages and drawings that just go off into nowhere. You think Evangeline's just shitting with us? Like this is some kind of test or something to make sure the younger sisters don't fuck up again?

And is this bitch serious with these instructions? On what planet can we not wear makeup to formal? Or have our hair done? I already have an appointment booked for an updo.

And I look terrible in white. Like a bloated maxi pad.

No way she's serious. No way.

~L

SUBJECT: Re: FW: Formal 2005
FROM: Allison Pattson <allipattson@mu.edu>
TO: Lily Adams <liladams@mu.edu>
DATE: Sunday, April 10, 2005

Where did she even find this packet? How does she expect us to know what's in it when half of it barely makes sense? And what in the world is "the darkening night"? It's mentioned on almost every page.

She's completely fucking with us.

And you do not look terrible in white.

Allison
Zeta Forever! <3

SUBJECT: Class Today
FROM: Lily Adams <liladams@mu.edu>
TO: Allison Pattson <allipattson@mu.edu>
DATE: Thursday, April 14, 2005

Didn't see you in class today. I went ahead and signed you in and out though. Dr. Young and his fucking attendance policy. You feeling okay?

I'm so fucking tired. Keep having weird dreams, and Evangeline keeps messaging me to see if I've read the packet yet.

I went back and looked at the packet again, and I swear to God, more of it made sense this time. Maybe I missed some of it before?

Anyway, my phone is all fucked up, and I can't see any of my texts, so email me or call me to let me know you're okay.

~L

SUBJECT: Re: Class Today
FROM: Allison Pattson <allipattson@mu.edu>
TO: Lily Adams <liladams@mu.edu>
DATE: Thursday, April 14, 2005

Sick. My head won't stop pounding, and my entire body hurts. My skin hurts. My bones hurt. Ugh. Maybe it's the flu or something?

I read the packet again, and you're right.

Something about it just feels . . . God. I don't know. It's hard to explain?

Like, I remember understanding more of it, but when I try and think about it, try to remember, my head feels like it's going to split in half. But I remember feeling *good* when I read it. Almost happier than I've ever felt before.

And something else, I think it made me cry. My face was wet. I don't know. Could just be the fever.

I'm going back to bed. I might not be at chapter this Sunday. I'll let Evangeline know, but she's going to be pissed. This is the second chapter I've missed this year.

Allison
Zeta Forever! <3

SUBJECT: Sunday's Chapter Meeting
FROM: Evangeline Murphy <evamurphy@mu.edu>
TO: zetaomicronzeta@yahoo.com
DATE: Friday, April 15, 2005

Dearest Sisters,

Bring your packet with you on Sunday. I expect you bitches to know most of it by now.

Wear white.

No makeup or jewelry. Nothing in your hair.

Our gathering together in true sisterhood will grow into loveliness. Together in the long hours of the darkening night.

Yours in Sisterhood,

Evangeline Murphy
President, Zeta Omicron Zeta
Beta Phi Chapter

SUBJECT: Chapter
FROM: Lily Adams <liladams@mu.edu>
TO: Allison Pattson <allipattson@mu.edu>
DATE: Monday, April 18, 2005

You were right. Evangeline was pissed, but it wasn't just at you. There were, like, six or seven girls who didn't come. Brittany, Mackenzie, Colleen, Tricia, and God . . . I can't remember who else. I hadn't really looked at the packet that much, so she was mostly just pissed at me. Honestly, I thought she was going to hit me at one point.

I need to talk to you. ASAP. I've tried calling a bunch of times, but my phone is still messed up so maybe the calls aren't going through?

We talked about the packet. Evangeline said she found it in the library. Part of some book? Said it would help us.

But then . . . Allison, I don't remember anything after that. Nothing.

Call me.

~L

SUBJECT: ANSWER YOUR PHONE
FROM: Lily Adams <liladams@mu.edu>
TO: Allison Pattson <allipattson@mu.edu>
DATE: Thursday, April 21, 2005

Allison?

~L

SUBJECT: Re: ANSWER YOUR PHONE
FROM: Allison Pattson <allipattson@mu.edu>
TO: Lily Adams <liladams@mu.edu>
DATE: Friday, April 22, 2005

Lily. Lovely Lily.

LIllilllilLLIIILLLLLLLL. Lilllyyyyyyyyyyyy.

Have you read it yet?

Have you read it?

The words inside.

LililllLLLillll. LIly. Illllong hours of the darkening night.

Lilliiill.

Allison
Zeta Forever! <3

SUBJECT: Re: Re: ANSWER YOUR PHONE
FROM: Lily Adams <liladams@mu.edu>
TO: Allison Pattson <allipattson@mu.edu>
DATE: Friday, April 22, 2005

You're freaking me the fuck out. This better be a joke.

~L

SUBJECT: Chapter/Formal
FROM: Evangeline Murphy <evamurphy@mu.edu>
TO: zetaomicronzeta@yahoo.com
DATE: Saturday, April 23, 2005

Dearest Sisters,

Formal is next Saturday night.

Follow your instructions.

Any sister who chooses not to listen will be removed. Try me. I've waited too long for this night. Too long. All of us have been waiting.

We will link hands and look into the long hours of the darkening night. Look down and down and down into what sleeps below.

How beautiful it will be.

Evangeline Murphy
President, Zeta Omicron Zeta
Beta Phi Chapter

SUBJECT: Re: Re: Re: ANSWER YOUR PHONE
FROM: Lily Adams <liladams@mu.edu>
TO: Allison Pattson <allipattson@mu.edu>
DATE: Monday, April 24, 2005

I went to the library to see if I could find the book. The one Evangeline photocopied.

I asked every person working in that place, but no one had ever heard of a book about the long hours of the darkening night. They looked at me like I was crazy.

Maybe I am crazy. I'm emailing you like you didn't send me weird shit. I'm dreaming about water. Dark green and cold, and it slips up over my mouth, my nose, and I can't breathe. I start to choke and then something wraps around my thighs and my waist, and it's like being swallowed, and I wake up and still can't breathe.

These emails from Evangeline . . . something's really, really wrong.

Still trying to call you. I went by your apartment and knocked and knocked, but no one answered.

Tell me where you are.

I'll take the packet with me to the library next time.

~L

SUBJECT: Re: Re: Re: Re: ANSWER YOUR PHONE
FROM: Allison Pattson <allipattson@mu.edu>
TO: Lily Adams <liladams@mu.edu>
DATE: Monday, April 24, 2005

Illllllll.

Lily.

You'll understand.

Have you read it yet? Have you read?

Illillylily.

We'll wake them up, and you'll be a flower.

It will devour us, and you'll be a flower.

What does it look like when the dead come back to life?

Is it like something holy?

Is it like something born among the stars?
Illilly.

Allison
Zeta Forever! <3

SUBJECT: Book
FROM: Lily Adams <liladams@mu.edu>
TO: Allison Pattson <allipattson@mu.edu>
DATE: Wednesday, April 26, 2005

I found the book yesterday.

I showed a woman at the library the packet, and she smiled, and her mouth had no teeth, and she brought me to a place I can't remember anymore. She said she knew Evangeline. That she'd found the book for her. That she'd helped her. Helped all of us. Before she left, she pressed her lips to my hair. I think she whispered something. I should know what she said, but I don't.

I dreamt about you last night. Dreamt you were at the bottom of the ocean, sleeping under the world, but it was so bright. Bright as the sun.

I read the book, but I don't remember.

Where are you? I thought I heard you this morning. Thought I heard Evangeline. So many voices. All together.

Has the long hour started?

I'm forgetting what I've typed. Did I just type that last question? Was that me?

I haven't been to class this week.

I'm coming to see you. I'm coming to your apartment.

~L

SUBJECT: Re: Book
FROM: Lily Adams <liladams@mu.edu>
TO: Allison Pattson <allipattson@mu.edu>
DATE: Wednesday, April 26, 2005

You weren't there.

Everywhere I look there's only water.

~L

SUBJECT: Re: Re: Book
FROM: Allison Pattson <allipattsom@mu.edu>
TO: Lily Adams <liladams@mu.edu>
DATE: Thursday, April 27, 2005

All in white, all in white, allinwhiteallinwhiteallinwhite.

Are you here yet?

We are waiting at the end of darkening night. At the end of the long hour.

So many are waiting.

Allison
Zeta Forever! <3

SUBJECT: Re: Re: Re: Book
FROM: Lily Adams <liladams@mu.edu>
TO: Allison Pattson <allipattson@mu.edu>
DATE: Saturday, April 29, 2005

I woke up with the taste of salt in my mouth.

How many days has it been?

I think I spoke to you. I think you were here.
Were you here, or did I go somewhere?

~L

SUBJECT: The Long Hour
FROM: Evangeline Murphy <evamurphy@mu.edu>
TO: zetaomicronzeta@yahoo.com
DATE: Saturday, April 29, 2005

Dearest Sisters,
Tomorrow.
Tomorrow, tomorrow, tomorrow.
We will meet inallwhiteinallwhiteinallwhite.
We will come to know.
We will be devoured. We will drown.
Oh!
Into the DarKEning Night!

Yours in Sisterhood,

Evangeline Murphy
President, Zeta Omicron Zeta
Beta Phi Chapter

SUBJECT: Today
FROM: Allison Pattson <allipattson@mu.edu>
TO: Lily Adams <liladams@mu.edu>
DATE: Sunday, April 30, 2005

There is blood on my sheets and in my hair, and there is a white dress.

I don't know where it came from.

But I know to put it on.

Death is something like counting hours. Isn't it? At the end of all of this leaning over and staring into the water and waiting for something to wake up, is that what I'll learn?

Down and down into darkness.

Alllinwhiteallllllinnwhiwhiteallinwhiite

Are they awake yet?

There is salt on my tongue and water and water and water.

Tell me it will be beautiful.

Tell me.

~L

Kristi DeMeester is the author of *Beneath*, a novel published by Word Horde Publications, and *Everything That's Underneath*, a short fiction collection from Apex Books. Her short fiction has appeared in approximately forty magazines and in Ellen Datlow's *The Year's Best Horror Volume 9*, Stephen Jones's *Best New Horror, Year's Best Weird Fiction Volumes 1, 3,* and *5*, and *Black Static, Pseudopod*, and several others. In her spare time, she alternates between telling people how to pronounce her last name and how to spell her first. Find her online at www.kristidemeester.com.

The Needle's Eye of Nothingness

Elliot Cooper

COLLEGE WAS SUPPOSED TO BE A TIME OF EXPLORATION, OF FINDING ONE'S unique core in a sea of expanding minds. It was meant to be about study, critical thinking, turning the inward eye while figuring out how the hell to navigate the outside world. It was high school on steroids and coffee.

It wasn't supposed to be about hoping to see Sam, the gorgeous TA from English lit, in the campus cafe, his eyes dark and as full of charisma as his flirtatious smile. But there he was, sitting alone and sipping from a steaming mug, lean and graceful in his smart shirt and suspenders. His brown pianist's fingers stroked the MU school crest on the ceramic while he pored over a notebook and open text.

"Are you gonna order anything?"

Aiden jerked at the voice from over his shoulder, his gaze met by an upperclassman in a purple Badgers hoodie and fuzzy pajama pants. His pale cheeks flushed hot, and he mumbled an apology as he looked back to the cashier, June. She sat next to him in Introduction to Dream Interpretation.

Pierced brow arched, June looked him over expectantly. "If you need a minute—"

"Just a coffee. Small. Black. To go. Please," he blurted out, retrieving his wallet from his pocket and nearly dropping it. He glanced at the booth again after he paid, thinking of what he'd say to Sam to finally break the ice outside the classroom.

Mind if I join you?

No, that was too forward. Too presumptive. Especially when it looked like Sam was studying or working. There was a protocol there about not inserting yourself where you didn't belong. It had to be something brief, something friendly said in passing.

I liked that doodle you left on my Sir Gawain essay. It looked like a cat made out of symbols. Very cool.

No, he couldn't overdo it. Every time he tried to act smooth, it blew up in his face. Like when he came out to his grandmother.

"So, Grandma, I'm actually a boy. And I know that's probably weird to you, but it's not a big deal, I promise. Just wanted you to know. And my name is Aiden now. And feel free to ask me any questions."

"So you're okay with going to hell, Aiden?"

He'd been expecting everything else—she wasn't the outwardly religious sort, for starters. But it had been stupid to assume he could think of all potential outcomes. He wouldn't repeat that mistake with Sam.

Aiden collected his drink when his order was called and let the heat soak into his fingers. He tried to walk casually, as if he were just scoping out a potential seat and just so happened to notice Sam.

Fancy meeting you here.

Come here often?

He mentally rolled his eyes at himself. This wasn't some cheesy meet cute in a contrived rom-com. It wasn't a noir film either. And he wasn't cool enough to pull off a line like that.

Just be yourself.

That's what he'd built his young adulthood around. It'd served him pretty well so far. He hadn't been struggling to make friends over the course of the fall semester, but he wasn't hoping to *just* make friends with Sam. Who was probably not single. And not queer. And not into trans guys with lingering body image issues. But he wouldn't know for sure unless he asked or was told. And asking and telling involved conversing. Words. Stuff an English major should be able to use with ease.

Sam smiled up at him, and Aiden realized with a wash of dread that he'd walked up to the guy's table without saying anything, like some sort of creeper.

"Oh, uh, hi, Sam." He sipped his coffee for something to do and winced as the liquid scalded the roof of his mouth.

"Aiden. Burning the midnight oil too?" Sam checked his watch and shrugged. "Or the ten-thirty oil."

He nodded, grateful Sam was better at small talk that didn't sound like a terrible pick-up line. "About to. Well, sort of. I'm supposed to be getting decent sleep for my dream journal assignment. But I don't have any morning classes tomorrow, so I can sleep in."

Sam tapped his pen against his notebook, looking weary. There were dark circles under his eyes Aiden hadn't noticed before. "Sleep is a luxury sometimes. That's college for you. This translation's been keeping me up for two weeks, but with the head of the Ancient Languages Department on a conference tour in Europe . . . I'm stuck with books and an irritable former classmate across the country for help with the tricky parts. It's like a puzzle."

"What language are you working with?"

"Sogothian." Sam gestured to the seat across from him and turned his book around. "It's an offshoot of Phoenician with a unique alphabet."

Aiden took the invitation to sit and pulled the book closer. The letters weren't exactly letters or hieroglyphs but some strange combination of both. They spiraled and curved across the thick, yellowed pages, lines growing larger and smaller as they tumbled around one another. One recurring symbol looked like a capital Q with extra flourishes, another like a jagged blade. Others resembled stars or Greek letters or cuneiform. But together, all of them drew his eye to the tight whorl on the left page where the words lost their spacing and dove down, shrinking into impossibly tiny curls like a nautilus shell. The letters began to shift, to move, to pull themselves into the pinpoint of blank space like water rushing down a drain. Dread crept over him, prickling the back of his neck with a sense of warning that he too would be pulled in, sucked through the needle's eye of nothingness amid so much twisting ink.

A hand pressed his, clacking his cup down onto the table's surface. He snapped his head up, blinking. Glancing back at the book, he saw the words were still, just ink on paper. Maybe he'd been pushing his sleep schedule too far after all, only getting three or four hours here and there, taking naps at random intervals.

"You almost spilled your coffee," Sam said, giving his fingers a little squeeze before pulling the book closer to himself again.

"Sorry." Aiden swallowed around an uncomfortable thickness in his throat, the sort of slimy feeling that usually followed too much crying or a lingering cold. He lifted his coffee to his lips and sipped, frowning at how much it had already cooled off. But it wasn't like Miskatonic University put loads of money into their cafe's supplies. He blinked at the book again but didn't let his eyes rest on the pages. Sam was a much more attractive subject anyway. "How do you know where to start? Reading it, I mean. It's not linear."

"It has an internal sort of logic once you learn the alphabet and some vocabulary. Mostly you go from the outside in, pick a thread and follow it. Sort of like Wikipedia or TV Tropes." He pointed to the book, but Aiden didn't take his eyes off Sam's face. "Like this one, for example. It starts off talking about the sky, the stars after they've fallen. Or here, this one, that tells me how the stars fell and why."

"But which one comes first?" Aiden frowned, feeling dense. It wasn't going to help him at all to look like a complete idiot. Sam's intelligence and his dedication to learning were two of the things Aiden admired. And he seriously doubted Sam would be interested in someone who wasn't at least on his wavelength.

"It doesn't matter. They both do. Neither do. You can read the piece in any order because it all happens regardless." Sam smiled, the flash of neat, white teeth earnest and captivating.

Aiden smiled too, caught up in Sam's expression and his obvious love of his subject. He hoped he'd find something similar before his college days were done. Sure, he loved literature, but he hadn't yet found a niche that called to him so strongly that he wanted to immerse himself.

After digging around in his leather messenger bag, Sam held out a highlighter-yellow index card. "Here, I want you to have this. It might help you with your studies."

Aiden took the card and looked at the Sogothian letters on one side, three waving lines of text intersecting one another with their ends curling together like a stylized eye. He flipped it over to the ruled side, not wanting to stare at the symbols too long, and found three lines of English in a neat, blocky print.

"It's something I try to keep in mind. An old Sogothian proverb, and the first thing I successfully translated on my own. Maybe it'll have some meaning for you too."

"Thanks." The English didn't make much sense either if Aiden was being honest with himself. Maybe Sam was too cerebral for him. But maybe, he thought as he flipped the card back over and took a more serious look at the

Sogothian letters again, figuring out what this proverb meant would help him unlock the mystery that was Sam.

"Hey, I hate to cut this short, but I just noticed the time," Sam said and began packing away his things. He flipped the book shut, displaying its cream leather cover embossed with an unusual multi-pointed star made up of smaller stars and Sogothian symbols.

"It's cool. I interrupted anyway. Thanks for telling me a little about your project. It sounds really fascinating. And complicated." Ducking his head sheepishly, Aiden shifted out of the booth and tucked the card in his back pocket. He smiled at Sam, knowing this was the perfect time to give the guy his number. For texting about . . . stuff. Ancient languages, at least, and maybe Arthurian legends if Sam wasn't sick of grading papers about them.

"I was grateful for a little distraction, I promise," Sam said. He stood and slung his bag over his shoulder, towering over Aiden with a fresh smile. "I was kind of hoping to see you outside of class anyway. Maybe we can study together some time? I don't really like being alone all the time—I've been told I'm an extrovert." Hands shoved in the pockets of his indigo skinny jeans, he shrugged.

"Yeah, sure. Where? When?" Aiden's heart thumped a quick-march beat. He knew he sounded too eager, too young, too everything wrong. But maybe that didn't matter to Sam.

"How about tomorrow night, around seven? Galeman? I know Brooks is more modern, but there's something about old columns and marble balconies in a library. Most of the collection I need is there too."

Aiden nodded, infinitely grateful he didn't yet have to fumble for a way to exchange phone numbers. It always felt contrived and awkward. "Sounds great. See you then."

They parted ways, and Aiden sipped his cold coffee all the way back to his dorm. Before he got to work on his English reading assignment, he pulled the yellow index card out of his pocket and read over the lines on the back again.

into the void we dance
like so many tangled threads
slipping under the writhing deep

It read like goth poetry—something his kid sister, Kenzie, would love.

Maybe Sam's screwing with me. So goth. Right. Who ever heard of such a language or civilization anyway?

Irritation creased his brow as he pulled up the browser on his laptop and did a search for *Sogothian*. The only thing that came up were a couple links to or about the Miskatonic University ancient languages library collection. Why would MU, a college in the United States, be the only place to have any connection to an extinct language supposedly from the middle east? And why would Sam have a bound book from the time period the language existed during? Aiden was no written language scholar, but he knew the primary form of written documentation back then had been on parchment scrolls, papyrus, and clay tablets.

Things weren't adding up, and Aiden wouldn't be taken for a fool. He'd been tricked and lied to before by people pretending to be his friends. Overhearing his "best friend" of four years call him a "tomboy who got her tits cut off" had been enough humiliation to last a lifetime. He wouldn't be duped by a friendly face again.

The Sogothian letters on the front of the card looked less sinister than the script in Sam's book. At least he could confirm the language was real, even if it didn't seem to be well researched or known. That could've been why Sam was so frustrated with his lack of human resources when it came to his translation work. If there were so few scholars who knew about the language, there were fewer still who'd bothered to study it.

I'm tired. I'm frustrated. I'm being too quick to judge.

He flipped the card back and forth a few times, trying to figure out which line of English matched up with which line of Sogothian. The more he read over the lines, the more he felt like they were listed in the wrong order. That had to be why they didn't make much sense.

slipping under the writhing deep

into the void we dance

like so many tangled threads

That made a little more sense, even if every line held a different metaphor. Or maybe it was supposed to start in the middle.

"Like so many tangled threads slipping under the writhing deep, into the void we dance," he read aloud. "Huh."

Sam was right—it doesn't matter which order you read the lines in. It makes the same amount of sense any way it's ordered, even putting the first line before the third or . . .

The door opened, and Marc eased in, clicking the door softly shut. He popped his dark brown head around the corner. "Oh, hey, man. Wasn't sure if you fell asleep with the light on again."

"Nah, just failing at concentrating. How'd it go at your study group?"

Marc huffed in annoyance as he set his full backpack down next to his bed. "Keye's giving me the run around—about going out and the group project. Everyone else is doing their parts without trying to control the whole damn thing. We agreed at the outset we'd split the work evenly based on skills and do everything by votes, no leader."

"Didn't you say one of the reasons you found her so sexy is her take-charge attitude?" Aiden smirked, twirling the card between his fingers.

Marc pointed a finger at him, eyebrows shooting up. "Hey, I didn't say my tastes were logical outside the bedroom." He ran his hands back over his close-cropped black hair and let out a sigh. "Not that I've had any success getting her any closer to the bedroom."

"She said she's aromantic—not easy."

"True. And I'm definitely romantic, so maybe she's hearing the 'go out' and thinking 'date' or something." Marc cocked his head to the side, eyeing Aiden's index card. "Whatcha got there?"

"Something Sam gave me. It's this ancient language he's studying for his master's."

"Sam, huh? Finally talked to him then. At least one of us has some balls. Uh, figurative balls. No offense."

Aiden smirked. "None taken."

Crossing the room, Marc held his hand out for the card and looked it over with a frown. "Do the guy a favor—keep him away from open mic night at the student center."

"He didn't write it. He translated it." It was pretty damn awful, but maybe that had been highbrow for the Sogothians. "He said it was a proverb."

"Aren't proverbs supposed to mean something? Y'know, highlight some truth about life or whatever." Marc handed the card back.

Aiden shrugged and looked the card over again. "Maybe it sounds better in Sogothian." He'd have to ask Sam for a transliteration. That could be a good conversation starter. Plus asking him about the book itself, which bothered Aiden less the more he thought about it. There had to have been scholars of the language throughout history—probably in secret archaeological organizations, given the limited scope of present day knowledge about the language—who could've easily made books. Transcribing old texts from crumbling statuary and scrolls would be an important task for such a small group, he could imagine. It added another layer of importance to Sam's passion: he was keeping knowledge alive.

"Get your boy to read it to you. Bet it sounds sexy." Marc laughed before he grabbed his toiletries and excused himself to head to the showers.

Aiden swiveled his desk chair back and forth, arms crossed, studying the Sogothian letters. "Like so many tangled threads."

The proverb could be describing the language itself. But that doesn't make for a good proverb, does it?

His eyes followed the lines of text where they wound around one another to form the central eye. Did the shape of the sentences affect the meaning of the passage? It really was a puzzle, like Sam said. Down the letters shrank where they formed the pupil-like segment, just like they had in the book. And once again, the letters began to shift, to swirl and pulse as if they were alive, leaking down into the empty space at their center like water in a vortex.

The door opened, and Aiden jerked his head to the side to blink at Marc, damp towel slung over his bare shoulder. He felt sick, but he wouldn't let on to Marc that anything was wrong. He didn't want another lecture on collegiate sleeping habits and the perils of sleep deprivation.

"Damn, that was fast."

"I guess so. You okay?" Marc hung his towel on the handle to his closet and put his toiletries away. "You look like you just got some shit news."

"Nah, just was falling asleep at my desk." The lie was easy when the truth felt too close to "you're losing it" territory. Everyone had heard the stories of MU students diving off the deep end, even if the college liked to ignore everything surrounding such reports. There were a lot of rumors about the school, mysterious incidences that never quite sounded like they could be real. Aiden had known that before he'd applied, before he'd decided to go Ivy League at his parents' insistence. He didn't think the number of campus counselors was a coincidence, but he also didn't put a lot of stock in the fantastical.

"Get some sleep, man. You don't want to start falling asleep in class or hallucinating."

"Yeah." Aiden set the card on his desk, his fingers shaking.

"I've got some questions about your research," Aiden blurted out as soon as he and Sam were tucked away in one of the Galeman Library reading rooms. He pulled his books out of his bag and set them in a neat stack next to his notebook and pen.

"I thought you might." Sam pulled out his own study materials and sat down across the heavy wooden table from Aiden.

"Sorry, I just couldn't stop thinking about the proverb. Which isn't really like a proverb at all. I mean, not one I've ever heard of. Which doesn't mean anything, but—"

Sam held up a hand. "Woah, slow down. It's okay. I know how weird it must look from the outside in. But I had a bit of a leg up on other Sogothian scholars since my family can trace its roots back to the Sogothian Empire. So I grew up knowing about it, seeing the language in old books, that sort of thing."

"There was a whole empire?" Aiden's face screwed up as he tried to wrap his mind around that concept. How could there be a whole empire lost to history, without so much as a footnote about it outside of MU? Was this some kind of Atlantis myth taken too far?

"A secret empire, yes. Most academics today would call it a cult in the style of the Greek and Roman cults. But it spread almost as far and wide as Alexander's reach, an empire within empires." Sam's face lit up as he spoke, his smile growing reverent, his hands animated.

"That's pretty cool actually." Aiden needed a moment to collect his thoughts. He wanted to ask about the moving letters without sounding like his grip on reality had slipped. But nothing came to mind as a good approach. He pointed at the book instead. "Um, about that. How old is it? Where'd it come from?"

"It's part of the school's collection, but no one really knows how old it is. Several hundred years, at least. That's part of why I'm trying to translate as much of it as possible—to unlock its secrets." He patted the book's leather cover affectionately. "It's not really much different from what you do in your lit classes. You read the text, mine it for meaning, for its inner truths, and translate them. Into essays, not another language, but all the same."

Satisfied with Sam's answers, there was only one more thing to ask. Aiden swallowed hard and pulled the yellow index card out of the pocket of his notebook, placing it on the table Sogothian side up.

"When you look at this, what do you see?" he asked, voice lowered as if they might be overheard by someone outside the little room. There was uncertainty still in his mind: had he imagined it? Once, and he could've written it off, but twice . . .

"I see a universal truth," Sam replied, eyes following the path of the letters.

Aiden jabbed his finger at the card. "Not . . . not metaphorically, not the meaning of the words. What do you *literally* see?"

"Knowledge."

Either Sam was playing obtuse or he didn't understand the question because it didn't make sense to anyone who wasn't repeatedly hallucinating. Aiden clenched his jaw, scratching at the rough stubble there. He hadn't shaved in at least four days, hadn't made time for it. He'd have to if he wanted to get himself back on track mentally. Taking care of himself would have to jump to top priority.

Sam tapped the card. "Knowledge slipping into the void."

"Yes! You see it too? The words *move*, right? It's not normal." Aiden's eyes went wide as he peered up at Sam.

"It's normal for Sogothian—the first step to comprehension. Not everyone's capable of seeing it, which is why there are so few Sogothian scholars. Well," Sam smiled wryly. "That and we tend to get carted away in white jackets if we discuss our findings openly."

Aiden's brow furrowed, and he turned the card around to look at it again, not feeling nearly as afraid as he had the night before. At least he wasn't alone in seeing what he'd seen.

"I can teach you the alphabet, get you started on vocabulary and grammar. If you're interested." Sam took his hand and gave it a gentle squeeze, his smile turning earnest, eyes filled with hope and excitement.

Cheeks burning, Aiden squeezed back, letting his hand linger in Sam's, feeling the warmth and softness of his skin. It was another moment he knew he should embrace, should take as a sign to press forward a little, make his interest known. But how could he when Sam had just shared an incredible secret with him?

"Yeah, that'd be cool. I mean, I don't know how much time I'll have for it right away, but . . . it's kinda like magic."

Sam nodded, his thumb running over the back of Aiden's hand. "It is. It's exactly like magic. And it can do things, change things about the world, reality, space, and time."

"I thought things were . . . well, it seemed like a lot of time passed in a few seconds when I was looking at the words, when they were moving." Aiden chuckled. "I thought I was imagining it."

"No, it can do that to you if you're untrained. It's like . . . think of a water slide? You'll just slip down, racing to the pool at the bottom. And how hard is it to climb back up?"

"Easy if you take the ladder."

Sam laughed, nodding and giving Aiden's hand another squeeze. "Exactly. The alphabet is the ladder."

"So . . . do you have to ride it down, all the way?" The hairs stood up on the back of Aiden's neck. That sounded terrifying, especially for a novice. How long would it take him to gain competence enough to not lose chunks of time to the words? Sam had been studying Sogothian for years on end.

"I can guide you if you want. Be your anchor. There's so much to learn, so much to explore."

Aiden looked down at their hands clasped together over the table, both of them leaning toward one another. There was something there, a connection beyond whatever aptitude they shared for a strange, ancient language. He wasn't sure if it was good or bad.

I don't care. I want it. I want to see where this goes. All of it.

He nodded, and before he could ask any more questions, Sam began spouting off random Sogothian words and explaining their English equivalents. It was a guttural language with an odd sensuality. Throaty but fluid. Harsh yet silky. He yanked the Sogothian book between them and opened it to a page Aiden hadn't seen yet.

"This is a teleportation sigil," Sam explained, smoothing the pages down with both hands.

"Tele—to where?" Aiden felt suddenly skeptical. Sure, the words had moved, he'd felt the odd lapse of time while looking at them, but Aiden wasn't ready to dive into the idea of magic being real with both feet.

"Another plane of existence, outside this one. I've traveled there, talked to beings older than anything in this world. They know so much, can do so much for us."

Aiden frowned, nervous again. "You're serious."

"Dead serious. Here, take my hands. You'll see." Sam reached out over the book, his smile bright and boyish.

What could it hurt? If it's bullshit, it's bullshit.

"Yeah, all right." He took Sam's hands and swallowed hard, peering down at the wheel-shaped Sogothian words while Sam recited them. The spokes pointed toward an empty center, that familiar blank heart all Sogothian writing shared. And if he looked close enough, he could see the letters angle down like narrow blades into the parchment, taking on a new dimension no writing should have.

His head felt pulled forward and his whole body behind it. The same sensation as when he'd fall asleep after too many nights of little sleep—like his entire being might be sucked through his mattress if he didn't wake immediately.

Darkness stretched in all directions: blue-blackness over a barren wasteland of jutting rocks and the buzz of silence. The air felt thick and hollow at once, pressing in on Aiden. He worked his jaw, trying to make his ears pop to dissipate the pain radiating to the center of his skull from both sides of his head.

"I want to keep this one." Sam's voice sounded muffled even though he stood right next to Aiden. "He's cute."

Through the dark, Aiden could just make out a strange shape like a winged statue. Only it moved, its eyes catching on some light source to flash at him, gold and menacing. The creature stepped forward into the lighter area Sam and Aiden occupied. Its face was like a man's surrounded by a squirming mane of tendrils, its body that of a huge lion with claws the size of daggers.

Aiden choked on a scream, coughing as he stumbled back onto his elbow and hand. The air was too heavy, too viscous and strange, for his lungs to handle. He scrambled away from the monstrous sphinx until his shoulders nudged something soft and far too forgiving to be a rock. Wetness seeped through his shirt as a thick, wormy appendage slithered across his chest and curled under his arm, yanking him back into the darkness toward a sucking sound.

"Sam! SAM!"

The sphinx's eyes flashed gold again and the tentacle withdrew.

Sam strolled over as if nothing were wrong. He held out a hand and hauled Aiden to his feet. "Stay in the light. Let my father have a look at you."

"Your f-f—"

"This one is full of fear," the sphinx announced in a bone-rattling rumble. It smiled with a maw full of shark's teeth while yellow eyes inspected Aiden intently, adding to the hammering dread in his chest. "Scars of anguish. Songs of hope . . . and dreams of you, Samael. He's no different from the others."

The more the sphinx spoke, the more pressure built in Aiden's head until his skull felt like it thrummed to the same drumbeat as his chest. He winced and pressed his palms to his forehead, the pain taking relentless hold.

"He's a human changeling," Sam said and pulled Aiden close, wrapping him in a soothing embrace. "He knows what it is to become."

The pain ebbed in the sphinx's silence, and Aiden clung to Sam, certain his life depended on it. He wanted to believe he was dreaming, having some kind of psychotic break, because everything seemed so terribly real, even if he felt like he was moving, breathing, and hearing through cotton.

"He feels incomplete to his senses. A horror unto himself." The sphinx purred and padded closer with heavy paw steps. "No wonder you show affection, sentiment."

I'm right here. Why can't you speak to—

"We can help you become. For a *price*." The sphinx's words lingered in the air, slinking into Aiden's ears like a living hiss.

It was tempting—the chance to strike a deal to fix what remained wrong about his body. Whatever Sam was, whatever his father was, they were powerful. If they could transport him to some alternate world, they could make good on any promise.

But *would* they?

Sam had been telling the truth about the sigil in the book, about where they'd go, what they'd meet. But what purpose did the traveling serve? Was he really the offspring of this inhuman monster looming over them? What was Sam really doing on Earth?

Aiden had wanted the teleportation to answer his questions, but now he had dozens more, each one leading down paths of thought more boggling than the last. And he could only trust Sam so much until he got a few real answers. Although if he were being reasonable, an island of rationality within his own mind, he knew he had no choice but to place his bets on Sam to protect him from whatever the fuck lurked in the darkness around them.

"I'm fine as I am," Aiden said, feeling as if he were speaking around marshmallows. He shifted in Sam's arms to gaze up at the sphinx. "What's going on? What is this place? Why bring me here?"

Twin yellow lights flashed over Aiden's face again, forcing him to blink and shield his eyes. "So many questions in every human. All of them with the same answer."

Aiden's head filled with jabs of pain again, and he curled instinctively against Sam, who stroked his back. Hot breath bathed his neck and ears, jetting down the collar of his shirt.

"They're filled with a lust for knowledge, Great One, but lack the capacity to contain it," Sam said, a hint of sadness in his voice. "I'll teach this one how to stretch and bend. Would you like that, Aiden?"

Cold sweat beaded on his skin as the gentle touch of the sphinx's icy tendrils caressed the back of his head. Its breath smelled of death and decay, of fresh cut grass and sickly sweet fruit. It smelled like everything that had ever lived or died. "I'd like to go back. *Please.*"

He'll eat me either way. Now or another time.

Aiden blinked up at the handsome man smiling down at him, the one he'd wanted to get to know, to let learn him in turn. The man he now knew too much and still nothing about. The man whose voice had been in his thoughts, guiding him as if it were his own.

How long had that been the case? How could he have missed something so simple? So obvious?

Because you already knew. You already understood the truth and accepted it.

No, he would have fought such an intrusion. Would have asserted his self inside just like he had in the outside world.

A hot, wet tongue lapped at his hair, startling a shout from his throat. Aiden squeezed his eyes shut and tried to wrest free of Sam's tightening grasp. "I'm not ready to die!"

But you're already dead.

"No!"

into the void we dance

slipping under the writhing deep

like so many tangled threads

"It doesn't mean anything!"

Yes and no. It means everything. And nothing.

"I don't care!" Aiden pushed and twisted, slipping away from Sam. He hadn't wanted to know, hadn't cared until Sam had planted the curiosity in his head.

Until Sam had tricked him into following him to some kind of evil dimension for who knew what. If only he had a weapon. A gun. A sword. Fire. Anything.

"Yet you care a great deal," the sphinx hissed, a whisper as it drew closer, flapping its huge leathery wings.

Aiden clutched his pain-racked head, doubling over. "I want to go back!"

You're already back.

Aiden opened his eyes, ears ringing, the sounds of his pulse and breathing all he could hear. Sam's hands held his fast, palms to sweaty palms, a sinister grin on his lips.

I'll show you so many things. So many wonders you've only understood in the deepest, darkest reaches of your mind.

"That's where we were," Aiden said, emotionless as understanding began to wash over him.

Come see where we are.

Aiden peered into the vast mahogany of Sam's eyes and saw the truth in them—his irises comprised of Sogothian script forever sinking inward. He felt the swift pull and sank into the inevitable undertow of empty fullness, bending and tumbling amid the crashing waves until he became one with them.

§

Elliot Cooper is all about happy endings and positive queer rep in genre fiction—specifically the subgenres of romance and erotica. His stories range from sweet to scorching hot, light to dark, humorous to serious, and everything in between. He loves to experiment with genre mash-ups and old favorite tropes, turning some on their heads, meeting others head-on.

Through Cryptic Caverns, the Shoggoths Come at Night

Liz Schriftsteller

IN THE AFTERMATH THAT FOLLOWED, KELSEY OFTEN ASKED ME QUESTIONS, many of which I couldn't answer. "Why" was the big one, but "how" and "when did it begin" were close cousins.

I suppose from a strictly chronological perspective, you could trace it all the way back to Asenath Waite herself and the residence hall that bears her name. It was a snare, baited with the promise of freedom, that closed 'round the naive women who fell into its trap, myself included. Perhaps it could've all been avoided if only we had never come to Miskatonic in the first place.

But in my mind, it will always begin with that first kiss.

I'm not sure if it was the drugs, the dorm, or the intoxicating rush of destiny, but whatever the cause, in that moment time folded in on itself, leaving my mind jumbled, my memories overlaid like a stack of shuffled papers.

I remember the smell—sickly sweet like we'd dipped a skunk in honey and set it on fire. The air hot and muggy, our exposed skin stuck to the cheap plastic chairs, more grey than white from the thin coating of grit and ash. It covered the bottom of my thighs and got under my fingernails when I ran my hands through her hair. Yuko's hair, black and shiny like her eyes, smelled like cherry blossoms, her tongue like smoke.

That's when it happened.

I saw it all, our entire timeline folded over and over again until it all became one irreversible tangle of destiny: Yuko underwater and me standing over her, looking down as her hair drifted among the kelp, the minnows nipping at her dead eyes.

And I was the minnow, nibbling her lips as they crumbled away on my tongue. And she was a creature in the water whose dark abyss held my own glossy reflection in its grip. Her eyes, the creature, the minnows, and me—all black, all of us underwater, tongues and breath and limbs intertwining, desperately clutching, unsure whether we were frantically trying to save each other or drag each other down.

I woke hours later in a pool of my own vomit, bits of dried sick clinging to the tendrils of my crusted, curly brown hair. My phone beeped incessantly a few feet away. I swatted at it, barely able to bring it to eye level.

ENG101MTEX—9:45AM

I switched it off, unable to remember what it meant. Later, once I drank about a fifth of Gatorade, it hit me.

Engineering 101. Midterm. Exam.

I had missed it.

Shit.

My mother dropped me off at Miskatonic University on the third weekend of August. We had driven thirteen long hours in the car together, wind whipping through the open windows to dry the sweat creeping down to the small of my back, sticking my legs to the pleather seat.

Mom was white-knuckle the whole way. If she were a cussing woman, she would've had little else to say in the way of conversation. Still, she was taking me, and for that, I was grateful. It was no easy feat to get her to agree to MU, but in the end, she relented.

My mother had three rules when it came time to pick out colleges: it had to be privately run, it had to have a significant Christian community, and it had to be affordable. It did not, however, have to be in-state.

That last part had to do with Liberty University, which was a mere two hours north across the Virginia border. It was her first pick when it came to schools but not mine. With those as her stipulations, I made it my mission to pick the absolute god's-honest farthest university from home, no matter where it might be.

Which is how I ended up here.

The campus itself was not as huge as I'd hoped, but the dense forest in the surrounding area made it feel more secluded. I was assigned to Waite Hall, an all-girls dormitory on the far side of campus from the main quad. It was built in the 1920s and only recently refurbished as a dormitory. It was an enormous building, five stories tall and over two hundred feet in length.

We found my dorm room and unloaded the car, sharing a private laugh at the Yankee kids and their yuppie parents whining about the ninety-degree heat. Back home in Carolina, it had already touched on 110. This was damn near pleasant, all things considered.

But then, it was time for her to leave.

I fingered the gold cross around my neck, the finish long worn away from years of pawing at it whenever my nerves were frayed. As much as I had yearned for this moment, now that it was finally here, I was having second thoughts about my resolve.

"Here, Bernie, I got you something." Mom reached into her oversized purse to pull out a small package wrapped in a wrinkled plastic bag. "It's a pocket-sized New Testament," she said before I could finish unwrapping it.

"Oh." I smiled. "Thanks, Mom."

"So you remember your roots." She brushed a loose strand of frizzed-out hair behind my ear. "You got good roots, Bernice. Don't you let any of them liberal hippie types cut 'em out from under you."

"Mom . . ."

"I'm just saying." She gave me a kiss on my forehead. "Oh, and these too." She rummaged around for a moment and produced two paper rolls of quarters, which smacked into my hand with surprising heft.

I sighed. "Thanks."

We said our goodbyes, and I waved her off to return to my room alone. I found an empty drawer in my bureau where I put the scripture and the quarters along with an accordion-folded sleeve of condoms from my sister, slipped devilishly into my bag with a scrawled note:

Be safe, have fun! ;)

I closed the drawer on them, each fundamentally useless in its own way. The laundry rooms had long been equipped with card readers for our flex accounts, their change slots disabled. The cross remained the only outward sign of my "roots," more out of habit than faith. And the condoms?

I emptied my suitcase out onto the bed and ran my fingers around the inner edge of the lining until I felt the hidden zipper. Carefully, I tugged until it pulled away, leaving exposed my most prized, most hidden possession. My fingers wrapped around the soft fabric, unearthing it from its containment. The light hit the fabric in a way I had never seen back in Carolina—the rainbow stripes more vibrant than ever in an environment where they could truly shine.

I pulled a few butterfly clips from my toiletries and hung it on the underside of the top bunk. I climbed onto the bare mattress and lay staring up at it until my eyelids drooped, and I fell asleep, grinning like an idiot, wild and free.

The door slammed open, jolting me from my sleep. The shadows on the ceiling slanted in a grid pattern from the fading light. For a moment, I wondered where my flag had gone until I remembered the beds were no longer bunked and hadn't been since that first week of class.

I turned over in the bed. "Yuko . . . ?"

"No, it's me," said Kelsey. "Where the fuck were you today?"

"Overslept," I mumbled.

"Yeah, no shit." She strode across the room and yanked the cord for the blinds, letting the last of the afternoon sun blaze into the room. "You been here all day?"

"Think so."

"Where's Yuko?"

"Fuck if I know." I rolled back over and plopped the pillow on top of my head. I wondered if Yuko had made it to her own exam. Guilt over last night's drunken debauchery pulsed beneath the forming migraine. Why had I kissed her? Or had she kissed me? I tried to remember the taste of her on my tongue, but it only reminded me that my mouth felt like something had crawled in there and died.

"Hey!" Kelsey yanked the pillow off my head and tossed it across the room. "I asked you a question."

"I wasn't listening."

She glared at me. "When did you last see her?"

"Last night. At the party."

"And she hasn't been back since?"

"Dunno. Don't think so. Why?"

Kelsey sat on the edge of the bed and ran sun-kissed fingers through her long blonde hair. "Asenath Waite's research."

I sat up, afraid to hear what I already knew she was going to say.

"It's missing."

That first night at MU, I kept waiting for a roommate who had yet to arrive. The RA assured me that I did indeed have one, an exchange student from the satellite campus in Kyoto, who would be arriving as soon as her plane landed. There was a frightful storm raging up the east coast that night, which was delaying flights.

Even my mom had to rent a hotel outside of New Haven since she was unable to make it any farther. I had hoped to wait up for my new roomie and make her feel at home, but in the end, I relented and went to bed, unable to keep my eyes open.

Thunder shook the building, waking me in the middle of the night. My alarm clock flashed 3:13 a.m., but my watch suggested it was closer to five. I wrapped a robe around me and headed out into the hall, half expecting the other girls to be there as well, bubbling with excitement over their first night away from home. But their doors were all shut, the corridor dark as I wandered down the lavish staircase to the main lobby.

My footsteps echoed on the tile flooring, which looked out of place beneath the cork bulletin boards covered in brightly colored maps of campus and wellness tips for a successful semester. Opposite the stairwell was a lounge with an ornate fireplace and monstrous grand piano. Above the mantle was the portrait of a young woman, tall and slim with an alabaster complexion and deep, wide-set eyes. Beneath it was a plaque with a simple engraved message:

We dedicate this building to the memory of Asenath Waite Derby, first of her kind to grace our beloved Miskatonic University.

"'First of her kind.' What do you suppose that means?"

I spun, my hand grabbing an oversized candelabra from atop the piano. I brandished it at the unseen figure in the darkness.

"Relax," she laughed. A scratching sound preceded a flicker of flame as the young woman struck a match. "Wouldn't want you to hurt yourself."

She leaned forward and lit the candelabra in my hand. Her blue eyes shown up at me as a sly smile settled into the corner of her full, pink lips. "You're the new girl, aren't you? The one from out of state, I mean."

"Yeah, I guess."

"I'm Kelsey Upton. Don't think we met earlier." She extended her hand, which I took with some trepidation.

"Bernice," I said. "Jackson."

"Storm wake you up?"

"Yeah."

"Yeah," she repeated. Her mocking smile teased in a way that might've be good-natured if it hadn't been our first encounter. "Me too."

Kelsey set the candelabra on the piano and crossed over to the couch. It wasn't until she sat that I noticed she carried a stack of yellowed papers and two leatherbound notebooks. She kicked her legs up on the cushions and spread a few sheets out on her lap.

"What're you doing?" I asked.

"Thought I'd get a jumpstart on some studying." She smiled but offered nothing further.

"Down here? In the middle of the night?"

"I find it gives me . . . inspiration." She glanced past me. I followed her gaze over my shoulder to the portrait of Asenath Waite.

"Whatever," I mumbled. "I'm going back to bed." I took a step toward the staircase and noticed something odd when my foot hit the tile. "Hey, Kelsey?"

"Mmm?"

"How'd you manage to sneak up on me?"

She turned over a page in the notebook. "What do you mean?"

"My footsteps echoed all the way down the hall. How did you manage to be so quiet?"

Kelsey frowned. "What are you talking about? Waite Hall doesn't echo."

"Yes it . . ." I took another step, but she was right.

Whatever sound had been following my footsteps was gone.

I threw on a sweatshirt and followed Kelsey across the hall to her dorm room. The chaos that was her research had gotten worse. Everywhere there were newspaper clippings, scraps of yellowed paper, and piles of archaic library books from the MU vaults. I guessed there were at least a few volumes smuggled out of the reference sections. Either that or her daddy had pulled some more strings with an extra donation to the endowment fund.

"Good lord, Kels," I muttered. "What the hell were you working on?"

"Here." She pointed at the middle of the room where a series of meandering lines drawn on several sheaves of graph paper was spread out on the floor. "Any of that look familiar to you?"

"Not in the slightest." I tilted my head and paced counterclockwise around the pile. "Wait. Is that . . . a map of the quad?"

"Not just the quad. The whole campus." Her eyes sparkled as she bent over her findings, tracing a path from the research labs on west campus down to our dorm. "There's an underground cavern system that stretches underneath the university. Yuko's been helping me map it out. I never dreamed how intricate it was, how far reaching. And look here . . ."

Kelsey pointed to another spot on the far right corner of the map. "I think that part leads to a tributary of the Miskatonic River." She grinned.

"So?" I frowned, unable to see her point.

"Don't you get it?" Her voice held a sharp edge, and I knew she was frustrated with me for not drawing my own conclusion. "The whole university has a direct path to the ocean. And . . ." she swallowed. "Vice versa."

I rolled my eyes. "Big deal. NASCAR was founded by a bunch of bootleggers."

Now it was Kelsey's turn to look confused. "What does that have to do with . . ."

"Prohibition. What you've got here is just a complicated system for college kids to homebrew some moonshine in the labs and run it out to sea without ever getting caught. That's all this is, Kels, not some grand conspiracy. If y'all had even a lick of sense—"

She raised her eyebrow, and I swallowed the rest of my sentence lest the rest of my accent spill out. I had done so well to keep it in line these past few months, but liquor and fatigue seemed to bring it out of me. After last night, I wasn't much able to keep ahold of it.

"Well," she said, ignoring my outburst, "that's one theory. But take a look at this." She pulled herself up and took a step back, gesturing at the layout of it.

"I am looking. What am I not seeing?"

Kelsey sighed. "Don't focus on one thing. Look out at the whole of it."

It was then that the map began to take shape, and I saw it for what it was. "Oh my god . . ." I breathed. "It's one big sigil."

She nodded.

"Did Yuko see this?"

"Yuko helped me piece it all together."

I caught her gaze, a knot forming in the pit of my stomach. "When was that exactly?"

"Last night. Sometime before the party."

I felt for a moment as if someone had grabbed the back of my head and pulled hard at my hair. My vision blurred, and I felt the ground shift under my feet. I hit the floor before I could even feel myself lose balance.

"Bernice!"

The graph paper and smooth wood under my palms was gone, and in their place, I grasped slick jagged rocks in a cavern of some sort.

"Bernice!" Kelsey called, and this time I was able to look up at her.

"I need you to keep it together, Bernice. Tell me. Tell me what's happening. What do you see?"

"I . . . you. I see you." The heady stench of brine and damp festering mold made me dizzy. Focus. I just needed to focus on one thing at a time.

She frowned, her hand reflexively moving up to brush back her long blonde hair. Only now, both were coated with a thin layer of black grit.

"You're . . ."

". . . safe."

In the moment it took for me to blink, I was back in the dorm room, sprawled out over the map. "What?" I mumbled.

"You're safe," she repeated, helping me up. "Probably just a side effect of whatever you two got into last night."

"Yeah."

"Yeah," she repeated. Her mocking smile teased in a way that might've be good-natured if it hadn't been our first encounter.

I shook my head, trying to dislodge the memory of her face in the darkness, holding out a match to the candelabra. It was so real, at once there and then again not. My heart raced as I tried to ground myself, force myself to come back to the present. This isn't right. *This isn't right this isn't right this isn't . . .*

"Right!"

"Whoa, whoa!" I felt Kelsey's hand on my shoulder, and I looked up to see her concerned face staring back at me. We were in her dorm again. I was kneeling on the floor, her hands gripping my arms to stop me from thrashing about.

I took a couple of breaths to steady myself but said nothing, too confused and embarrassed to think straight.

"Bernice . . . ?" she ventured.

"Yeah?"

"Your eyes . . ." I looked over her shoulder toward the floor-length mirror. My reflection was normal, save for my pupils. They had dilated more than ever before, completely pushing out the brown until there was nothing more than perfectly round black dots floating in the whites of my eyes.

Kelsey's hands trembled as she looked at me. "What the hell did you do?"

What the hell *didn't* I do? Yuko was the most beautiful girl I'd ever seen, and somehow, I'd ended up with her as a roommate. I'd have done anything to get her attention, but living with her presented a separate set of challenges. I had every opportunity in the world to talk to her and absolutely nothing to say.

She'd unbunked the beds as soon as she moved in, and they now sat on opposite sides of our narrow room with only about five feet of clearance between them. "Spitting distance," my sister would say. The nights were unbearably hot in that tiny room, even with the box fan propped up in the open window. She couldn't decide whether it was better to point it in or out, the blades doing little more than circulating the damp air.

Yuko sat cross-legged on her bed, bent over a textbook laid open across her lap. She wore a thin tank top and running shorts, which crept up her legs every time she shifted. Her iPod rested beside her thigh, its thin, white cord bright against her dark hair, winding down from her slender neck to the bed below.

I cleared my throat. "So . . . uh . . . what're you here for?"

"Hmm?" Yuko's fingers dipped behind her left ear to dislodge the earbud.

"Er . . . you know, what are you studying?"

She frowned. I couldn't tell if she was irritated by my interruption or if something was getting lost in translation.

"I'm in the engineering school," I said, already starting that nervous babble I never seemed to grow out of. "Or I hope to be anyway. They make you take Intro to weed out anybody who ain't too serious about it." I cringed inwardly and made a mental note to check my accent. "But anyway, what about you?"

"Marine biology." She turned back to her book but left the earbud out, which I took as an invitation to continue.

"Oh, no way! I love marine life." I smiled in a way I hoped was nonchalant but was probably trying way too hard.

"Is that so."

"Oh, yeah. My family traveled down to Kitty Hawk all the time when I was a kid. I loved going down to the water, looking at all the fish."

"Mm."

"Is that biology that you're reading now?" I was bothering her—I knew I was bothering her—but I couldn't stop talking. It was the longest conversation we'd had since she moved in, and I was determined to get to know something, anything, about her.

"It is English."

"Well, I'm sure it's in English but—"

"Literature."

"Ah." I shifted uncomfortably in the silence that followed. "So . . ."

"Have you heard the legend of the Kraken?"

"The . . . like the squid-thingy?"

"Hai. It is." She traced her finger along the lines of poetry as she spoke. "Below the thunders of the upper deep; far, far beneath in the abysmal sea, his ancient, dreamless, uninvaded sleep, the Kraken sleepeth."

She looked up. For the first time, I felt the full force of her attention on me. Her eyes were black and glossy as an oil slick, drawing me in.

For a moment, I forgot to breathe. "It's . . . uh . . . pretty," I managed.

"Beautiful," she agreed. "It is a common story. Many cultures have similar tales of sea monsters. In my country, we have the Akkorokamui. There are even shrines to it in our Shinto religion."

"You mean people worship it?"

"In a way. Many cultures worship the dark unknown."

We sat there a second too long before I realized that I was staring at her. "If you say so." I broke her gaze abruptly, my cheeks burning. When I glanced back up at her, she was smirking, an inviting coyness that left my head spinning.

"I do. That is why I came here. To see what universal truths I may find."

I shrugged. "I mean, I guess that's the whole point of college. Learning things you wouldn't otherwise know. You, uh . . ." I cleared my throat, hoping she wouldn't notice my awkwardness. "You let me know if there's anything I can do to help. You know. With your research."

Her smirk blossomed into a smile, the first I had seen since she arrived. "I will."

Thunder shook the building, waking me in the middle of the night. I turned toward my alarm clock, but it wasn't there. This wasn't my room. This wasn't my bed. Across the room, Kelsey sat at her desk, pouring over a stack of papers with half-scribbled notes.

"Kelsey . . . ?"

She turned to face me with a look of relief. "Oh good, you're awake."

"Where . . ." No, wait, I knew where I was this time. I shifted on her bed. "What time is it?"

"Midnight, thereabouts. The day after the party," she added. "Just in case you're wondering."

I pawed her nightstand for the bottle of aspirin she kept beside her prescriptions. "How'd you know I'd be asking that?"

"Just a hunch." She crossed over to the bed and put her hand to my forehead. "Yeah, better take some more of that." She nodded toward the bottle. "You've been in and out of consciousness all night. Never seem to know where you are or what's going on."

"I don't remember that."

"Probably for the best. At one point, you kept shaking, rambling about something you saw in the shadows."

I swallowed the pills with a grimace. "What was it?"

"No idea. Neither did you by the sound of it. Just that it was black and shapeless, like a bubbling puddle of oil. If I had Asenath Waite's notebooks, I could probably look it up, but Yuko still hasn't come back. Here." She unwrapped a packet of toaster pastries and handed me one. The dry, frosted graham crackers crumbled away in my mouth, barely held together by a sugary paste in the center.

I gagged.

"Eat it," Kelsey insisted. "You need to keep your strength up." She tossed me a Gatorade from her minifridge.

"I just want to go back to bed."

"Not just yet." She headed for her closet where she pulled out her coat. "We have to find Yuko. And you," she added, "better get your shit together. Try to remember where you last saw her, what you talked about. I think that'll help us track her down."

I sipped the drink in my hand, letting the salty, syrupy citrus wash down the diabetes crackers. "Yeah, but where do we start?"

Kelsey held up the notes with her makeshift cartography. "Where else? Now come on. Before you have another episode."

I managed to make it all the way down into the catacombs before the smell finally got to me. I stumbled, my palms hitting the slick rocks underfoot as I fell.

"Bernice!" I looked up at Kelsey, confusion sweeping over me as I struggled to stop from jumping into another memory.

"I need you to keep it together, Bernice. Tell me. Tell me what's happening. What do you see?"

"I . . . you. I see you." The heady stench of brine and damp festering mold made me dizzy. Focus. I just needed to focus on one thing at a time.

She frowned, her hand reflexively moving up to brush back her long blonde hair.

"You're not slipping again, are you?"

I shook my head. "No, I don't think so. I guess it was just déjà vu." That's what it felt like, but it seemed as real as when my memories took hold and propelled me back into the past. Had my brain also been yanking me into the future?

Kelsey grabbed my hands and helped guide me to my feet. We walked on toward the mouth of the cavern until we passed under a beam of light that had broken through. Her grip tightened around my hand as she swallowed a gasp.

"What is it?" I couldn't keep the panic from my voice.

"Nothing." Her thin-lipped smile was unconvincing. "You're all right. You're going to be all right."

I struggled against her grip, desperate to catch a glimpse of my reflection in the water. I saw that my pupils had dilated so much that they'd pushed to the edge of my eyelids. The whole of my eyes were full black, as dark and empty as a shark's. Kelsey clamped her hand over my mouth before I could scream.

"Focus!" she hissed. "You've got to fight it!"

"I can't! Oh god, Kelsey! What the hell!"

I was exhausted by the time I got back to the room from study group. Engineering had been a bitch so far, but I felt confident enough that I could knock the midterm on its ass. Now all I needed to do was get a good night's sleep and . . .

I opened the door to see Yuko half-naked in the room. "Oh god, sorry, sorry!"

"No, no, come in!" She waved me in, and I shut the door behind me. "You can help me with the zipper." She stepped into a black cocktail dress and slipped her arms through the straps.

My pulse quickened at the smell of her perfume, her bare back exposed to me while my fingers fumbled with the fabric. "What's the occasion?" I asked.

"Raging kegger at Phi Lambda." She winked at me. "Plus Kelsey and I just had a breakthrough moment in our research. I'd say that's cause for a celebration."

"Oh right. Her." I trudged over to my bed and pulled out the pajamas from underneath my pillow.

She eyed me from across the room. "Why don't you come with? Cut loose a little."

"Can't. Got a midterm tomorrow."

"So do I." She grinned. "Come on. One drink. What's the harm?"

I caught the full brunt of her gaze when our eyes locked. There was something different about her lately. At first, I thought it was her English, which had grown by leaps and bounds over the course of the semester. But looking at her now, I could see it was something else. Her brown eyes were so black I could hardly tell where her pupils ended and her irises began.

"Will Kelsey be there?"

Yuko scoffed. "What's your problem with Kelsey anyway?"

"I don't know. I don't trust her, I guess. She kind of gives me the creeps with those ancient notebooks of hers." I broke her gaze, unsure how much I should say. "I mean, you hang out with her. What's even in those?"

"I don't know," Yuko admitted. She crossed over to her desk and opened the bottom drawer. Gingerly she pulled out one of Kelsey's leather-bound journals. "What do you say we find out?"

I leaned forward and retched, chunks of blueberry toaster pastry and citrus sports drink hitting the rocks with projectile force and splattering onto my shins.

"Oh god!" Kelsey jumped out of the way, and I heard her gag behind me as I forcibly emptied the contents of my stomach.

"I . . ." I heaved, the edges of the memory starting to bleed back into view. "I know where Yuko is."

"You're gonna eat it in those heels," I said.

Yuko's smile blossomed as she glanced over her shoulder at me. "Thank you."

I laughed. "I mean, you're going to fall." I followed her down the staircase to the grand parlor where I had first met Kelsey so many nights ago.

"Oh. Isn't that when other people find you attractive?"

"That's 'they're going to eat you up.'"

She shrugged. "Close enough."

"Seriously though, you sure you don't want to change?"

"A breakthrough like this can't wait." Yuko held open the notebook and ran a finger over the page. "It says here that there's a hidden switch inside the fireplace. Would you mind?"

She gestured to a crevice in the upper right corner that was just barely visible. I stuck my hand out and felt around until I discovered a small latch, which I unhooked. "This is the part where the whole thing spins around and traps me inside, isn't it?"

Yuko laughed. "Nothing so dramatic."

There was a click and with it the slightest breeze that carried a faint odor of musty sea air. I pawed at the back panel of the fireplace, which swung backward revealing a passageway.

Yuko's face glowed with excitement. "Shall we?"

"Let me see that map." I yanked the notes away from Kelsey and rotated them until I found what I was looking for. "Here. Look, we came in through the catacombs, near the entrance to the river. But that's not the only way in."

Kelsey peered over my shoulder as I traced the paths under various parts of campus. "I don't understand. Yuko and I walked all up and down these caverns. I never saw any doorways."

"They're hidden. You have to have the notebook to know where the latches are. She showed me one that goes from Waite Hall to the woods across from the Phi Lambda house." I pointed to a spot on the map. "That's where I last saw her."

"Lead the way."

"Chikusho!"

I grabbed Yuko before she could fall, her foot caught on a rock in the caverns below campus.

"Told you you were gonna eat it." I smiled as she held my arm. "Although, to be fair, you did make it all the way there and most of the way back without tripping."

She grimaced as she rubbed her swollen ankle. "I think I . . . broke it? Is that the word?"

I glanced down. "Nah, probably just sprained it."

"That's what I meant."

I leaned over and brushed a strand of black hair from her face, stealing another kiss. My head swam from the heady rush of pot and liquor coursing through me from the party. She kissed back, her fingers cupping the back of my head and pulling me closer. Our tongues twirled, her teeth on my lips, biting until she drew blood.

"Oo! Not so rough!" I pulled back, my gaze meeting her eyes. The blackness that was her pupils had spread until the whole of her eyes were covered. "Oh, my god . . ."

Yuko reared back, hissing, no longer my roommate but some unearthly creature of the night. I stumbled backward as she lunged at me, and we tumbled to the ground, limbs intertwined in a tearing, grasping embrace. Somehow, my arm broke free, and I pawed in the darkness for anything I might use to get her off me. My hand settled around a rock, which I swung at her head. There was a crack, followed by a sickening squish.

She went limp.

I shoved her lifeless body off me where it rolled down into a pool of stagnant cloudy water. I watched her sink below the surface where her black hair intermingled with the dark green kelp. Minnows scattered from the greenery and swarmed her face, nibbling at her dead lips. I felt hundreds of eyes behind me, watching me, watching her. I couldn't tell if they belonged to one being or many; I only knew that they were there, creeping closer. After a moment of staring into the darkness, their visages became clearer—shapeless, oozing, bubbling, and slithering with rows upon rows of jagged teeth.

We stood over the pool where Yuko's body lay decomposing under the surface. Kelsey had gathered Asenath Waite's scattered notebooks without a word as I related in trembling tones what I remembered from our struggle last night.

"I know it was self-defense but . . ." I shivered, unable to finish my sentence.

"That's not important now. What's important is that we stop it from happening to you. Your eyes went all black too, but you were able to fight it. Why?"

"I don't know . . ." I fiddled with the gold cross around my neck to calm my nerves.

Kelsey glanced from the cross to me and raised an eyebrow.

"You think . . . ?"

"Hell, I don't know, Bernice. Maybe it has nothing to do with it; maybe you can't be cured at all. But if there is something that'll save you, I'm betting it's in these books."

"What do we do 'til you find it?"

"Seal up the tunnel entrances, as many as we can find. Disrupt the sigil pathways so it doesn't summon any more of them. And Bernice?"

"Yeah?"

"Here's hoping you haven't forgotten how to pray."

Liz Schriftsteller hails from North Carolina, but these days, "home" is anywhere the wifi automatically connects. Her published fiction includes works found in *Daily Science Fiction*, *Havok Magazine*, and *The Arcanist*. When not writing, she enjoys going to the theater, binge-reading stacks of comics, and over-analyzing the plot elements of her favorite TV shows. Follow her on twitter @LizSchriftstell or online at lizschirftsteller.wordpress.com.

Official Inquiry into the Waite-Gilman-Carter Antarctic Expedition

KG McAbee

I raced down the corridor of Curwen Hall at top speed. I was going to be late to the hearings. This did not bode well for my upcoming tenure-track discussions, but I put that out of my mind as, arms full, I careened around a corner.

"Oof!" complained the brick wall into whom I'd just barreled.

As the air expelled from my chest, I threw my arms around the wall to keep myself from falling, in the process depositing my briefcase and three folders onto the polished wooden floor. The briefcase fell with a satisfying clunk, but the folders sprang open, contents left to the vagaries of fate—that is, they scattered to the winds.

"Bloody blast and damn," I said, and believe me, it was heartfelt.

"Professor, are you okay?" asked the young man masquerading as a brick wall. Tall, blond, massive, broken-nosed, not a student I recognized. Indeed, if he'd been dressed in anything but jeans and a sleeveless T-shirt with the insignia of the Miskatonic lacrosse team, the Fighting Cephalopods, he would have been the dead spit of how I imagine King Canute. Well, perhaps Hardicanute.

"I am quite well, I believe, but I fear my papers are far from it." I made a helpless gesture at my dispersed paperwork.

"Oh, sorry. Let me get them for you," he replied. He set about doing so, stuffing random sheets into the three folders I had just spent an hour organizing to my liking.

"Ah," I said as he stood before me, holding out my papers in one hand. He resembled nothing so much as a clueless border collie who had managed to corral a herd of turtles in lieu of sheep. Before I could actually seize the folders, he dropped them in mid-air and stooped to retrieve my errant briefcase that, somehow, he had just noticed, even though it had been at my feet the entire time.

"Oops!" he shouted in glee and leapt upon the skittering papers yet again, managing to make them even more disorganized.

At last, he stood before me, all but wagging his tail.

I took the three folders and stuffed them into my already overburdened briefcase before he decided to play catch with them again.

"Thank you," I said. I pulled out my pocket watch—yes, it is an affectation, but it belonged to my grandfather—and sighed.

"Something wrong, sir?" asked the young man.

I looked up—and up—to a pair of mild blue eyes. Any inclination I'd had to remonstrate dissolved into those pellucid depths.

"I'm due at a meeting in eleven minutes," I said. "It appears I shall be late as the library is clear across campus."

"Not a prob, Prof."

He grabbed my briefcase with three fingers of one hand, tucked the other hand under my arm and—I believe the term I seek is *hustled*—hustled me down the corridor toward the double doors, talking all the while.

"I've got my bike just outside. We can hop on and be at the library building in no time flat."

I allowed myself to be propelled out the door and down the steps—I truly did wish not to be late. But at the bottom of the steps, I had second thoughts, followed at once by third.

I had expected a two-wheeled vehicle. I was not mistaken. I had imagined a stately ride, very Mr. Chips, and regretted that Miskatonic faculty did not wear don's gowns. I had not expected . . .

"Is *that* your *bike*?" I pointed with trembling hand.

"Oh, yeah. Ain't she a beauty? Indian Chieftain Dark Horse. Top of the line. Set my old man back a bit, I'm guessing."

"Guessing?" I breathed. I guessed this monstrous beast had set his father back somewhat more than the yearly rental of my tiny apartment, even throwing in my ancient Renault, currently residing with a local mechanic who spent more time with her than I did. "Be that as it may, I cannot risk myself on the back of your motorcycle, Mr. . . .?"

"Oh, I'm sorry." He thrust out a hand that entirely engulfed mine with room left over for several more. "Randy Carter. Freshman. And you're Professor Eldin Franklyn. I've signed up for your class in theoretical grimoires next semester."

"If I get to teach it," I began after I retrieved my hand, thankfully undamaged. "I can't possibly—"

Before I was able to explain precisely what I could not possibly do, I found myself perched behind Mr. Carter on his monstrous motorcycle, my overstuffed briefcase clutched to my bosom with one hand. He did something esoteric to buttons and switches and such, the thing roared and rumbled, and I hung onto the seat with my unencumbered hand as we raced across campus toward the Armitage Library Building. Mr. Carter ignored screams of protest, shaken fists, road signs—indeed, roads themselves—as we rushed past the Zann Music Hall, the Pickman Center for the Arts, the Ashton Smith Astrophysics Building—closed for renovations after a recent botched attempt at opening a wormhole—bisected the lacrosse field to the great consternation of the practicing team, took a hard right and bounced across the grass quadrangle, dodged and wove past students and faculty, and finally pulled up in front of the library.

I tottered from the great beast, took a breath, and pulled out my watch.

Five minutes to spare.

"My undying thanks," I said over my shoulder to Mr. Carter as I dashed up the steps. I ran down the hall and up a short flight of stairs. Through double doors, down a long corridor, and I arrived at the conference room door, gasping for breath.

"Professor Franklyn." Dr. Harlan Peasbody gave me a frosty nod as he pushed past me and entered. Rank hath its privileges—and no one was as rank as Peasbody.

"Hey, Professor?" asked a voice. "Mind if I sit with you?"

I turned to see Randy Carter towering over me. The lad was not even out of breath.

"Well . . ." I began, not wishing to be rude.

"Because Dad paid for the trip, you see, and he asked me to attend the hearing since he can't make it," Carter finished.

I recognized the name at last. Randolph Spencer Carter was one of the biggest donors to Miskatonic University. Ergo, this boy must be his son.

"Certainly," I said. I led him to the table where the other three faculty members sat, ignoring their glares, and waved him to a seat beside me scant seconds before Dean Hengist rapped his gavel on the table.

"Faculty and honored guesths, come to order pleathe."

Yes. He lisps. This verbal quirk I blame on his total lack of front teeth due to an unfortunate shoggoth encounter some years ago.

"I will now turn the gavel over to our esthteemed vithiting profethor of ancient studies, Doctor Jothiah Llanfer. Doctor?"

I breathed a soft sigh of relief that we would not be subjected to more lisping and began to unpack and sort the contents of my briefcase. I confess, I paid little attention to Llanfer, a noxious blowhard from Wales whose blathering on was little improvement over being forced to listen to Hengist.

"Professor?"

I turned and raised an eyebrow at Carter.

"What's that?" he whispered.

What indeed? A wooden box, perhaps six by four by two, sat in pride of place on the long table set across from our own. In fact, perhaps I should set the scene a bit more.

A typical conference room in the Danforth Wing of the library with three parallel tables set perpendicular to the door we'd just entered. Hengist the Dean, Peasbody the Arrogant, Llanfer the Blowhard, and myself, with young Carter beside me, sat at a table on the right as one entered. In the center of the room was a similar table, littered with the aforementioned wooden box plus other bits and bobs of unrecognizable flotsam and, I had no doubt, jetsam. Beyond this and facing us was the final table, where sat, I supposed, three members of the WGC Expedition with notes spread before them.

Surviving members of the expedition, one must naturally assume. I knew, of the fifteen who left for Antarctica, only three had returned.

Still, for a Miskatonic-sponsored expedition, that is far from the worst ratio I've seen. The Pabodie-Lake Expedition of 1931, sponsored by the university and the Nathaniel Derby Pickman Foundation, had set off with fourteen; two returned. The Starkweather-Moore Expedition, some years later, disappeared to the last man. So to have one-fifth of this particular group return in relatively good health—physically, at least—was something of a coup, a feather in the Miskatonic cap.

Dr. Llanfer tapped the gavel and coughed. "Shall we come to order please? We have much to hear."

The long box on the center table chose that moment to shudder and emit a kind of rattling growl.

I confess, I jumped. Used as I am to such things happening here at Miskatonic University—so different from Oxford it was still a bit of a surprise.

A lean man with a wizened face rose from his seat at the far table, stepped around, and put one hand on the box. It settled down, almost as if it were a dog soothed by its master. I nearly expected him to say something like, "There, boy."

He returned to his seat and opened a notebook.

Dr. Llanfer cleared his throat again. I seemed to detect some small hint of concern.

"Dr. Waite. Perhaps you would care to begin the proceedings?"

So this was Doctor Ezekiel Hezekiah Waite, PhD, FRGS, MSc, MLitt, MDiv, et al., ad inf. As long as I've been at the university, I've never had the opportunity to meet the legendary doctor who tended to make flying stop-offs, scattering his newly acquired finds and information, to receive a new degree or two and dash off on another adventure. Tall, lean, his dolichocephalic head was covered in shorn grey stubble, his eyes shielded by the darkest of glasses, his long-fingered hands—I could see how covered in scars they were from clear across the room—toying with a pen. He was dressed not in the de rigueur professorial attire of leather-elbow-patched jacket and khakis but in a charcoal-colored boiler suit as were his two team members. This gave them the appearance of some covert paramilitary force—not unintentional, I'm sure. Waite had the reputation of riding roughshod over, well, everyone and everything in his path.

"Hey, Prof?"

I turned to face young Randy. He had a quizzical look in his clear blue eyes.

"Yes?"

"That box on the table?"

"I see it."

"It did just move, right?"

I nodded, and he settled back in his chair, satisfied.

I was beginning to grow fond of the boy.

Dr. Waite rose again to his feet and stepped back around to the center table. He ignored the long box and went instead to a tottery pile of flat rocks stacked in decreasing size, the small topmost rock being barely larger than a half-sheet of notepaper. Waite removed the smallest rock—it appeared to be about as thick as the bottom of a beer glass—and held it up so that we could make out the image.

"This," began the good doctor, "was the first indication we found of the lost Starkweather Expedition."

I stifled a brief sense of disappointment. Instead of some manly baritone, the doctor's voice tended more toward the sophomoric tenor with the occasional inadvertent squeak.

"We found this in our first excavations into the lower levels of the prehistoric underground city first discovered in 1931."

"Cool!" said young Randy Carter. "I didn't know there was a lost city in the Arctic."

I could clearly hear the crackle of ancient bones as the heads at our table turned in the boy's direction. Dr. Hengist gave a short cough of disapproval. Dr. Llanfer contented himself with a glare. Dr. Peasbody snorted.

But Dr. Waite was of sterner stuff.

"*Antarctic*, young man. Quite the other end of the globe—if you were indeed aware that the world is round." His acerbic tones would have wilted the most eager professor begging for tenure.

It had as little effect on young Carter as had the Hengist cough, the Llanfer glare, or the Peasbody snort.

"Sorry, sir," Randy said cheerfully. "Didn't mean to interrupt. It's just cool, you know? A lost city and all. And I'll remember, I promise. South pole, not north."

My heart warmed even more to the boy. How many of us professorial types could be so cool under such pressure?

"Excellent," said Dr. Waite in as snide a tone as a squeaky tenor could provide. "Now if I am allowed to continue . . ."

And continue he did, for something like an hour and three-quarters. I will take pity on you and condense his information if I may be so bold.

The WGC Expedition's primary purpose was to investigate the disappearance of the previous one some seventy years ago led by Amos Starkweather; that expedition was based on information of yet an earlier expedition. The two surviving members of the first expedition—one of whom had died in a madhouse—had refused to discuss their findings in public. Miskatonic Library had many of their secret journals in storage, I understand, locked in archives with the original copy of the *Necronomicon*, the Pnakotic Manuscripts, and other such forbidden writings. Suffice to say, a city predating the Cambrian-Ordovician boundary extinction event existed below the surface in the Antarctic. Where it was, who built it, and why it was abandoned were the primary questions to be answered, and it seemed Dr. Waite and his team had answered them, or at least some of them. The relics littering the center table were evidence of success.

I listened with one ear while I examined the collection with rather more interest. In addition to the pile of irregular flat rocks and the long wooden box, there were numerous shriveled, starfish-shaped objects that seemed to be organic but appeared desiccated or even mummified; an old, leather-bound journal of some sort, rather the worse for wear; and oddly, a pile of matted furs covered in dark stains. I was contemplating the journal when a voice broke into my reverie.

"Doctor Waite?"

It was dear Randy again.

"Yes?" snapped the doctor, irritation in every line of his lean body.

"Is that Dyer's journal?"

"I believe I just stated that it was."

"Can I read it? Please?"

A collective gasp was followed by a buzz like an angry hive of bees.

Dr. Llanfer glared—at inoffensive me!

"Professor Franklyn, if you cannot control your . . . assistant, pray remove him from the room."

"Oh, I'm not the prof's assistant," Randy laughed. "Heck, wish I was, but I'm just a freshman." The boy rose to his full six feet four and gave his disarming grin. "I'm Randy Carter. My dad, Randolph Spencer Carter, helped fund this expedition, and he wanted me to sit in and report back to him."

The angry buzz died away to be replaced by an awed silence. After all, not only had Carter Senior funded this particular expedition, he had likewise funded two buildings, the lacrosse field, an addition to the library, and the gods alone knew what else.

"So I thought I'd like to look at that journal a little, ya know?" Randy concluded, his voice dropping like a stone into the sudden silence.

Dr. Waite seized the journal, stalked to our table and slammed it down in front of Randy. I could see the man was torn between righteous indignation—a mere freshman, by all that's holy!—and concern for his future funding.

"Perhaps, *Mister* Carter"—Waite snorted—"you might share any insights you manage to obtain from this priceless historical record once you've studied it. No doubt over beer and pizza."

"Well, it is getting close to lunch, so if you guys are planning to order some," Randy said cheerfully, "make mine mushroom and pepperoni."

I had to cough to cover my smile at this latest blasphemy.

"Perhapths," said Dr. Hengist, "we sthould indeed take a thmall rethess." He banged his gavel and stood up.

The long box on the table seized upon that instant to shake again. This time, Waite set both hands on it, and I was almost sure I could hear him utter some sort of nonsense syllables, something like *tekeli-li* or sounds along those lines.

But this time, his soothing had no effect. The nervous box began to bounce on the table, making sharp smacks as the two wooden objects came into contact. The pile of flat stones now decided to enter into the proceedings; it shook, shivered, and threatened to topple at any moment. The other two men who were with Waite, neither of whom had been introduced, had spoken or indeed moved, now leaped to their feet and dashed around the table. One, a short man who must once have been chubby or even fat but whose skin now hung in folds about his face, threw both arms across the box. The other, a somewhat taller man, reached to rescue the pile of stones.

Alas, too late. The stones themselves seemed to give an exultant leap. The top two went left, the next ones jagged right, and the entire obelisk scattered across the tabletop, some even escaping to the floor. But none of them remained in their scattered positions. Instead, a kind of whirlwind arose, a whirlwind of rock shards. Each of them returned to their former pile, in order small to big, but not sitting on the table. Instead, they rose and hovered in a kind of cone, spinning in a frenzied vortex.

Meanwhile, the box was causing even more of a ruckus, and I was sure I could detect answering calls from within, odd pipings that could just be interpreted as those nonsense words Dr. Waite had now begun shouting: "Tekeli-li! Tekeli-li!"

I glanced around, and I feel no one can blame me if I admit I was seeking the nearest exit. I began gathering my papers in as composed a fashion as I could muster. I have been in many a meeting at Miskatonic and have found that often a hasty retreat is the better part of valor.

The hastier the better in my considered opinion. I turned to tell young Carter it was time to go. In all conscience, I could not leave him behind. I had begun to like the boy.

And after all, he had a very rich father.

His chair was empty. Where . . .?

"Hey, Dr. Waite, you need some help?"

Randy was scrambling over the table. On the other side, he jumped off the dais and leaped next to the bouncing box and the toppling stones.

I abandoned my papers and briefcase and shoved my chair back, muttering to myself about the stupidity of my own actions. My chair rammed into Dr. Hengist, who appeared on the same quest as myself—that is, escape. But the old man surprised me. He stumbled past and, instead of heading for the door, tottered down toward the melee in the middle of the room.

I suppose he realized the point of the old adage, that no one lives forever, and thought perhaps his legacy would shine all the brighter if he, in effect, went down with his ship. Sadly, the ancient dodderer became the first casualty.

Just as Dr. Hengist stepped off the dais, almost as if he'd left holy ground, the topmost rock in the tornado left its comrades and sped toward him. The thin sliver of rock struck him just below the chin, taking his head off as neatly as a fillet knife. A plume of misty blood shot up and speckled the ceiling as the headless body collapsed.

The head itself whirled around counterclockwise and plopped onto the table in front of me, just missing my briefcase. His eyes, a surprised look in their cloudy depths, blinked twice as if warning me to try a different route.

I nodded my thanks and ducked under the table to find Dr. Llanfer.

"What in heaven's name is happening?" he shouted. Shouted because the cacophony of bouncing box, whirling stones, eldritch shouts, and screams of fear made normal tones useless.

As I had no idea, I simply shook my head and scrambled past him to the other side of the table. With extreme caution, keeping an eye out for wayward rocks, I gingerly reached one foot onto the floor. My head stayed intact, so my other foot joined the first and—stooping, I admit—I ran toward young Carter.

Well, it was more of a duck-walk, but I went. Credit where credit is due.

Just as I reached him, the screeching scream of nails being torn from their sockets echoed through the room. The top of the long wooden box tore itself loose and rose majestically upward to hover halfway to the ceiling. The rock shards were still darting here and there. I chanced a glance over my shoulder, expecting to see more decapitated heads, but Peasbody and Llanfer had wisely ducked below it. I could see them huddled together, their screams nearly as irritating as the other uproar in the room.

I reached Randy and tugged his shirttail.

"Yeah, Prof?" He grinned down at me. "What are you doing on the floor? Are you hurt?"

I pointed over my shoulder.

"Oh wow. Is that Dr. Hengist's head?"

I nodded. "Shall we depart?" I shouted.

Randy shrugged, reached down and grabbed the collar of my jacket, using it to hoist me to my feet. I needed the assistance.

"I don't think we can do anything to help here, do you?" he yelled as he smartly dodged a flying rock shard, pulling me sideways with him. Really, the boy's reaction time is remarkable.

"Assuredly not! The door, my boy, the door!"

"But shouldn't we help the other professors?"

"Should? Yes. Can we? Debatable."

As we were discussing in shouts, I was pushing the dear boy toward the door. We reached it, and I grabbed the knob only to draw back in pain. The metal was blazing hot. I waggled my hand in pain.

A rock came whizzing past my head and embedded itself into the wood of the door. I feared the varnish would never be the same.

Randy, with great perspicacity, stripped off his shirt and wrapped it around the knob. He turned and jiggled it a bit, and the door opened a crack.

"No!" came a despairing scream behind us, accompanied by other shouts and moans with no decipherable words—the sounds of minds driven mad with fear. I could certainly sympathize as I was fast driving down that road myself.

Although I had no desire to do so, my curiosity overcame me, and I turned to look.

Some strange semi-gravitational—or perhaps not, physics is not my forte—mayhap a kind of non-Euclidian force had the three professors and two assistants suspended in mid-air. Twist, turn, and struggle though they might, they all seemed to be floating inevitably toward the yawning maw of the now-open box. I was wondering how in the world the box thought it could hold them all, being little larger than a small coffin, when my question was answered in the most hideous way imaginable. Out of the box rose a kind of vortex seemingly composed of black smoke interspersed with streaks of odd, alien colors. Such things are fairly commonplace at Miskatonic, I have learned.

I looked up at Randy Carter. "Out, my boy, out!"

He put his shoulder to the recalcitrant door and gave a mighty shove. The door slid open by inches until it was large enough for us to slip through. The dear boy shoved me first, and I stumbled over the thing that had been blocking the door and dropped to my knees.

A dead body. Not someone I recognized, but he was dressed in the same kind of serviceable boiler suit that Waite and his assistants had been wearing. Crouching beside the man's shoulders, I could make out a tiny sigil on the breast pocket, stitched in grey silk and almost invisible unless one were but a few inches away, as I was.

My heart would have frozen in fear if it had not already been well past that stage.

The silken image was a starfish shape, much like those shriveled fossils brought back by Waite and displayed on the table with the other objects. I am far from an expert on the Elder Ones, the Mi-Go, or even the Star Spawn of You-Know-Who, but this image did not bode well for the earth.

"You okay, Prof?" asked young Randy as he hauled me to my feet.

"I am. Did anyone else escape?"

"Nope, don't think so," he said. "Let's give 'er another look, want to?"

We peered through the crack between door and wall. The smoky vortex that had been drawing the others to it through the air had, it seemed, succeeded. We were just in time to see the final sacrifice, Dr. Llanfer, sucked into its depths with a despairing cry.

But wait! Dr. Waite still survived, just visible in the ever-darkening room, his arms held out to his side, and he screamed, screaming "tekeli-li" over and over. Then a snaky tendril of black smoke, shot through with arcane colors, whipped around his waist and drew him into the box, no doubt to some dread universe where he would be eternally consumed and regurgitated to be eaten again and again and again by some Nyarlethotepian mass, bubbling at the center of creation . . .

Really, these Ancient Old Ones have distressing dietary habits.

"Trouble, Professor Franklyn?" asked a voice behind me.

I turned, a vast relief surging through me.

"Commander Phillips!" I shouted.

The stocky woman, a grin on her broad face, reached out and enveloped my hand in a strong grip. Behind her, a team of calm and competent-looking women and men held various devices and equipment, all of which appeared to either flash, beep, hum, bleat, or all four.

"What seems to be the problem this time?" asked the commander. "Someone chanting what he shouldn't or summoning something nasty?"

A crack echoed behind me. I chanced a quick glance.

The door had split down the middle, and wisps of black smoke were leaking out.

"Ah, got it," snapped the commander. "Inter-dimensional portal to a pocket dimension. Stand aside, you two, and give the professionals some room."

She took both Randy and me by the arms and dragged us out of the way. They set to work placing their equipment in a semicircle about the door to the now-accursed conference room. I gave her a brief rundown of the recent events.

"Waite, hey? Bumptious little beast, never can see the forest for the trees." Phillips turned to rap out some incomprehensible orders and continued, "He's always bringing things back he shouldn't, like a badly trained dog dragging in trash from the compost heap. Last time it was—"

Before she could continue this fascinating line of conversation, a gentle boom interrupted her. I turned to look at what had caused it and fell into a dark pit . . .

A week later, I was propped up in my bed, eating some disgusting pap in the college infirmary when young Randy Carter dropped by for his daily visit.

"Hey, you're looking great, Prof!" he exclaimed.

Since he'd said the same thing each of the three days since I'd awoken, my head bandaged, I took his comment with more than a few grains of salt. But I admit, I was feeling much better and told him so.

"That's wonderful, sir," he said, plopping down in a chair which gave a squeak of concern at his weight. "Commander Phillips and Doctor Asenath both said you'd be okay, but I wasn't sure. That was some knock you took."

"An errant bit of wood from the wall that was, at that moment, exploding, I hear?"

He nodded. "The doc said she'd decided you were well enough to be told what happened. Yep, the commander's team had set up a containment field around the wormhole—"

"Wait, what?" I held up my hand, nearly upsetting my luncheon tray. "Wormhole?"

"Something like one anyway. At least, that's what the team has decided." A blush suffused his face. "Wow, those guys on the Esoteric Containment Squad are awesome, huh? I'm thinking of quitting the lacrosse team and trying out for it."

"Dangerous work," I said. "Have you discussed it with your father?"

"Not yet, but how can he turn me down? After all, grandpa Randolph got up to some pretty scary and dangerous things when he was a student here, so I guess I can follow in the family footsteps, you know?" Randy leaned forward, and the chair gave another squeak of dismay. "Would you . . . I mean, do you mind . . . could you put in a word for me to my dad, sir?"

I reached over and patted him on the shoulder. "It's the least I can do, dear boy, after saving my life, but I don't know if the word of a minor professor would carry much weight."

"Minor!" shouted a robust voice.

I looked to the door, filled nearly to its edges with the stocky figure of Commander Minerva Phillips. She strode to the bed—I am sure I merely imagined the floor shaking—and disclosed the fragile figure of Doctor Asenath behind her, dressed in regulation white lab coat with a stethoscope hanging from one pocket.

"I'd hardly call the new dean of students and president of Miskatonic University a minor professor," Minerva Phillips boomed.

Dr. Asenath winced. "Minnie, please! We do have some ill students down the hall."

"Sorry, sorry, Bridget." Minerva lowered her voice to a dull roar. "Anyway, I'm just here to congratulate Eldin on the promotion."

I was, to say the least, stunned. A thought struck me. "No one else wants it, I assume?"

"Dear boy, no such thing!" she said stoutly. "To be honest, no one else is available with your seniority. The recent, uh, loss of staff, you understand. So the job is yours if you want it."

"Cool!" said Randy Carter.

I felt I could not in all honesty disagree with the dear boy.

KG McAbee has had a bunch of books and nearly a hundred short stories published, some of them quite readable. She lives in a 200-year-old haunted log cabin in South Carolina, takes her geekdom seriously, loves dogs and iced tea, and believes the words "Stan Lee" are interchangeable with "The Almighty." She writes steampunk, fantasy, science fiction, horror, pulp, westerns, and the occasional comic. She's a member of Horror Writers Association, Sisters in Crime, The Heinlein Society, and International Thriller Writers and is an Artist in Residence-Literature with the South Carolina Arts Commission. She's won a Dream Realm award for fantasy, a Black Orchid Novella award for mystery, and an honorable mention from Writers of the Future for a steampunk/zombie mashup novella called *Undead Under London*. Feel free to drop her an email at kgmcabee@gmail.com or visit her website: www.kgmcabeebooks.com

Wyrd Science

Brenda Kezar

INSIDE THE YELLOW PLASTIC CAGE, A FEW OF THE MICE DRIFTED OFF TO sleep. Others rolled onto their backs and kicked their little legs frantically in the air. One snapped at the hunks of corncob bedding as if they were to blame. One slid bonelessly off the little plastic clubhouse inside and crumpled in a heap. The plastic walls fogged with their dying breaths, and the air filled with the tang of urine. As one gasped for air, it thrust its paw, pink and hand-like, against the side of the cage and glared at her accusingly.

Diane hated to watch them die. She glanced at the clock, the gas gauge, her own hands, and then at Joyce, her mentor. Joyce stared back at her, arms crossed, eyes narrowed, gauging her, judging her.

"Where did you work before?" Joyce asked.

"I was a stay-at-home mom of five, but my husband . . ." Diane paused, shook her head. "Now I'm learning to do the single mom thing." She would not go into the details with her new boss. Her finances were a mess. There would be no spousal support, no child support, and her husband was going to prison for a very long time. Good riddance, but it meant she and the kids were on their own. Not only was his income gone, but he'd also forged her name on accounts, and his creditors were coming after her.

Worse still, her daughter, Olivia, had been diagnosed with thalassemia and would need regular blood transfusions and lots of expensive medication. "Quite manageable," the doctors had reassured. Sure. Perfectly manageable as long as you have fantastic health insurance. She sighed. At least it wasn't cancer or leukemia, and at least the diagnosis had come after her Misk U benefits had kicked in.

The animal technician job at the medical school research division, with its amazing pay and incredible health benefits, was almost as good as winning the lottery.

As they wheeled the carcasses to the disposal room, she tried to change the subject. They passed a door with a pin-pad lock and a large, red-lettered warning sign: "Authorized Personnel Only, BSL Containment Area."

"When do I train for in there?" she asked, jerking her head toward the door as they passed.

"You don't." Joyce frowned. "Only senior people get clearance for BSL. Ruth worked there before she retired, and Margie had to move up and take her place."

Diane had assumed *she* was Ruth's replacement, but apparently, she was Margie's replacement. "Well, at least someone got a promotion out of the deal."

"Promotion?" Joyce smirked. "I guess you could call it that."

"What kind of research goes on in there? Is it scary stuff like smallpox?"

"What goes on in there is none of your business."

Diane frowned. "Don't I have a right to know, just in case?"

"In case of what?"

"I don't know. You see it in movies all the time. An Ebola monkey gets loose—"

Joyce laughed. "You don't have to worry about anything like that. And no, you don't have a right to know. The research is top secret, so no one can steal their ideas."

They disposed of the carcasses, washed up, and went to the break room for lunch. Two students, research assistants, wolfed their lunches in a hurry to get back to their experiments. Four animal technicians sat nearby. Diane remembered the blonde one's name, Jennifer, but couldn't remember the names of the other two. The fourth one she had never met before.

"I'm Diane." Diane smiled at the unknown tech. "The newbie."

The unknown tech gave her a quick, stiff smile. "I'm Tina." She turned back to the others.

"Nice to meet you, Tina," Diane's smile faded.

Tina ignored her. "So I started putting the order away, and I found three dead ones in the shipping container. I checked the purchase order, and each mouse cost two thousand dollars. Six thousand dollars' worth of mice, dead on arrival. Heads are going to roll."

Diane laughed and tried again. "Those must be some mice! For that price, they should be smart enough to do research on themselves!"

Tina scowled at her. "They're transgenic. They are genetically modified to be used as models for human disease." She turned back to the others and rolled her eyes. They talked in lower tones as they cleared their plates and left the break room.

"Friendly bunch." Diane shook her head.

Joyce unwrapped her sandwich and shrugged. "People come and go. No sense in getting attached." She peeked inside the sandwich and wrinkled her nose. "Damn. They put banana peppers on it again."

She noticed Diane watching her, waiting for her to continue, and sighed. "It's all the death. It burns people out. And working in BSL is even worse. It takes a special person to handle working here. Who knows if you're that person yet?"

After lunch, Diane retreated to the solitary quiet of her mouse colony room and pushed lunch out of her mind. She had more important things to worry about, like Olivia's diagnosis.

While she worried, she changed cages. Four cage racks filled the room, each one like a rack of clear post office boxes, seven cages wide by ten cages high, seventy cages per side. She removed a cage of five male mice from a slot and placed it on the stainless-steel top of the changing station. She removed the lid from the plastic, shoebox-like cage, picked one mouse up by the tail, and dropped it into the clean cage, still lost in her own thoughts. As she picked up the next mouse, one of the remaining mice jumped out of the dirty cage, onto the changing station.

She dropped the mouse she held into the clean cage and tried to catch the one scampering across the changing table. Meanwhile, the mouse she had just put into the clean cage coiled and launched itself out. It hit the changing station, paused, and jumped again, straight to the tile floor.

The mouse shook its head and scampered beneath the closest cage rack. Diane grabbed the mouse loose on the changing station, finished moving it and its siblings to the clean cage, and replaced the lid to make sure none of them escaped while she went after their brother.

She tore the room apart. She looked under the cage racks, under the changing station, even under the step stool. After half an hour of crawling around on the floor, she sat back on her heels perplexed. "Where the hell did it go? It didn't just vanish into thin air!"

As if in response, the mouse crawled out of the wheel housing of a cage rack and darted beneath the door leading into the anteroom.

She leapt to her feet and threw open the door as the mouse ran through the anteroom and straight under the outer door into the main hallway.

Diane gasped, threw the door to the hallway open, and glanced both ways. Fortunately, no one was around. The mouse bypassed the doors to the other colony rooms and continued its half-hopping run down the hallway. She grabbed a cage and lid and rushed after it. The door slammed behind her, causing the mouse to veer and duck beneath the nearest door.

Stenciled in block lettering on the door were the words "To Docks." She opened the door and walked into a small room with two additional doors: one labelled "Shipping," the other "Receiving." On the floor halfway between lay a single mouse turd. She paused and chewed her lip, unsure what to do. A narrow plastic bin, like a magazine holder, hung on the wall next to the shipping door. The paperwork inside was stamped "BSL 4."

No way was she going in there. On the other hand, she would lose her job for sure if she had to admit she not only lost a mouse but had also let it roam the facility and possibly contaminate a shipment prepared to go out. No job, no insurance.

If they were shipping animals out, it had to be secure. The shipping company personnel couldn't be exposed to BSL 4. Besides, there was nothing on the door that said "Warning, Biohazard." If it was dangerous to go in there, they would either have warning signs or the door would be locked.

She reached out, and the knob turned easily in her hand. She pushed the door open, and a bright rectangle of light fell into a dimly lit room filled with several two-foot by two-foot wooden crates. Her mouse sat frozen in the beam of light. She smiled in relief and rushed in, cage at the ready.

The door slammed behind her, plunging the room into semi-darkness. It took a moment for her eyes to adjust. She wrinkled her nose. The room reeked of damp earth and decay, like a rotting swamp.

The slamming door prompted no movement from the mouse. It huddled in the same spot as when she first spotted it, its eyes bugging and shining in the low light. She frowned. Was it still alive, or had the strain of the chase and the noise caused it to die of shock? She took a step forward but paused. Something rustled in one of the crates, and a scraping noise, like claws dragged slowly across concrete, filled the room.

From among the shadowy boxes, a rope uncoiled across the floor. No, not a rope, a . . . tentacle? A few inches from the petrified mouse, the tentacle stopped. The mouse trembled but made no effort to run away. The tip of the tentacle lifted, like a snake testing the air, and darted forward. It coiled around the mouse and snatched it into the darkness of the crates. The air filled with moaning, and the crates shook as if the occupants of the other crates were protesting their brother's forbidden snack. The swamp smell grew overpowering.

She fumbled for the doorknob. The moaning ceased, and the scraping resumed, only now it was *many* claws dragging across concrete. She twisted the knob: left, right, left, not daring to look over her shoulder. The door opened, and she dove into the hall. Just before the door slammed shut, she glimpsed seven tentacles exploring the space where she had just stood.

She sat in the industrial-green bathroom stall, her head in her hands. She wanted to run away, to never see this strange place again, but the pay, the benefits. She knew people who would sell their souls for the benefits this job offered. How could she walk away?

What the hell were they researching anyway? Aliens? Creatures from another dimension? She wanted to ask Joyce, but she didn't dare. Joyce would want to know what she was doing back there where she did not belong.

What was she going to do? She had been out of the job market so long; the only other job offer she had gotten was from a local shoe store, offering minimal benefits and pay so lousy she would barely be able to afford the house payment. She would have to get a second job. With the university job, she was home by five every day and could have dinner with the kids. And the medical coverage!

She straightened and steeled herself. She would tough it out and avoid the damn loading docks, and she wouldn't have to worry about taking care of whatever was in the BSL for a few years at least. Not that she *ever* wanted to take care of it, but she would cross that bridge when she came to it. She had to worry about the here and now, and this job was crucial for making the here and now work. At least whatever was in those crates had solved the problem of the roaming mouse.

She stepped out of the stall, grabbed a paper towel, and washed her face. She leaned against the counter and faced herself in the mirror. "You can do this," she said to her reflection. "The kids are depending on you."

She forced a smile and went back to work.

The next day, while working in her colony room, the fire alarm lights on the walls began to flash. Reminding herself to stay calm, she closed the mouse cage she had been working with and returned it to the bank of cages in the rack. She opened the door to the anteroom, but a scream in the hall froze her in her tracks.

Heart pounding, she put her face to the small window in the door and peered into the hallway. The screaming stopped and was replaced by a clicking-clattering noise. She couldn't see anything because her panting fogged the window, so she opened the door a crack and peered out.

The body of an animal tech lay face down on the floor, propping the BSL door open. Several small, red creatures sat on her back. The creatures looked like prawns with giant crab claws they were using to pick at and eat from a wound on the tech's back.

Stunned, Diane stepped into the hall and walked toward the BSL. As she drew closer, she saw the small prawns hadn't brought the animal tech down. A spider-like thing clung to the tech's face, and its long, multi-jointed legs reached around the woman's head in a murderous hug.

Prawns wandered, exploring the hall. One of the closer ones spotted Diane, threw its giant crab claws into the air, and ran toward her. Reflexively, she stomped it. It crunched beneath her foot and left a wad of sticky, snot-like goo on the bottom of her shoe. The crunch caused half a dozen others to stop and look her direction.

At that moment, Joyce popped her head out of the nearest room.

"Shit." She ran down the hall toward Diane and the fallen tech. The prawns tried to meet her. Joyce rushed past most of them but accidentally stepped on one and slid, banana-peel style, for a few feet.

Diane almost laughed and stuffed her fist in her mouth to prevent it. While Joyce dropped to her knees to check on the downed tech, Diane stomped more of the prawns. “What the hell are these things?”

Joyce shook her head. “They are just food for some of the research animals.”

Diane’s stomach lurched. Food? Food for something bigger, meaner?

Joyce grabbed the downed tech’s arms and dragged her out of the way, and the BSL door swung shut with a clang. She pulled her phone out of her pocket and dialed five numbers, a campus number. There was only a moment’s pause. “Yes. 6685, Joyce Neumburger. Yes. Yes. Tango Delta. Yes. One known. Yes. Received.” She disconnected and dropped the phone back in her pocket.

“Cleanup and Containment are on their way, but we’ve got to split up and make sure nothing else is out here. Vivian was the only one in BSL today.”

“Nothing else?” Diane startled herself with the shrillness of her voice. “What else could be out here?”

“There’s nothing in there that has opposable thumbs, so the colony rooms should be okay. We need to check the halls and the cage wash rooms.” She pointed down the farthest hall. “You go that way, I’ll go this way, and we’ll meet in the middle.”

The main part of the facility consisted of a hallway that made a square. Along the square were doors to colony rooms. In lieu of a colony door, on the southeast corner was the BSL section door where they were standing. The northeast corner of the square was a door that led to the dirty-cage wash room where the dirty cages and equipment ended up before washing. The northwest corner of the square was a door that led to the clean-cage room where the clean equipment waited for use after being washed and sanitized. While the colony room doors had standard doorknobs, the doors to the cage-washing rooms were automatic to accommodate cartloads of equipment.

Joyce headed down the hall toward the dirty-cage wash room while Diane approached the corner of the far hall, leading to the clean-cage room. As she neared the corner, she imitated the cop shows she habitually watched and pressed herself to the inside wall. She popped her head quickly around the corner and drew it back. Although it looked good on television, it didn’t do a thing for her. All she had seen was a blurred glimpse of the hallway.

Slowly, she peered around the corner again, an inch at a time. The hallway appeared empty. She stepped around the corner and stopped, listening. On the far side of the hallway, she heard the automatic doors whoosh open. Joyce was already into the dirty room. Or she *hoped* it was Joyce that had triggered the door.

She slinked down the hall, scanning every section of the pale-green, cinder-block walls, every bit of speckled, industrial tile flooring, every inch of ceiling. To her relief, nothing seemed out of the ordinary.

She stopped just before the "auto-open zone" of the clean-cage room doors and tried to look through the glass windows set in the big stainless-steel doors, but she couldn't see much besides the rows of clean carts stored inside. She took a deep breath and stepped forward.

The doors to the clean side whooshed open, and she stood, waiting. The cage wash staff and work-study students had gone to lunch. Nothing moved inside the room.

The cage washers sat idle. They were big enough to drive a Mini Cooper inside and had sliding doors on both the dirty and the clean sides for loading and unloading. The doors on the clean side stood open.

She crossed to the cage washers and the little door in-between which led to the dirty side. Through the window in the door, she could see Joyce crouching, checking under the carts loaded with dirty cages. She realized she should do the same with the clean carts.

She turned and froze. Hiding beneath the water-bottle-filling machine sat a squid-like thing the size of a chubby cat with thin, jellyfish-like tentacles. She couldn't tell the length of the tentacles because they were stuffed into the drain. Since it was the clean side, the drain led to the city sewer system. Her heart sank as she realized what the creature was doing: its tentacles were down the drain because it was trying to escape.

She glanced around. She had no weapons. The closest things were a rag mop and bucket, a water hose, and a squeegee. She grabbed the mop and shoved it beneath the machine. The creature reared up, hissed, and waved its tentacles at her. She jabbed at the creature, and it knocked the mop head aside. She swung it back, smacking the squid. It screamed, wrapped its tentacles around the mop, and tried to yank it out of her hands. She hung on, and they played tug of war, pushing and pulling until the thing was no longer beneath the machine. The creature stopped trying to reach her and started thrashing and squealing. She thought it was reacting to the light, but she realized it had gotten its tentacles tangled in the cotton strands of the mop and was trying frantically to get loose.

Inspiration struck. She lifted the creature from the floor and carried it, mop and all, into the open cage washer. While it was busy trying to disentangle itself, she let go of the mop, stepped back, and hit the close button on the cage washer. The doors rattled shut.

She reached out to start the two-hundred-eighty-degree wash water but paused with her hand over the button. She thought back to her escaped mouse and to Tina's two-thousand-dollar mice. The thing was obviously a research animal. If she hit the button and the hot water killed it, she might destroy someone's research. It was contained and couldn't hurt anyone. Let the professionals decide what to do with it.

Responding to the noise of the thrashing creature caught in the cage washer, Joyce rushed through the connecting door between the rooms. "What is it?"

"I don't have a damn clue. It looks like a squid."

Joyce scowled. "I need more than that."

Diane recoiled. *How many kinds of tentacled-things were there in the facility?* "Like a cat-sized squid with man-o'-war tentacles."

Joyce's jaw dropped. "And you trapped it in there?" She licked her lips and eyed Diane with concern. "Did it touch you?"

"No. Why?" Diane asked, fear rising again.

Joyce smiled, maybe the first real smile Diane had seen. "Damn. Pretty impressive."

At that moment, the room doors whooshed open, and a crew of three people in full biohazard gear stepped through.

"The threat in this section has been contained," Joyce said. "BSL still needs to be cleared."

The lead biohazard person nodded and stepped back out. He waved his hand, and the half-dozen soldiers waiting in the hallway disappeared down the hall. The biohazard people moved to the cage washer while Joyce led Diane to the break room.

"What the hell was that thing?" Diane asked. "And what about the thing that killed the animal tech? It looked like something from those Alien movies!"

"The squid's real name is a series of unpronounceable characters from another language. We just call it a dwarf stinger." Joyce crossed her arms. "As for the hugger, where do you think they got the idea for the movies? Didn't you ever think it was odd how many actors, directors, and musicians have degrees in particle physics or quantum mechanics? A lot of Misk U alumni live and work in Hollywood!"

"How is this all secret?" Diane shook her head. "Doesn't the government regulate this?

"Most of it is *for* the government," Joyce snorted. "The biggest hurdle for research is usually funding. We don't have that problem here. Between the government and our star-level alumni supporting their alma mater, this is the most well-funded university on the planet."

A man in a black suit stepped into the break room. "Agent Conroy wants to see you both in the conference room immediately."

Agent Conroy talked privately with Joyce first and then sent her back to work and called Diane into the conference room for the "incident debriefing." Conroy was a sour-faced, scowling man with ruddy skin.

He started before she even sat down. "When you were hired, you signed a non-disclosure agreement. That agreement still applies after you leave. As you can imagine, the consequences of violating it by telling anyone what you've seen while employed here are quite serious." He paused as if giving her a moment to understand the gravity of his words. It wasn't necessary. After what she had been told about the government backing the bizarre research, she knew that if she opened her mouth, she might be made to disappear.

As if reading her mind, he continued, "The government would consider it treason, so we expect you to honor the agreement. Now," he tapped a folder on his desk, "we do allow you to use Miskatonic as an employment reference if you wish, but you cannot discuss the research or animals kept here beyond the standard research mice. Any questions?"

"Yes," her heart sank. "But after all I've just been through, why am I being fired?"

He scowled. His eyebrows shot up, and his face softened. He frowned again. "Aren't . . . you . . . quitting?"

"I'm responsible for raising five kids on my own and drowning in debt. You think a couple of monsters are going to scare me away from financial security? You know what's really scary? Not having health insurance," she snorted. "Get the bill for a couple of blood transfusions or an MRI, and you'll know fear." Her hands were shaking, but she kept them in her lap.

A light came into his eyes, and a smile played at the corner of his lips.

"Interesting. You want to continue your employment. In that case, I have to give you kudos for your quick response to the crisis. Most people would have crumbled, but instead, you showed real ingenuity, bravery, and . . . promise. You neutralized the danger while preserving irreplaceable research stock."

Diane wasn't sure she liked where this was going.

"And since you're eager to stay, I have a proposition. As you know, there's now an opening in BSL—"

"No thanks," Diane interrupted.

"Let me finish. We will start slow. One day a week in BSL. And those hours will be at the standard starting wage for BSL of course."

Diane leaned forward. "Standard starting wage?"

Conroy tented his fingers like he knew he had her. "A hundred dollars an hour."

Diane collapsed back into her chair. Eight hundred dollars in a single day. After two days of BSL, she could pay her mortgage every month. The other two days every month would pay their utilities and the hospital co-pays. Her regular pay workdays could go toward paying off the debt that scumbag Jimmy had saddled them with. Things *could* be okay after all. It was a dangerous job, sure, but lots of people worked dangerous jobs: cops, firefighters, soldiers, crab fisherman. Hers was just dangerous in an unusual way.

She smiled queasily. "When do I start?"

"Pending background check and psychological exams." He stood and held out his hand, "Welcome to Security Clearance Alpha at Misk U."

§

Brenda Kezar is a horror and fantasy writer from the dark tundra of North Dakota. She is a proud member of the Horror Writers Association and a past participant in HWA Fright Club (but she can't talk about that). Her short stories have appeared in *Daily Science Fiction*, *Silverthought*, *Bonded by Blood V*, *Penumbra eMag*, *Zombidays: Festivities of the Flesheaters*, and others. To read more, visit: www.BrendaKezar.com

Something Beautiful

Nate Southard

ONE WEEK BEFORE SHE ESCAPED, REGGIE SAW THE FIRST OF THEM STANDING in the west quad. At the time, she didn't realize what it meant. He was just a kid, maybe eighteen or nineteen. Almost certainly a freshman. A T-shirt from some band she didn't recognize, jeans that sagged off his hips. Sideburns that said he was experimenting with facial hair in lieu of a personality.

He stood in the grass a few feet from the sidewalk, back straight and shoulders up. Perfectly still. His posture caught her attention first. Had she ever seen anyone stand like that? Maybe once. There had been a party her first year at Miskatonic, a couple hundred kids in a basement just off campus. She'd scarfed down a handful of mushrooms with some of her girlfriends. An hour later, she'd walked through the crowd, as everyone changed colors, to find Barb facing the wall, back so straight it looked like someone had inserted a metal rod in her spine.

"Barb?" she'd asked. "You okay?"

And her friend had smiled. "It's a whole other world. It's so beautiful."

The mushrooms had been pretty damn good.

For a moment, she thought the kid standing on the west quad was having a similar experience. She stepped closer. She was already preparing advice, something about telling the boy to hang on, ride it out, and maybe don't try hallucinogenics before noon on a Wednesday. His face stopped her though. Instead of a look of wonder or interest or even panic, he wore no expression at all. She searched for any trace of feeling, any kind of reaction, but he gave her nothing. For a second, she wondered if he was real. Maybe the art students had set up one of their projects again. If that was the case, they'd really upped their skills.

"Hey, there," she said. "You all right?"

The boy gave no reaction. His eyes didn't track, and his lips didn't twitch. Had he even blinked? She put a hand on his shoulder, thinking she'd feel like a real idiot when she touched hard plastic, but the touch confirmed he was real.

Her nerves tingled a little, the first moment when concern began smoldering within her. She considered the canister of pepper spray on her key ring and dismissed it. Plenty of folks in the quad. If the guy tried to start something, it would get squashed almost immediately. "C'mon. Talk to me. You in there?" Waving her hand in front of his face garnered no reaction.

She took a step in front of him but jumped back when something crunched under her shoe. His glasses now cracked and pressed into the quad.

"Crap. Sorry, guy." Her gaze rose to his face again. "You're really starting to creep me out, okay? Wake up."

Still he refused to move. Only the closest examination showed his chest expanding and contracting.

Reggie shook her head. "Whatever, guy. Ride it out. Get your crap together."

She started to walk away, but a sound stopped her. At first, she couldn't recognize it. Something forceful yet muffled, like a pitcher of water slowly poured on the ground. The scent reached her nose a second later, and she looked down to see the wet stain spreading in the crotch of his jeans before trailing down one leg of his pants.

"Jesus, guy!" She turned and left, walking at a determined pace before the kid either revealed his joke or collapsed to the quad.

"Dude was probably research science. Those guys are all nut jobs. Or drama. Performance art or something."

Alex pulled a takeout container from the bag and placed it in front of her. He licked soy sauce from his finger as she opened the lid and let the smell of pork and vegetables waft up her nose. A lot better than the last smell she remembered.

"You really think he was a drama major?" Reggie asked.

"Sure. Maybe the department got tired of putting on plays they have to advertise by saying everyone who's ever seen it went crazy."

She shuddered. "Not cool."

"But pretty funny. Remember a few years back? That one cast had nervous breakdowns during rehearsals."

"They were doing *Rent*."

"Sure. Crazy *Rent*."

Reggie shoveled a forkful of kung pao into her mouth. It tasted slightly metallic, same as all the other food in the area. At first, she'd thought it had something to do with the water, but it applied to everything. Candy bars, potato chips, breath mints: it didn't matter. After a few semesters, she'd grown used to it. "Whatever his deal was, the guy was there when I left class an hour later. No one was even paying attention to him."

"He should thank you then. At least he had an audience for a minute."

"If he knew I was there, they should cast that guy in every play for the rest of time. He didn't even seem to notice me."

"Probably a good thing."

"Yeah?"

"Sure," Alex said. "The alternative is that he set the whole thing up, so he could trick a woman into watching him piss himself. I mean, people got fetishes."

"Gross."

"Agreed. Just sayin'."

"I wish you hadn't."

"Me too. Kinda."

"I just . . . I hope this isn't the start of some . . . thing."

Alex smiled. "A thing?"

"You know. Like a bunch of idealists start protesting over something, whatever this week's cause is, and it ends up in a riot from one end of campus to the other."

"That's progressive of you."

"I have midterms next week. Progressive will need to wait. Let me do okay in Applied Physics, and maybe we'll see. I'll throw down for a vegan or whatever. I have . . . principles."

"Sure you do, sweetie."

Reggie tried to frown but failed to keep the smile from cracking her expression. She pushed more food into her mouth and concentrated on chewing.

"It'll be fine," Alex said. "Just take care of you, okay?"

"Yep," she said. "That's what I do."

The next morning, Reggie felt her nerves tingle as she stepped onto campus. For a while, she kept her eyes on the sidewalk. Only when she chastised herself for being ridiculous, swore up and down there was nothing to fear, did she lift her head and start looking where she was going. She scolded herself again when she considered taking a different route to the physics building, one that would take her past the west quad.

"He won't be there," she said. "Nope. Totally won't."

Still, she held her breath as she rounded the astronomy building. Her gaze tracked downward, and she had to force it otherwise.

He wasn't there. The spot he'd occupied the day before sat empty, just a patch of grass between two ancient trees. Reggie felt her breath ease past her lips, and her next inhalation tasted a little sweeter. Good. Either the kid's acid had worn off or he'd decided his performance was over. Maybe Alex had been right, and he'd just wanted a chance to wet himself in front of someone. She resented the fact it had been her, but at least he wasn't back for an encore.

Reggie made it halfway down the quad and had almost completely disregarded the strange freshman and his statue routine when she saw the two girls. They stood in the middle of the lawn, almost shoulder to shoulder. Neither moved. Reggie slowed to a stop, and something cold filled her.

"No way."

She wanted to shake it off, ignore it and continue along her way. It wasn't her concern. If it was the drama department trying to stir up a buzz, she was too smart to fall for it. Even as she stepped off the sidewalk and started toward the pair, she kept thinking she didn't care. She kept repeating the lie in her mind until she stepped in front of the two girls, gave them a disapproving glare, and spoke.

"Seriously, what the hell is this?"

They remained silent. As far as Reggie could tell, neither knew she was there. She looked closer, examining their pupils. They didn't look pinned or excessively dilated, so maybe they weren't jacked up on some strange mushroom or designer drug. Somehow that made things worse. A sudden anger flared within her. They were screwing with her, with everyone. What other explanation was there? The idea that someone would find a stunt like this worthwhile—hell, they probably thought it was *hilarious*—made her want to slap the girls one after the other. She'd make them pay attention to her, and then she'd tell them to stop acting like such goddamn children.

"Look, maybe you think this is cute, but it's really just annoying. Got it? Maybe consider pulling your heads out of your—"

Their eyes didn't move to meet hers. Something about their faces looked off, and it took Reggie a second to tell they were both crying, tears tracing down their cheeks to their chins.

"Shit. Hey. You okay? What's wrong? Sorry, I didn't . . . what's wrong?"

One of the girls trembled. She was all freckles and pale skin, hair full of curls so tight they were almost kinks. Her hands jerked into fists, shaking at her sides, and her lips parted into a smile. They moved again, and Reggie thought she heard words. Faint, almost a simple breath, but she'd heard them.

"It's so pretty."

"What is?"

But the girl didn't say anything. Instead, she reached out a hand and took hold of her friend's. Their fingers laced, and they squeezed hard enough to pop their knuckles white. Reggie thought she heard the grinding of bones and joints.

The other girl spoke, her voice all but overcome with emotion. "It is. The most beautiful thing I've ever seen."

Reggie looked over her shoulder before she could stop herself. Behind her, one of the many buildings on campus she'd never entered loomed. It was old, a structure of carved and arching pale stone. The windows, set behind iron bars, were panes of black that reflected the trees and quad. She'd always assumed the building housed offices, professors and teaching assistants toiling away at their various tasks.

She turned to the girls again. "Seriously, are you two on something? I'm not judging, but be careful, okay?

Neither girl registered her presence. The one on the right, all blond bangs, reached out with her free hand. No, she reached up as if trying to catch an incoming baseball. Her friend threw both arms around her and hugged her tight. Through it all, their gaze stayed locked on the building. Or something beyond it.

"It's coming," the pale girl said. "It's coming this way."

"It is. Oh, God."

Their smiles grew; tears sluiced from their eyes. Reggie felt cold again. Freezing. An electric sensation raced up her neck. The first sign of panic, of fear turning into something like terror.

Reggie stepped around the embracing pair and hurried across the quad. She refused to look back.

As she tried to settle into her favorite spot in the lecture hall—to the right and a little less than halfway back—Reggie still felt distracted. The questions refused to slow. Around her, students set up their laptops while she pulled a notebook and pen from her backpack. Not for the first time, she reminded herself to find a new battery for her computer, one to replace the garbage that wouldn't make it through a single lecture.

"How are we doing today?" Professor Barrow said as he stepped to the front of the class, set down his briefcase, and pulled out a small sheaf of papers. "Is it a glorious Wednesday or what?

The hall responded with a few polite chuckles. Someone in the back shouted, "I'm hungover!"

"That makes two of us," Barrow said. The chuckles broke into a second of genuine laughter. He retrieved a few clear plastic sheets and set the first one on the overhead projector. "All right. This is our last session before the midterm, so let's get to the sexy bits."

Reggie put pen to paper and started copying the first lecture sheet. She kept an ear tuned to the professor and looked up occasionally. It helped that Professor Barrow didn't drone. His voice rose and fell, took sharp turns. He spoke with the emotion of someone who had never lost interest in their chosen field, who hadn't been broken on the wheel of academia and its politics. He remained enthusiastic, passionate, and she respected him for it. A few minutes passed, and she felt the dread slough away. She was a student again, and she was learning, and that made everything all right.

Perhaps ten minutes into the lecture, she looked up at something that snagged her attention. A student in the first row leaned toward his screen. Something about his posture looked off, and she quickly realized he was staring as though something was wrong. As she watched, he bunched his sleeve around the heel of his hand and wiped at the display. Again, he leaned in, and from her angle, Reggie could see him squint.

Things started clicking into place. Her mind tried to sort directions and then discard them. That electric sensation returned, making her squirm in her seat. She shook her head without realizing it, the word *no* repeating in her brain like a skipping record. *No, no, no, no, no . . .*

The student in the front row turned and looked over his shoulder, toward the back of the lecture hall. Reggie spent an instant praying he'd turn back around, but he threw an arm over the back of his chair, and his face went slack. Even from a distance, she could see the sense of wonder fill his eyes.

"Mr. Cannon?" the professor said. The student didn't turn. "I'm over here, Mr. Cannon. Do you need me to show a little leg?"

The class laughed, but Reggie saw a few of them turn to see what had stolen the man's attention. She started to turn as well, but the electric panic in her body froze her.

Cannon stood, climbing from his chair and letting his hands fall to his sides. His laptop clattered to the floor, the cracking of plastic like a gunshot in the echoing hall. His eyes never left the back wall. Slowly, he leaned forward and craned his neck, looking like a masthead. His mouth spread into an awed grin.

Reggie watched, covering her mouth with one hand to keep a scream in place. Three other students had started staring, and one of them was already out of her seat, standing on it as though it might give her a better view.

Several others searched for whatever the quartet saw, and others simply watched, no doubt wondering what in hell was wrong with them. An uncomfortable, buzzing murmur filled the hall. When Reggie closed her eyes, it surged in volume. She imagined she could feel it crawling along her skin, a fear that skittered around in search of a soft opening. Shaking her head, she fought to will it all away. She found herself on the edge of panic, her toes wriggling over the precipice, and it took all her willpower to keep from stepping. Giving in would be so easy, but she fought to remain calm.

The sound died down. Reggie opened her eyes again, and what she saw threatened to shove her over the edge into full-blown terror. Nearly a dozen students now stared at the room's rear wall. One of them, a man, moaned in a way that sounded either blissful or horrified. A woman fell to her knees, reaching out with both hands as sobs racked her body.

Professor Barrow tried to rein in the class. Reggie knew he was saying something, gesturing with purpose, but she couldn't make it out. The rush of blood to her skull filled her ears with static.

Her breath coming faster and faster, Reggie shoved her notebook into her backpack. If more people started staring at whatever the hell it was, she wasn't going to wait around to watch them. She didn't want to be a spectator to the world going insane. Climbing from her seat, she refused to give in to the fear that energized her. When she wanted to shove aside the man standing at the end of her row of seats, she instead stepped around him as delicately as she could. Once she reached the aisle and stairs, she climbed steadily, not running. Eyes down. No way in hell was she going to look up.

Behind her, the professor shouted something about class not being over, but she failed to make herself believe him. Instead, as she threw open the door and escaped the hall, she wondered if there was a reason to attend the midterm.

"I want to go see," Alex said.

The words stunned Reggie. She looked up from the textbook she'd been trying to convince herself she needed to read. For several seconds, she replayed what Alex had said, trying to decide if he'd really meant it. How could he?

"You're not serious."

"I'm serious."

"You're not."

"Come on!" He left the kitchen, a beer in each hand, and sat down beside her. "How many times do you get to see mass hysteria up close and personal?"

She took the beer. The cold booze helped tamp down the annoyance she felt rise within her. "I've seen it once. Believe me, it was enough."

"But I haven't gotten to see it at all. I was on campus today. I didn't see so much as a protestor."

"Did you go by the west quad? There were two girls there."

"Yeah, I did. Nothing. Nada. Bupkus and other words that mean zero. It was just a quad. Grass and trees and a circle of patchouli kids with dreads and a hacky sack. The place was so stereotypical college I almost cried."

"Good," Reggie said. "Stereotypical is good. Boring is good. I've had more excitement today than I want to experience for a few more semesters at least."

He collapsed backward, all but lying down on the sofa, and sipped. "Look, your midterm is Friday. You have two days to get ready for it, and besides, you know you're going to ace the damn thing. When are you going to encounter something like this again?"

"Around here? Probably next week."

"Exactly! We hear all these stories about Miskatonic, like it's this place where things go wacky every other day. Buildings get closed, faculty disappear—"

"The historical library goes missing."

"The historical library goes missing! One day it's there, and the next day it's a hole in the ground, right? We hear that kind of thing all the time, and we tell ourselves we come here because we have scholarships and because it's got the best faculty and facilities in the world, but we know the truth: we came here because we wanted to see if all the stories and rumors are true. I know it, and you know it.

"But guess what? We've been here for years, and nothing cool's happened. The drama department went wacky once, but that was after they got hold of some bad Molly. The new library hasn't grown legs and walked away, and every professor we've had has stayed right there at the front of the class through every semester. This place is . . . it's supposed to be a hundred different shades of freaky, but it's just boring. I'm bored. We're sitting here sipping beers and studying, and it's only eight o'clock. Jesus, we're young! Why are we using our butts to hold down the couch?"

For a long moment, she watched Alex, lips in a firm line and one eyebrow arched.

"I'm sensing disagreement," he said.

"So why don't we go out dancing? Or hit a bar? Why do you want to go to campus to look for weird shit?"

"Because it's weird shit. That's the beginning, middle, and end of what I'm saying. Isn't any part of you curious?"

"No. A tiny part of me doesn't care. The rest is frightened."

"So we go to campus, look around, and prove to ourselves that nothing's wrong."

"Alex, something is very, very wrong."

"Don't you want to know what?"

"*No!* Why do you think I want to know? This isn't rewriting physics or biology. This isn't some discovery that's going to fix the world. Whatever is happening on campus is weird, and it's scary, and no, I don't want to know what it is!"

Alex leaned forward, elbows on his knees, and stared at the mouth of his beer bottle. His lips twisted into a thoughtful knot. "Maybe it's all of those things," he said.

"What?"

"Sure, why not? Miskatonic, right? Yeah, maybe whatever it is, is scary. But maybe it's also important. Maybe it is a thing that can change the world. We don't know, but . . . I mean, you know where we are. It totally could be."

Reggie felt her teeth grinding as she inspected the idea, turning it around in her head and examining its contours, the shape and dimensions. The possibilities.

"Dammit," she said and set down her beer.

"What direction has everyone been looking?" Alex asked.

Sitting in the car's passenger seat, Reggie sorted the directions in her brain before pointing at an angle to the right. "That way," she said. "Don't look in that direction."

"Seriously?"

"Yeah, I'm super serious. Super-duper."

"Okay then. You ready?"

"Ready is relative. I don't know. I guess."

"Here we go." Alex opened his door and all but bounced out from behind the wheel. Reggie watched him skip around the car's hood and felt a stab of annoyance between the nerves and dread.

"You coming?" he asked.

She stepped free of the car. Alex was looking around, all but hopping in place.

"Could you maybe not look so excited?" she asked

"But I am excited."

"Maybe, like, don't act like it?"

"Come on. We're investigating a strange phenomenon. That's pretty cool, right?"

"It doesn't feel cool."

"Now see, that's just—"

Alex froze, looking at something over her shoulder, and she felt a sudden riot of terror. She clamped both hands down on his arms, gave him a quick, harsh shake.

"Hey? Hey!"

"What?"

Relief washed over her, quick and all-encompassing. "Jesus, Alex. I thought I'd lost you there. What is it?"

He answered by pointing in the direction he'd been looking.

Reggie turned. There was an adult, easily in her forties, and her clothes marked her as a professor. A satchel hung across her body, but her hands were iron fists at her sides. Slowly, she rocked forward and back. Her mouth worked soundlessly, but Reggie suspected she'd hear words if she got close enough. *It's beautiful,* maybe.

"You weren't lying," Alex said.

"Not even a little."

He stepped closer, bent as though he were taking in a museum piece. "This is nuts. I don't think she even realizes we're here."

"She doesn't."

"But why? What's so incredible that you forget everything else?"

Reggie rolled her eyes. How many times had she wondered that over the last few days? "I don't know. Pretty sure I don't want to know."

Alex circled her. She watched as he waved his eyes in front of the woman's face, clapped. He snapped his fingers next to her ears. When he'd either finished or grown bored, he sat on the sidewalk in front of her, legs folded beneath him, covering his mouth with a hand.

"This is . . . it doesn't make any sense. Like none."

"Excellent hypothesis, doctor."

"Oh, quiet. I mean, look at her. This is kind of amazing, right?"

"Sure, but mostly scary."

"Scary things can be amazing."

"If you say so."

He unfolded and popped to his feet. Quickly, he turned in a circle, searching the immediate area. "Let's head to the quad."

Alex started down the sidewalk, but Reggie couldn't make her legs work. When he turned around to look at her, amusement lit up his face. "Come on," he said, and she could hear the notes of his voice. They told her he was having fun, that she was bringing him down. Her annoyance shifted into anger, but fear still held court.

She found her keys and slipped the canister of pepper spray into her fist. What help it would be, she had no clue, but it made her feel a little better as she followed Alex.

A stone wall separated the walk from the quad, the sidewalk sloping upward until it leveled off, and the quad welcomed pedestrians to campus. As they climbed, Reggie concentrated on her breathing, kept telling herself things would be fine or at least that she'd be prepared. One or two, maybe half a dozen, but that was it. Thinking that kept words like *outbreak* and *epidemic* from her mind. Anything else was manageable. Anything else, with enough mental contortions, she could explain.

The quad came into view, and she felt dizzy. The world dipped and spun. The ground tilted beneath her, and she grabbed the top of the wall, now waist high.

Dozens. She tried to count and almost immediately lost track, but easily three dozen people stood in the quad. They occupied the grass and the sidewalk. One stood halfway down the steps that fronted the Hammond Building. They remained frozen, staring into the distance. Some stood with hands at their sides. Others reached out. Some swayed, their mouths opening and closing. The man who stood closest to her, no more than ten feet away, wept openly, sobs racking his body. He looked as though he was caught in a religious fervor, gazing upon . . . something. Reggie killed the question before she could consider it further. Questions wanted answers, and if the answers didn't simply appear, she might go looking for them. Looking was the last thing she wanted to do.

Alex all but ran into the crowd. He turned every which way at once, a ridiculous grin on his face, one of both amazement and curiosity. As Reggie watched, he flung his arms wide.

"Will you look at this? Dammit, will you look at this?"

"I see it."

He practically skipped from one frozen person to the next. He leaned in close to a woman barely into her twenties. "Hey! I'm right here!" he said. She gave no response, but her lips quivered. Either love or horror filled her eyes. Reggie couldn't tell which.

"Don't be a jerk," she said, but Alex had started tickling the girl's nose. Reggie hurried over to slap away his hand.

"What?"

"Asshat."

"I'm just—"

"I know. Try to be something other than a complete tool, okay? You're not exactly being scientific."

He looked hurt, insulted. "How can . . . what causes this? And look at it! There aren't any cops here, no EMTs. This is . . . it's being ignored, right? Why? We can't be the only people who have noticed this. Sure, maybe a few days ago, but now? Now this is big. You can't just ignore this, but that's exactly what they're doing. It's . . . doesn't it confirm everything? All the stories and stuff, they're true. This place is insane, and somebody knows it."

Alex put his nose to the woman's cheek, shook his head. "My God, all of it's true."

Reggie began to protest, but her teeth clacked shut before she could utter a syllable. Maybe it wasn't all true, but some of it had to be. She stood in the center of several dozen people who refused to move, who stared into the distance at something she couldn't see. All of them staring at the *same* thing. And then there was the rest of it. Standing in the still quad, she could hear the murmurs, the gasps. The shuddering breaths as they watched in awe. She smelled their sweat and the ammonia of their urine. A rougher smell from something else. Reggie didn't want to think about it, but she couldn't ignore it.

She spent a moment looking at the grass and trees, thinking about how, a few days earlier, that had been the quad. When it hadn't filled her with dread every time she walked nearby. Just grass and trees, that was all. That was gone now. The simple luxury of the mundane had disappeared.

"Can we go?" she asked. The time to leave had come and gone.

When Alex didn't answer, she looked up to make sure he'd heard. It happened so fast she didn't have time to feel fear, time for dread to fill her like ice water into a pitcher. She called out, received silence in response, and looked up to find Alex staring into the distance. Reggie whimpered. She ground her teeth as the whimper started melting into a screech.

She grabbed his shoulders and shook him. His head banged back and forth, whipping with his neck, but his eyes didn't close. He didn't blink or make a sound or even acknowledge her existence. As soon as his head fell still, he resumed staring at nothing. At something.

"Alex!" She cracked a hand across his cheek, but it didn't do anything. More shaking brought her the same result. She kept saying his name, her voice breaking as her shouts became screams. Alex only stared, something so thoroughly amazing him that it had rendered the rest of the world static.

Reggie backed away, looking at her friend through a blur of tears, and she remembered the pepper spray. She primed the trigger, praying it might work but finding her thoughts a scrambled mess. Holding her breath, she aimed the canister and Alex and fired.

"Jesus Christ!"

Recoiling from the jet of burning liquid, he howled as though he'd been splattered with hot grease. Both hands flailed, and he crashed to the ground.

She felt such relief that she forgot to stop spraying. The wind shifted, and the spray blew back at her. Even whipping her head to the side failed to save her completely, and the world went blurry behind a veil of searing pain. She shoved the heels of both hands to her eyes, and the pain eased the slightest bit.

Hands clawed at her. Alex. She blinked, and he came into focus, though pockets of her vision looked smeared. "We have to go," he said. "Can you drive?"

"Go where? Ow."

"Anywhere. Anywhere but here."

Again, she blinked. Her eyes kept welling with tears, but she thought she could manage the car. Maybe slowly, but she could get them away from the quad.

"Yeah."

Holding onto each other, they stumbled through the quad, bumping into people who never noticed, who only cared about something she couldn't see. Beside her, Alex whimpered and hissed and whimpered again. Every breath was a terrified, shuddering thing.

He fell into the car's passenger seat and handed over the keys. Without a word, she stabbed them into the ignition, started the engine, and swung the car around and fled.

They made it three blocks, wiping her eyes with her sleeve every few seconds, before she dared to ask, "What did you see?"

Alex sobbed. "It was . . . horrible. And beautiful. Something I can't . . . just keep going."

Reggie checked the rearview mirror without thinking. With her tearful, burning eyes, she saw the streetlights melt, saw campus recede into a distance that was much too far. Behind the smear that dominated her vision, she caught an impression of a silver disc rising into the sky, a cold sun that dominated everything else. Something moved in front of it, a bulk larger than any mountain. Chains pulled, and as the bulk shifted, she thought maybe it was dragging something. Or it was being dragged.

She blinked, and her vision began to clear. She jerked her eyes forward and concentrated on the road, refusing to look back. "Don't do it," she said.

"What?"

"Don't ever look again. Never."

"I won't."

Reggie accelerated, blasting past her apartment, needing nothing but distance and thinking that distance might never be enough. She thought about the immense, struggling thing she'd caught the slightest glimpse of in the rearview and felt a chilling urge to look again.

"No," she said, and she ground her teeth and shook her head.

"It was beautiful," Alex said.

"I don't care."

Nate Southard is the author of *Bad Dogs*, *Porcelain*, *Will the Sun Ever Come Out Again?*, *Red Sky*, *Lights Out*, and *Just Like Hell*. When he isn't writing scary stories, he's probably cooking. Usually Thai food or fried chicken. He loves fried chicken.

Nate lives in Austin, Texas with his girlfriend, a dog, and two cats. The cats are total assholes.

www.natesouthard.com

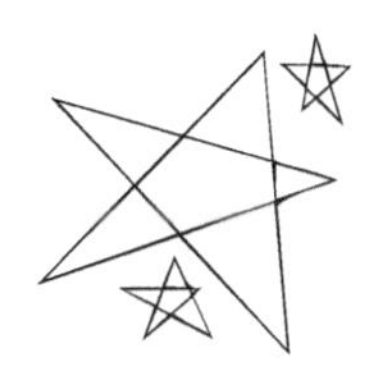

The Steeplechase

Scott R Jones

IN THE CHILL PRE-DAWN LIGHT, THREE MILES INTO A PUNISHING FIVE-mile run along the crumbled banks of the frozen Miskatonic, Benjamin Lowry could almost convince himself that the terrors of the night before were just that. Night terrors, the same as they ever were since he'd been a kid. The same oppressive atmosphere, the liquid leadenness to the air, the awful, black gravity that threatened to flatten the furniture, reduce all within sight and sense to crushed molecules, to nothing. His body transformed to cold, living stone cursed with hyper-alertness, a kind of migraine consciousness that absorbed everything in excruciating detail. The hooded figures which boiled up out of the shadowed corners or, worse, simply opened the door to the room and entered to surround his bed in postures of palpable malice.

Night terrors. A classic presentation no different from thousands of other sufferers, according to the research, but no less debilitating for that.

Ben knew he'd been fortunate. His parents had taken the issue seriously; the official diagnosis of sleep paralysis had come early, as had the meds and the sessions with a prominent psychiatrist upstate. By the age of twelve, he was sleeping normally, and he'd stopped taking the clonazepam. Perhaps he even dreamed, though he could never recall. He had thought that for the best. Dreams, even the relatively sane ones he'd read about or heard from friends in strange detail, were malformed things best avoided. Lizard cities, houses that seemed familiar but contained extra rooms, places that were one place but also others at the same time. Who could enjoy such nightly aberrations of reality and call them quirky—or fun?

Now though, two years into his bachelor's degree, the night terrors had returned. *The stress,* he thought. Exhausting himself with his mechanical engineering studies had only gone so far toward mitigating the effects, and he didn't dare get back on the pills for fear of losing the edge he'd been cultivating since high school. Ben had always been driven, and he had no doubt that he did himself harm with his current course load, but to slow down now was unthinkable.

He bore the nightly ordeal as well as he could. Ben was a practical person with what his psychiatrist had called a level, even-tempered mind. He knew the root causes of his affliction, and he could survive the spectacular effects, he told himself. And when the terrors passed and his body was returned to him, he could do what he was doing now. He could run. Run, because returning to sleep was not an option.

A pale winter sun had just begun to line the eastern skyline when Ben's phone chimed softly. Attempting to pull it from the armband holster with half-frozen fingers was too much for his inner ear to process at speed, and he managed to lose first his balance and then his footing on a patch of black ice on the Garrison Street Bridge. The shock to his tailbone as he made contact with the antique cobblestones set his teeth on edge.

Cringing, Ben half-slid, half-crawled, to the side of the bridge. He pulled the phone from its holster to find a text from Chet Williams, which made the injury hardly seem worth the effort. Williams travelled in circles far from the frat houses of Miskatonic University, was in fact working on his master's in religious studies, of all things, but in recent months had taken to imagining himself as an undercover anthropologist of the collegiate set with a specialization in "bro culture." Even knowing this, Ben often found his friend's adopted mannerisms irritating. The popped collars, the bravado, the untapped talent for beer pong. He was on the ground though, in pain, and his run was effectively over. Ben groaned and answered.

Hey bro u up?

Running. 2 miles from campus.

In this weather? U crazy.

Getting coffee @ new place on the quad

I'm buying. 10 min?

Ben stood up, muscles aching in the cold. He could feel the bruises already spreading across his right glute. Warmth and company, even Chet's, suddenly seemed a better deal than this.

Sure.

"Well, I'm just gonna say it 'cause I know you won't. You look like shit, bro."

"Thanks."

"Seriously though? Why do you do this to yourself?"

"All work and no play makes Ben a dull boy?"

"Oh, Benny. Ben. How long have we known each other? You were *always* a dull boy, son."

"What? Two years. Was that actually a serious question?"

"It was. It absolutely was. I'm concerned for you, man."

"Okay, well," Ben sighed. *How to even begin with this,* he thought. "I mean, I've gotta stay fit, right?"

"Mmhm."

"And it's good for the stress. I've got some things happening. Issues."

"True confession: I didn't buy you that overpriced coffee to be friendly, friend. I'm bored and require tales, falsehoods, campus gossip. Lay some sexual braggadocio on me. Gimme your exploits. Whatever you got. Hit me."

So Ben hit him. Slowly at first, unsure of how much to reveal, but after a few minutes, he could feel an odd species of release growing in his chest, filling up the space, expanding his ribs and pushing more and more words into the air between them. He imagined the space growing darker around them, imagined his nightly visitors somehow listening from the shadows beneath the table, from behind the swinging doors to the men's restroom. It didn't matter though because he was talking about it in the daylight, and talking felt good. Like running while somehow sitting still. The same almost physical relief. And then he was done, the air lightening as silence descended. Chet's eyes were wide.

"Jesus. Man, that's unreal. You're not shitting me?"

"Ask me that again but slowly. Why would I make up something like this."

"Can't argue with that." Chet thought for a moment, his eyes moving about the room. Really, the guy was frighteningly intelligent, and Ben guessed that the spastic eye tracking was the outward sign of deep connections being made in Chet's mental space. He'd seen something about that on the Discovery Channel, hadn't he? He sipped at his espresso, tried to enjoy it.

"I want you to see somebody," Chet finally said.

"No more girls, man."

"Not like that. Yes, she's a *she*. Such a *she*!" Ben immediately knew Chet had slept with her. "But that's beside the point. I mean, you need to see her in her professional capacity." Chet took out his device, began tapping at it. "There." Ben's phone pinged, but he didn't reach for it. Chet shot him a sour look.

"Her name's Desiree Escarrá. She's a doctor, runs the new multidisciplinary sleep study for MU. They're getting some interesting results, new therapies. Lasers! All good things."

"Never heard of it. Or her."

"Don't be an asshole, Benny. She's got deep funding from the Peaslee bunch. And why *would* you hear about it? This is soft science, man, nowhere near your territory. The stuff of dreams, like, literally."

"I'd like to be done with those. Literally."

Chet's smile turned wry. "Shit, son, if what you told me is true, I don't half blame ya."

"Yeah. I'm just so tired."

"Real talk? Dizzy can help you. Call that number, bro." Ben nodded half-hearted agreement. Chet smiled and downed the dregs of his coffee.

"You ever hear of the Four Noble Postures of Buddhism, Benny?"

"No, but I'm guessing I'm about to."

"There's lying down. Sitting. Standing. And walking."

"So running is out for Buddhists."

"For you too, maybe. Consider it. Did I mention you look like shit?"

He called the number eventually. Another week of terrors, culminating in a particularly destructive night that had seemed to last an eternity, leaving him exhausted and useless the next day, made him pick up his phone and look up the study. An appointment had been made, and now he was here at the Hypnos Sleep Institute.

Ben had seen smaller versions of the print that hung on a wall in the spacious and spare waiting area. Much smaller versions. He wondered idly how large the original painting was and hoped it was not much over the print. Any larger and the beings depicted would threaten to overwhelm his composure. The horse's head thrust between the curtains, for instance, the eyes showing a crazed white, was almost worse than the hunched, smoky demon squatting atop the distressed sleeper. Almost.

Why would they even have something like this here? he thought. *Who* are *these people?*

"Like it?" A feminine voice from behind him broke his nervous reverie. He turned to find a plain-seeming woman with olive skin and dark hair, carrying a tablet and dressed in a lavender clinic smock and pleated pants.

"I'm not sure," he replied. "Goya, isn't it? I was just thinking it felt a little odd to see it in a clinic?"

The woman laughed. "Ahh, because we're healers, you mean. And it's a Fuseli actually. *The Nightmare.* At Hypnos, we feel it's important to know the myths behind the science, Mister . . . ?"

"I'm Ben. Ben Lowry."

"Ahh, Chet's friend! And my two o'clock. I'm Desiree Escarrá, the director."

"Really? I thought . . ."

"You thought what?"

"Well, the way Chet spoke about you, I . . ."

The director narrowed her eyes, and the ghost of a smile passed over her face. "You thought I'd be one of Chet's prizes?"

"Look, I'm sorry. It's just that he has a type."

"Just the one, huh? How do you know I'm not? Your friend's a smart guy, right? Mature? Varied interests? Give him some credit."

"Chet? Varied? I mean, I guess so. I don't really know him all that well," Ben stammered. He could feel his face heating up. "Look, Doctor, I really *am* sorry, I should—"

"You should forget it. And *relax*. Doctor's orders." She smiled and flicked a finger across her tablet. "I've just been reviewing the intake form you filled out online. I hope you won't mind a little more grilling? There's a personal interview. We can run some physical tests while we're doing that, to save time."

"I do like efficiency."

Desiree laughed again and proceeded to lead him down a hall. "Yes, I gathered that from Chet. You like to have your life in order, don't you, Mr. Lowry?"

"It helps me find my socks in the morning, I guess."

"Here we are." She'd brought him into a dimly lit room; one wall featured a small sideboard on top of which two laptops and an array of esoteric equipment hummed lightly. *Is that a helmet?* Ben thought and chided himself for a fool. Of course it was a helmet. There was also a zero-gravity chair in the room's center, and after taking his coat, Desiree directed Ben to it. "Would it be nice for you to relax about your socks a bit, Mr. Lowry?"

"I'm not sure what you mean."

"I mean, allow some room for chaos in your life." There was something in her tone; he tensed and immediately felt a fresh flush of shame. How Desiree noticed this, he couldn't imagine, but she had. "I'm sorry. I didn't mean to upset you. I should have said *spontaneity*."

"Oh. Yes, of course. Sure." He was being paranoid and knew it. Ben resolved to ease into the process. If he was to heal, he'd need to allow things to happen for once.

She confirmed this intuition immediately. "Mmhm. Well, to do that, you need to relax. Give yourself *permission* to do so. Roll up your sleeve there." She fitted a blood pressure cuff to his upper arm and began inflating it. "And sleep, obviously, which you have *not* been doing."

"No."

"But of course, that's *technically* incorrect. Sleep paralysis and the accompanying terrors are a *form* of sleep. Did your psychiatrist ever go over the neural science with you?"

"I'm not sure there was much science to go over at the time. I was a kid. It was early days for this kind of stuff. Just drugs and counselling for me."

"Your BP is a little high, 150 over 90, but that's well within tolerances. Okay, well, with SP you have REM sleep latencies that are far shorter than normal and usually deeply fragmented. Certain neural populations are hyper-activated, others under-activated. Overlap of the REM and waking states occurs. There's vestibular-motor disorientation during this overlap, hence the paralysis. The sufferer is awake but dreaming, unable to move, and this creates a fearful emotional state which conditions the dream experience along cultural narrative lines. A fight or flight response that can't be acted upon, which as you know is a vicious circle.

"This helmet is basically a neural driver." Desiree lifted the rig and ran a finger along the inside of the helmet. "There's a ring of low-level cold lasers here for transcranial penetration. We engage the pineal gland and parietal lobe with these, and the frequencies of the spectrum goggles are calibrated to your brainwaves. We want to engage a number of neural systems obviously, but the real beauty of the helmet is the stability it lends to your shortened REM sleep periods."

As she placed the device over his scalp and began fitting it, her fingers brushed the tops of his ears and pressed into the hollow at the base of his skull. Her touch was assured and carried with it a feeling of expertise . . . and excitement? Desiree clearly had a passion for the work she did, but no, he was making something out of nothing. Ben imagined he was building up a charge on his skin somehow and took a deep breath to dispel it.

"Good. People forget how important healthy breathing technique is to sleep. Do you meditate at all, Mr. Lowry?"

"That's never been my . . . no. Chet tried to get me to a yoga class, but it's . . . huh. You know something, I only just made the connection, but it's too much like sleep paralysis. Savannah and all that."

"*Savasana.*"

"Right."

"The *corpse pose*, it's called."

"What? Jesus. No wonder I hated it."

Desiree laughed again, and Ben found himself enjoying the sound more and more. For a specialist in a bleak field, she had a remarkable cheeriness, an excellent bedside manner.

"Our psych team believes that SP has real and demonstrable negative effects on all life functions. I'm not surprised that yoga disturbs you." She left his side and stepped to the sideboard to consult a screen. "These are good readings. Your alpha waves are strong, steady. And I like what I'm seeing in the beta two *and* three. We'll have a calibration for you in a few moments."

"Okay, but I'm not really *seeing* anything in these goggles."

"Good. That means it's working."

"Seriously?"

"Yes, seriously. And you won't, not really. During the hypnagogic stage of sleep, just before you drift off, you *may* notice a wash of color on the back of your eyelids that's a little more intense than usual.

"Our research has homed in on the fight or flight response. The helmet stabilizes the erratic REM cycle and gives the dreamer the option to actually *flee* the night terror, end the paralysis. Nine times out of ten, we've seen full awakening and returning motor function within moments of initial paralysis."

"And the tenth time?"

"I'd rather not condition your responses, Mr. Lowry."

"Oh, come on. What's the harm? Either I experience what others have or I don't. So long as I'm cured, I don't mind either way."

"Fair point. All right. Subjects who *don't* awaken have reported sensations of flight and a headlong rush toward a new dream. Prismatic clouds, impossible architecture, floating chrysanthemum constructions, all within a deep grey space that's been described as calming. Many find it pleasurable. The opposite of a quicksand dream; a sense of freedom and weightlessness."

"Sounds fantastic," Ben sighed. "If that happens, fine, and if not, okay. Because it's not for me. Dreaming, I mean. If this thing can let me sleep through the night, then that's enough."

"Oh, you'll sleep." She lifted the rig from his scalp and brought the room lights up. "You'll sleep like a king."

"Do you get a lot of royalty through Hypnos? I mean, why Miskatonic, if you don't mind me asking?"

"I could say funding and leave it at that. The Peaslee Foundation has been generous, very interested in the work. But really, it's the students and faculty. Historically, Miskatonic has catered to a population with certain sensitivities, and we find they make the best subjects for study." She handed Ben his coat and opened the door to the hall. "We're done for now. I'll need you to return here this evening. I'll want to monitor you for the next few nights. This is a sleep study after all. You've made arrangements?"

"Yes. I figured I'd be sleeping here. I'm sorry, but *certain sensitivities*? What does that mean?"

"You don't know?" She shot him a puzzled look. "Ah, but then it's not the kind of thing they'd put in the brochure, is it? Nightmares, Mr. Lowry. Miskatonic has the highest incidence of nightmare sufferers in the Ivy League."

Ben goggled at the information. "Who would even record that? How would you get those numbers?"

"Oh, they've kept careful track here, Mr. Lowry. Miskatonic has had a vested interest in dreams and dreaming for decades. There's a lot to be harvested here. Now, I've got to prep for my three o'clock, so I'll see you out."

She led him back to the atrium with the Fuseli. The print again threatened to overwhelm him with its imagery. She placed a firm hand on his shoulder at the door.

"Goodbye, Mr. Lowry. We'll see you tonight."

Ben tried to sleep.

Getting comfortable in the clinic bedroom would have been simple were it not for the treatment rig. He made a number of attempts, shifting the pillows, adding more, or taking them away. He found a decent position and drifted off, but the hours of effort just to get to that place were enough to keep him waking up and jittery through the night. He reflected that at least insomnia was an improvement over demons and immobility.

The next night was better. The next night was *uneventful.* Ben slept, *really* slept, and awoke with the sun, refreshed. His morning run (normally a desperate, panting affair after a night of terrors) seemed to energize him. Doctor Escarrá was pleased with his progress and let him return to his dorm with a home rig with instructions to check in with her after a week had passed.

After a few nights of deep, dreamless sleep, his appetite returned; he was mildly surprised that he hadn't noticed it leave in the first place. His studies became easier. He felt sharper, fitter, more efficient. Even Chet noticed when they met for coffee again.

"You look less like shit these days, bro."

"I *feel* less like shit," Ben said. "Bro."

"Oh ho! Nice. We'll get you back into the true college lifestyle in no time now. Keggers, coeds, half-assed Nietzchean jam sessions. The works. Your collar will pop automatically when you're fully acclimated." Chet feigned wiping at a proud tear. "I hope I'm there to hear it. My boy. They grow up so *fast.*"

Ben smiled. "I'll consider it. Say, I wanted to ask you something actually . . ."

"Hit me."

"I'm heading over to Hypnos in a few. Doctor Escarrá wants to check me over, see if my rig needs recalibrating."

"Oh yeah? Is that what's in the box? Can I see it?"

"Um. Sure. I guess." Ben lifted it from the floor and set it on the table. He was about to open the box but felt a vague embarrassment. "I'm not going to take it out though, man. It's probably delicate."

Chet shot him a sideways look. "You sleep in it. How delicate can it be? But okay, I get it. I'll look but won't touch."

Ben opened the box, and Chet peered in.

"Man. That's some nice work. They've tightened up the design considerably since the prototype."

"Yeah, that's, uh . . . that's actually what I wanted to ask you about, kind of, Chet. How do you know Doctor Escarrá again?"

"I thought that was obvious. Dizzy and I dated for a couple of months last year."

"Sure, no. I mean, yeah, obviously I gathered that, but she seems . . . I was stupid actually. I asked."

"Not my type, right?" Chet smirked. "Guess she shut you down on that front?"

"Kinda."

"Look, straight up? I was asked to do some consulting work for her group before they really got going. And she impressed me. Smart, funny, driven. I was sold."

Ben nodded.

"Besides," Chet went on, "what do you think, that I'm, like, actually *shallow* or something? Dude."

"No, man, nothing like that. I just . . . wait. You did consulting for Hypnos? On what?"

Chet sighed. "Recall that beneath this charming letter-sweatered exterior beats the heart of a near-fanatical religious studies major, son." In a way, it was fascinating to watch the adopted persona drop away from his friend, Ben thought, though he had to admit it also made him uneasy. "Why do people believe as they do? What drives that impulse to worship? And perhaps most importantly, what gods *own* that worship?"

"That's a strange way to put it. And a little backward? I would have thought . . ."

Chet cut Ben off with an actual scowl. "It's just possible you think too much, so how about you read my thesis and get straightened the fuck out, son."

"Huh."

Chet recovered with a chuckle. "Okay! Wow! That was *harsh*. Sorry. Look, Hypnos is multi-disciplinary, dreams have long held this weird intermediary space in all types of faith culture, and Desiree just wanted the group to get right with god, after a fashion."

"After a fashion?"

"Think of it as a blessing."

"You consulted on a *blessing*."

"Well, I *consulted* on getting her access to the Special Collections at Orne and a little translation work. How's that? Satisfied?"

It was Ben's turn to scowl. The exchange had made him feel foreign to himself, his environment, and friends. Dislocated. So much of his simple life of hard work and hard science depended on people being who they appeared to be, and Chet's sudden vehemence on things spiritual had thrown him off his ease.

"Hey, forget it, bro." Chet checked his phone. "Aren't you going to be late?"

"Well, this is no good," Desiree said as she frowned at her screens.

"What? What is it?"

"You're not *dreaming* at *all*, Mr. Lowry."

"I thought we wanted that. I *want* that."

"You *think* you want that, Mr. Lowry. But I'm sure you know that REM sleep is integral to your health. You don't have to *remember* your dreams, but they need to be there for optimal brain function. They *have* to be there. I'd be remiss in my oath if I let things continue like this for you."

Ben felt sheepish, as if he'd stopped dreaming deliberately to be difficult, which was untrue. He hated to disappoint her, he realized.

"Okay. I'd rather not get between you and Hippocrates, Doctor."

"Oh, him. Very funny, Mr. Lowry."

"What do I have to do?"

"You? Nothing. Sleep here tonight. I'm putting you on the Steeplechase, and we'll see if that loosens you up."

"Pardon?"

"It's a deep-cycle, parietal lobe engagement program. You're going to run, Mr. Lowry. That dream of rushing we talked about, remember? We need to get you up and moving in REM, so to speak. You'll enjoy these dreams. They're very goal oriented. Run, jump, flee, fly. A real oneiric workout."

"Chet said I should give up running."

"The Noble Postures thing? Well, the Buddha never had anything to run *from*. And I'm pretty sure you're not him, so . . ."

"All right. Ready, set, go? Like that?"

"Exactly like that, Mr. Lowry."

Ben ran.

It seemed he had barely fallen asleep under the rig that night before he was running, running, tearing along at ridiculous speeds through something like the environment that Desiree Escarrá had described. There were columns of smoking light and shadow to either side of his rushing awareness. Jewel-like constructions that flashed and folded in and out of themselves rose from a vague floor before him, forcing a leap over or a slide beneath as they spun wildly and disappeared behind him.

The Steeplechase, he thought. *This is it. This is what Desiree meant.*

Up, over, through, faster, and faster. Multi-hued clouds of some obscure matter shook, grew, and collapsed in the spaces above, rained down fleeting ideas, concepts, equations that evaporated the moment he focused on them.

Ben ran. Ran and whooped with pleasure. Through the columns, which he now sensed spreading beyond him in vast shuddering leagues, he could sense other runners. Bursts of light and sound came to him from the fields of columns, sharp prismatic explosions and a kind of ecstatic rattling that spurred him on. He was lucid, he realized in surprise. He was dreaming and loving it.

Ben ran like he had never run before. He poured on more speed, willed whatever acted as his legs in the dream to pump faster. He was a floating point of consciousness, he knew, but the bodily sensations were present even so. The faster he ran, the deeper those sensations became and the more pleasure he felt. Each leap, each slide and dodge, sent ripples of energy over his dream body that registered as a delicious chill.

He ran, and the columns began to bleed into each other, transformed into a corrugated tunnel of throbbing light. It was amazing, a thrill of absolute freedom. Ben closed his eyes in profound gratitude for Chet, for Desiree and the Hypnos Institute: a good friend, a great doctor, a healing place. He dreamed that tears leaked from the corners of his eyes to streak his temples and fly off into the distances behind. This therapy wasn't just going to cure him; this was world-changing stuff.

Ben opened his eyes and realized immediately that he shouldn't have been able to close them in the first place. Wasn't that correct? Could you stop *seeing* a dream you were having? Had that ever happened before to him, to anyone?

Wait, he thought. *Stop.*

He ran on. Willing himself to stop did nothing. If anything, his speed only increased. The walls still rushed by, the jeweled barriers spun and shone as before, but they were steadily fading to an unsteady vagueness. The other runners too were gone now, and the joyful popping, whizzing sound of their passage was replaced with something on a different frequency, a low insectile drone that began to build as the oneiric landscape bled away.

Ben ran, fear blossoming in his mind. It felt as if he was racing to the very edge of the universe now, that he would crash into a wall of nothingness any second.

Stop! Stop it! Wake up!

To his sides, they arrived. The shapes from his room, in their hoods and coiling blackness. Moving too in a way they never had while he lay like stone in his bed. The figures, a dozen, maybe more, dopplering away behind him, were at least as fast as he was, he knew. Something about the way their segmented darkness reached forward and grasped at the air to pull themselves along made him feel they were toying with him. Were they even hooded? What was he *actually* seeing? A carapace? Something to hide their features. Armor? They paced him, and their speed was shocking.

Oh god, Ben thought. *They're* hunting *me.*

At the thought, the dream state quaked and roared, and his sight screamed in stark refusal at the scene that shattered the greyness. He passed from the dream space into snow, the flashing of bare trees, a reeling sky choked with star trails above. He could not feel his feet, but he could hear them crunch the crusted snowpack and ice below in a furious rhythm. With a sick, clawing motion, he reached for the rig that he knew was still clamped to his skull, tore it away by the bare wiring that trailed behind.

Because I'm moving *now! I'm prey because I'm moving.*

"No! Stop!" he screamed into the winter air. Where was he? A forest. Still in Arkham? Nowhere.

"Make it stop! I want to wake up!"

He didn't see Chet's arm rocket from his right until just before it caught him across the throat. His feet left the ground and seemed to fly off into the maddening sky for a moment before his naked back crashed to the snow. Ben threw up and pissed himself simultaneously, and a crackling, shining blackness filled his vision. He heard Chet's voice.

"Gross, bro."

"But well within tolerances," came the voice of Doctor Escarrá, and in the next moment, she was there, straddling him, pinning his body to the ground. Ben moaned, and Chet laughed at the sound.

"Told you he'd be great, Diz."

"Yes. You're awake, Ben. Your rig is ruined, but forget about that. You won't need it now." He felt her lips at his ear, laughing. "They *love* you, Ben. They've wanted you for years, but after tonight? What a chase!"

"They're all around us now. They're like horses and beetles and smoke, the servants of Hypnos. We still don't know what they harvest from dreamers like you, not *exactly*, but we'll find out. We'll find out why you're so desired. He's an inscrutable god with inscrutable needs."

"Inscrutable as *fuck*, son."

"We'll find out. For science. For the love of Hypnos. You'll run the Steeplechase for his servant's sport, Ben. You're a member of our stable now." He felt the weight of her lift, heard their hurrying steps in the snow as the pair retreated. Fresh tears coursed down his face and froze there.

"Every night, you'll *run*. Welcome to the institute."

By the time the chittering shapes fell upon him, his vision had cleared enough to glimpse, and guess at, what they pulled from his stony form.

§

Scott R Jones is a writer, artisanal information transference agent, and naturalized sorcerer from Victoria, British Columbia. He once wrote a book detailing an auto-ethnographical approach to religious themes and practices derived from the Cthulhu Mythos and has had some pleasant trouble living that down ever since. He edits anthologies for Martian Migraine Press and writes stories for others, which they seem to like. His beard is sentient, but the jury is still out on the rest of him. In these trying times, he urges one and all to Keep It R'lyeh, whatever that is.

From the Inbox of Madness

Gina Marie Guadagnino

SUBJECT: ROOMMATE PROBLEM, PLEASE HELP
FROM: chloeandjim79@yahoo.com
TO: president@mu.edu
DATE: Wednesday, February 6, 2019 at 9:15 AM

Dear President Algernon Wayland,

I am sorry to be writing to you like this, but I heard you speak during Parent's Weekend back in the fall, and I don't know who else to reach out to at this point—we are at our wit's end! We were woken up at 5:00 am California time by our son, Jeremy Bauer, who is a freshman living in Howard Hall, and his living situation is getting to be intolerable because his roommate is acting crazy! Rory McBride (that's the roommate) will be keeping all kind of strange hours, staying up until really late at night, peeling back the wallpaper and drawing all these various symbols on the wall (and by the way, because it is not Jeremy doing this, we expect to be getting our housing deposit back in full). Jeremy says that he keeps waking up to find Rory staring at him and muttering things in some other language! Rory is also lighting a lot of candles, and I do not want Jeremy getting into trouble. He keeps telling Rory to put them out, so they don't break the fire code. Rory just keeps ignoring Jeremy or will be yelling at him in that other language. This is really unacceptable!

Jeremy has talked to the RA, but the RA just keeps telling him to wear earplugs and get an eye mask if the sound and light bother him! For the amount that we are paying for tuition and housing fees, I don't feel like Jeremy should have to do all that when the roommate is the one who is behaving this strange way. Furthermore, Jeremy can't sleep when he thinks Rory is staring at him, and he is way too tired in the mornings, and his grades are starting to suffer. I have called the housing office a couple of times, and they don't seem to want to do anything about this. I am very upset about the lack of customer service, and even though in your speech you talked about caring for the students, your housing office doesn't seem to be very caring in this situation! They told me they cannot talk to me or my husband about the case because of privacy reasons and that Jeremy needs to file a complaint, but I don't understand what is so private when Jeremy is the one telling me all of this stuff anyway!

I would like to make an appointment to call you. We live in Malibu, CA, so there is a three-hour time difference, but I am available all day today and tomorrow. I can be reached at 310-483-0394.

Thank you,
Chloe and Jim Bauer

SUBJECT: Fwd: ROOMMATE PROBLEM, PLEASE HELP
FROM: evangeline.ambrose@mu.edu
TO: gregory.priven@mu.edu
CC: sophie.lamonte@mu.edu
DATE: Wednesday, February 6, 2019 at 9:52 AM

Hi Greg,

From the sound of it, these two have already contacted your office, so sorry if I'm duplicating efforts here. Obviously, the Office of the President does not want to step on toes if this is already being handled by Residential Life, but please do send me a quick status update on this situation. I am also looping in Sophie from the Wellness Center to see if Rory is on the radar over there. Sophie, can you please weigh in?

Thanks to you both,
Eva

Evangeline Ambrose
Chief of Staff
Office of the President

SUBJECT: URGENT STUDENT FINANCIAL AID ISSUE
FROM: jeyesh99@gmail.com
TO: president@mu.edu
DATE: Wednesday, February 6, 2019 at 10:01 AM

Hello Mr. President,

My name is Jeyesh Agarwal, and I was accepted to Miskatonic University where I am hoping to complete a degree in Library Studies (Student ID: MU10492848). It has been my dream to attend Miskatonic University for as long as I can remember, and when I received your letter of admissions, my mother and I were crying together tears of joy that all my hard work and effort had paid off.

However, our tears of joy soon turned to tears of sorrow when we got to the part of the letter that contained my financial aid offer. Mr. President, how can I describe our disappointment to discover that my scholarship allotment would not even cover room and board and that I would be expected to come up with the remaining $250,000 to cover my four-year tuition? My family simply does not have that kind of money. My father abandoned us, and my mother brought my three sisters and me to America for a better life. She is a single parent who works hard, but we receive no support from my father who we have not heard from in years. I am unable to apply for FAFSA as a non-US citizen, and I could not ask my mother to co-sign on a loan of such great magnitude.

I am writing to you today to plead for your assistance in increasing my financial aid allotment. As a prospective student in Library Studies, there is simply no better college in the world for me to attend, and ever since I first came to realize that Library Studies is my passion, I understood that Miskatonic is the university of my dreams. Mr. President, I know this may sound incredible to you, but it is literally the university of my dreams. When I sleep, I actually dream of walking through the fabled library there, and I can hear the books calling out to me with such force that I am compelled to take them down off the shelves and read them. How cruel and how unfair it seems to be so close to realizing these dreams, yet those dreams are dashed because of the "mundanity of money."

If there is anything I can do to change your mind or prove my worthiness to you, I am willing to do it. I read in your mission statement on the Miskatonic website that you want to make the university more affordable. Well, now is your chance! Please, Mr. President, show your compassion!

With sincere respect and regards,
Jeyesh Agarwal

SUBJECT: Fwd: URGENT STUDENT FINANCIAL AID ISSUE
FROM: evangeline.ambrose@mu.edu
TO: michael.martinez@mu.edu
DATE: Wednesday, February 6, 2019 at 10:10 AM

Hi Mickey,

Another financial aid request—'tis the season, yes? Could you and your team please take a quick look into Jeyesh Agarwal's account (MU10492848) and see if he qualifies for any of the international or DREAMER scholarships? It sounds from his letter like he hasn't explored those options. Is he eligible for any of the library fellowships? It seem like that is really his passion! :)

Cheers,
Eva

SUBJECT: MISSING STUDENT (CODE ORANGE)
FROM: paul.belafonte@mu.edu
TO: president@mu.edu, algernon.wayland@mu.edu, nora.moreno@mu.edu, sophie.lamonte@mu.edu
CC: evangeline.ambrose@mu.edu, gregory.priven@mu.edu, piers.sandersen@mu.edu
DATE: Wednesday, February 6, 2019 at 10:15 AM

This is an alert regarding an investigation currently in progress.

Situation:

On Wednesday, February 6, 2019 in Mason Hall at approximately 3:35 am, sophomore student Carmen Villanova (MU 17839538) awoke and attempted to open the door to the bathroom in her dorm room. The door was locked, but she observed a red light coming from underneath, and she could hear voices. She knocked on the door but heard no response. She noted that her roommate, sophomore Hannah Jameson (MU 17365227), was not in her bed and assumed that Jameson was in the bathroom with an overnight guest. Villanova went back to bed and waited until 3:50 am when she noticed that the light had grown brighter and the voices louder. She knocked again and called to Jameson to open the door. The light intensified, and Villanova says that she then passed out due to what she described as an "incandescent flash."

At approximately 4:17 am, Villanova regained consciousness on the floor of her dorm and attempted to open the bathroom door again. It was still locked, but the light was gone as were the voices. Villanova continued to knock on the door and call for Jameson. After approximately five minutes with no response, she awoke her Resident Advisor, senior Caroline Norris (MU 15028484). RA Norris also knocked on the door and called to Jameson that if she did not open the door, Facilities Management would. When there was no answer, RA Norris contacted Facilities Management, in accordance with Chapter 6 Section 12 of the Resident Advisor Manual, and instructed Manager on Duty William Graham to open the door. None of MoD Graham's keys would open the door, and he was forced to remove it from the hinges. There was no one inside the bathroom. The light bulbs were shattered, and a large pool of viscous red liquid was congealing on the floor. There was a note written on the bathroom mirror in the red liquid, which read: "Goodbye. Do not look for me. He is coming. H.J." There is no other point of egress besides the bathroom door. The red liquid was contained to a single area with no droplets, splatter, smears, or tracks.

Actions and Next Steps:

On Wednesday, February 6, 2019 at 4:37 am, RA Norris alerted Officer Serena Goldstein of Miskatonic University Campus Safety. At 5:00 am, after investigating the scene, Officer Goldstein contacted the Essex County Police Department to file a missing persons report and to begin an investigation. At 9:45 am, I received notification from the ECPD that the red liquid was not blood, human or otherwise, and has yet to be identified.

At this time, Carmen Villanova and Caroline Norris are currently answering questions at the Arkham Precinct with Officer Goldstein and Corey Hillman, Associate Director of Health and Wellness. In accordance with University Policy, Senior Vice President for University Life Nora Moreno has notified Hannah Jameson's family and has put them in touch with the Arkham Precinct of the ECPD.

The university will not comment on inquiries regarding this incident, in accordance with Chapter 2 Section 3 of Miskatonic University Bylaws as this is an open police investigation.

I will distribute further information when it becomes available as the case progresses. If you have any further questions, please contact me directly.

Paul Belafonte
Commander, Campus Public Safety

SUBJECT: Fwd: MISSING STUDENT (CODE ORANGE)
FROM: evangeline.ambrose@mu.edu
TO: piers.sandersen@mu.edu
DATE: Wednesday, February 6, 2019 at 10:19 AM

Fuck. You guys okay over there? Did you know her? What can I do? xoxo

SUBJECT: Fwd: MISSING STUDENT (CODE ORANGE)
FROM: evangeline.ambrose@mu.edu
TO: algernon.wayland@mu.edu
DATE: Wednesday, February 6, 2019 at 10:20 AM

Algey, Paul just called about this. He wanted to let you know this is very similar to a case from 1986, only that one was in one of the music practice rooms in West Block. The student was found less than 24 hours later. I'm adding this to our 11:00 am briefing session, and we can go over the details then. Paul will be available to conference in. - Eva

SUBJECT: Re: Fwd: MISSING STUDENT (CODE ORANGE)
FROM: piers.sandersen@mu.edu
TO: evangeline.ambrose@mu.edu
DATE: Wednesday, February 6, 2019 at 10:23 AM

Nothing, really. It's eerily quiet. The RA and the roommate are still at the precinct, and the ECPD are long gone. They cleared out around 7:00 am and sealed the door with crime scene tape. I had a meeting with the staff over here, very subdued. Nothing to do but watch and hope. I didn't "know her-know her," but I recognized her, yes. Shit like this is the worst part of the job. Thanks for reaching out, hon.

Piers Sandersen
Director of Residential Life
Mason Hall

SUBJECT: Fwd: POST DOCTORAL APPLICATION
FROM: evangeline.ambrose@mu.edu
TO: algernon.wayland@mu.edu
DATE: Wednesday, February 6, 2019 at 10:30 AM

Algey, I am printing these for your review at our 11.

------------ Forwarded message ------------
SUBJECT: POST DOCTORAL APPLICATION
FROM: aiz9@princeton.edu
TO: president@mu.edu
DATE: Wednesday, February 6, 2019 at 10:15 AM

Dear Professor Wayland,

I would like to submit my application for any postdoctoral positions you might have available in your Applied Mathematics Lab at Miskatonic University. As a scholar of non-Euclidean geometry, I was fascinated when I heard you speak on the panel "Flexible Structures: Theorizing Parameters of the Void" at the Northeastern Conference on Experimental Mathematics last month, and I would be excited for the opportunity to work with you.

I believe that if you review my CV, attached below, you will find that my work is very much in keeping with the initiatives of your lab group. Please also find attached a copy of my doctoral dissertation, entitled "The Hyperbolic Vacuum: A Study of Saccheri Quadrilaterals in Zero Gravity."

Best regards,
Alvin Zabarsky, PhD

SUBJECT: PETITION TO CHANGE THE NAME OF HOWARD HALL
FROM: slj284@mu.edu
TO: president@mu.edu, chairman@mu.edu
DATE: Wednesday, February 6, 2019 at 11:15 AM

Dear President Algernon Wayland & Chairman of the Board Franklin Reed,

At its founding, Miskatonic University limited admissions to white men: a distinct irony, given Miskatonic's location on land stolen from Algonquian tribes. Over the years, the university has made great strides in overcoming its oppressive colonial origins, breaking down barriers to access, and fostering a more diverse campus environment. Today, Miskatonic is home to students, faculty, administrators, and staff of nearly every race, gender identity, sexual identity, level of ability, and national origin.

In the spirit of furthering Miskatonic University's continued trajectory of equity, diversity, and inclusion, we, the undersigned, demand to change the name of the dormitory Howard Hall. Named for one of Miskatonic University's founding trustees, Philip L. Howard, Howard Hall is the oldest dormitory on campus. Its residents represent a cross-section of Miskatonic's diverse population, and it is therefore unacceptable to assign women, people of color, LGBTQIA students, and international students to live somewhere named after a noted racist, jingoist, misogynist, and homophobe.

Our petition demands that the president and the board of trustees consider the following:

1. Changing the name of the dormitory from Howard Hall and renaming it to honor a woman, person of color, or member of the LGBTQIA+ community who has contributed to Miskatonic's embrace of diverse populations.

2. Holding a town hall event to hear suggestions from the Miskatonic University community regarding renaming recommendations.

3. The removal of the bust of P.L. Howard from the courtyard.

4. Replace the bust of P.L. Howard with another sculpture thematically congruent with Miskatonic University's stated goals of equity, diversity, and inclusion.

We would welcome the opportunity to discuss this petition at the upcoming meeting of the Miskatonic University Board of Trustees on March 20th. Thank you for what we hope will be a swift and positive response.

Sondra Jackson, MU Class of 2018
Graduate Student Senator

SUBJECT: Re: Fwd: URGENT STUDENT FINANCIAL AID ISSUE
FROM: michael.martinez@mu.edu
TO: evangeline.ambrose@mu.edu, jessica.kurtz@mu.edu
DATE: Wednesday, February 6, 2019 at 11:20 AM

Good morning!

Eva, I received your message regarding Jeyesh Agarwal. I was looking at his file, and his GPA and SAT scores are not quite high enough to qualify him for any of the funding in the DREAMER pool. As you know, this year we had the lowest acceptance rate in over 75 years—19%—and the highest number of international and resident-alien student applicants ever. As a result, minimum grade thresholds for those funding streams have been highly competitive, and with a 3.6 GPA, Jeyesh was outside the range.

That said, it is my understanding that there are still unawarded Library Studies Fellowships, so I am looping in Jessica Kurtz. Jessica, I am attaching Jeyesh's application. While his GPA is slightly lower than the other applicants under consideration, given the impassioned language of his personal essay and his obviously researched familiarity with the Library Studies program, I will leave this to your discretion. The deadline for acceptance is this Friday; we'll need to get the ball rolling on the paperwork today or tomorrow if you accept him. Let me know how you want to proceed.

Thanks,
Mickey

Michael Martinez
Associate Vice President for Financial Aid
Miskatonic University

SUBJECT: Fwd: PETITION TO CHANGE THE NAME OF HOWARD HALL
FROM: kiara.holyoke@mu.edu
TO: evangeline.ambrose@mu.edu
DATE: Wednesday, February 6, 2019 at 11:24 AM

I ALWAYS SAID THIS DAY WOULD COME! VINDICATION, BITCHES!

(Good thing we were ahead of the curve on this one, eh?)

Kiara Holyoke
Chief of Staff
Office of the Chairman of the Board

SUBJECT: Fwd: PETITION TO CHANGE THE NAME OF HOWARD HALL
FLAGGED AS IMPORTANT
FROM: kiara.holyoke@mu.edu
TO: president@mu.edu, gladys.channing@mu.edu, gregory.priven@mu.edu, francis.mcgill@mu.edu, pippa.montez@mu.edu, walter.desoto@mu.edu
DATE: Wednesday, February 6, 2019 at 11:45 AM

I am writing on behalf of Chairman Reed, regarding this petition. As several of you are already aware, the Board of Trustees Real Estate and Facilities Committee was prepared to vote on a proposal to rename Howard Hall to Saltonstall Hall in honor of Marianne Saltonstall, great-granddaughter of Eli Saltonstall and one of the first women to be admitted to Miskatonic University in the 1870s. Although the Saltonstall family endowment has contributed greatly to the university's development for two centuries, there has never been a building named after them.

In addition to being one of the first women to receive a BA (then known as an MA, Mistress of Arts) from Miskatonic, Marianne Saltonstall went on to received her PhD from MU and eventually taught in the Classics Department. Although personally silent on the subject of her own sexuality, her academic focus on the poems of Sappho and the fact that she never married but instead lived with her lifelong "companion" Phaedra Humbolt have led subsequent scholars to hold up Saltonstall as an LGBT icon. It is for these reasons that the REF Committee will be voting on this topic next month. Gladys Channing, the Chair (copied here), has indicated that informal response to the proposal has been favorable, and the motion is likely to be carried.

Chairman Reed therefore suggests that this group agree upon one the following courses of action, listed below in order of his preference:

1. We thank them for their input and promise to add the topic to the agenda for the next REF Committee meeting.

2. We let them know that the topic of renaming Howard Hall is already on the REF Committee agenda for next month and that we will be in touch with them following that meeting.

3. We put them in touch with Gladys who can discuss the issues raised and gauge whether to tell them it can go on the agenda.

4. We do not respond and let them be pleasantly surprised by the results of the REF Committee Meeting.

Please respond at your earliest convenience.

Best,
Kiara Holyoke
Chief of Staff
Office of the Chairman of the Board

SUBJECT: Re: Fwd: ROOMMATE PROBLEM, PLEASE HELP
FROM: gregory.priven@mu.edu
TO: evangeline.ambrose@mu.edu
CC: sophie.lamonte@mu.edu, francis.mcgill@mu.edu
DATE: Wednesday, February 6, 2019 at 11:50 AM

Hi Eva,

Apologies in advance for what is going to be a very lengthy message, but all this has been going on for quite some time. We are very familiar with the Bauer family. Frankly, I'm surprised it took them this long to escalate things to the OotP as they have been contacting our office on and off since October. Fran McGill, who I've copied here, was dealing with them after that first snow in December when they were calling upset that Jeremy's dorm was too cold. For the record, the issue turned out to be that Rory had gone away for the weekend and turned off the heating unit in their suite. Jeremy, being from Southern California, was not familiar with what the heating unit was or how it worked. For what it's worth, on that occasion, they escalated the issue to building management right away; at no time did Jeremy contact the RA, call the Facilities Helpline, or ask the front desk. Fran sent Facilities over, and they dealt with the problem immediately. Since that time, the Bauers have been reaching out to her whenever Jeremy has an issue as though she is their personal concierge. Fran, to her credit, has been handling it with her customary grace and aplomb.

Regarding the situation with Rory, a little background here. From what their RA has told Fran, it seems they have had trouble communicating from day 1. Rory is a night owl; Jeremy is an early riser. Rory is an omnivore; Jeremy is vegan. Rory invites friends over; Jeremy is shy. You get the drift. Their RA has done the standard roommate contract and mediation with them, but Rory keeps pushing the bounds of their agreement, and Jeremy, who is extremely nonconfrontational, keeps going to his parents rather than confronting Rory directly or going to the RA. His parents then go to Fran, and Fran has been working with the RA. So we keep getting bogged down in these communication loops.

Fran tells me that this latest issue with Rory's nocturnal behavior likely has something to do with the performance art collective he recently joined and is therefore probably harmless—if annoying. All this has resulted in the Bauers' insistence that we move Jeremy to a single (without additional fees obviously!). This, as you know, is impossible this late in the academic year. Their alternative proposal is that we remove Rory from the room, which we naturally can't do. Aside from the candle thing (which no one has caught him doing, btw), Rory is not actually breaking any rules. It is not actually against Residential Life policy for him to write or draw on the walls as long as he paints at the end of the semester. I have no idea what they are talking about vis a vis him peeling the wallpaper as Howard Hall has not had wallpaper since the 1940s. Fran has spoken with the Bauers about this, and I spoke with them yesterday as well. Long story short, they are going to keep writing and calling until they get an answer they like, and unless Rory commits an actual violation, they're just not going to get one.

As far as a response, I am happy to reply to them and bcc you. I don't think it would help matters to open up a channel to President Wayland or let them get the impression that appealing to the highest power they can conjure will get them results. I hope that this clarifies the situation somewhat and again apologize for such a lengthy email.

All best,
Greg

Gregory Priven
Vice President for Residential Life

SUBJECT: Re: Fwd: PETITION TO CHANGE THE NAME OF HOWARD HALL
FROM: francis.mcgill@mu.edu
TO: evangeline.ambrose@mu.edu
DATE: Wednesday, February 6, 2019 at 11:59 AM

Did you know about this? I maybe would have liked a heads up, considering that this is my constituency.

Fran McGill
Director for Residential Life
Howard Hall

SUBJECT: Re: Re: Fwd: ROOMMATE PROBLEM, PLEASE HELP
FROM: evangeline.ambrose@mu.edu
TO: gregory.priven@mu.edu
CC: sophie.lamonte@mu.edu, francis.mcgill@mu.edu
DATE: Wednesday, February 6, 2019 at 12:09 PM

Hi Greg,
Yes, if you could please reply and bcc me, that would be great. Thanks.

Eva

SUBJECT: Re: Re: Fwd: PETITION TO CHANGE THE NAME OF HOWARD HALL
FROM: evangeline.ambrose@mu.edu

TO: francis.mcgill@mu.edu
BCC: kiara.holyoke@mu.edu
DATE: Wednesday, February 6, 2019 at 12:17 PM

I knew that Gladys had proposed it, but I didn't know if it had made it to the final agenda. The agenda for that committee is generally circulated to Walter and Greg a week before the meeting. I didn't want to flag it to you without something tangible, and the last thing I heard was that it was possible but not confirmed.

SUBJECT: Re: Fwd: Petition to Change the Name of Howard Hall
FROM: gladys.channing@mu.edu
TO: president@mu.edu, gregory.priven@mu.edu, francis.mcgill@mu.edu, pippa.montez@mu.edu, walter.desoto@mu.edu kiara.holyoke@mu.edu, chairman@mu.edu
DATE: Wednesday, February 6, 2019 at 12:45 PM

If I had my druthers, I would rather tell them it's already on the agenda. I am not in favor of perpetuating the fiction that campus change only occurs when the students advocate for it. Some of us have served on this board diligently for years and should be allowed to (gracefully, of course) take credit when the changes we have fought for come to fruition. To that end, my preference would be for Franklin to put them in touch with me. I am happy to have a word. Or two.

Gladys

Gladys Tolbert Channing
MU BA '67

SUBJECT: Re: Re: Fwd: PETITION TO CHANGE THE NAME OF HOWARD HALL
FROM: pippa.montez@mu.edu
TO: president@mu.edu, gladys.channing@mu.edu, gregory.priven@mu.edu, francis.mcgill@mu.edu, walter.desoto@mu.edu kiara.holyoke@mu.edu, chairman@mu.edu
DATE: Wednesday, February 6, 2019 at 1:01 PM

As I have stated numerous times before, I do not believe that every petition deserves a response. There have been subdued grumblings about Howard Hall for years. I say we ignore and let them be pleasantly surprised. That way, should the motion not be carried, we are not putting ourselves in the position of having to backpedal or watch ourselves get skewered in the student press about "business as usual." We are already getting a lot of heat about our sanctuary stance. I think we should avoid stating positions—particularly when the outcome is uncertain—that could galvanize the group enough to stage a sit-in or occupy the Hoyt Building again.

Pippa Montez
Vice President for Public Relations

SUBJECT: Re: Re: Re: Fwd: ROOMMATE PROBLEM, PLEASE HELP
FROM: sophie.lamonte@mu.edu
TO: evangeline.ambrose@mu.edu
CC: gregory.priven@mu.edu, francis.mcgill@mu.edu
DATE: Wednesday, February 6, 2019 at 1:17 PM

Dear All,

Sorry for the delay in weighing in. As Greg and Eva know, things have been quite difficult in my office this morning.

Greg—you should go ahead and respond to the parents as discussed, but for your background (absolutely NOT to be shared with the Bauers or anyone outside this email thread), this is now the third time Rory has been flagged to our attention in as many days. His astronomy professor and his academic advisor both suggested wellness checks for Rory following some disturbing behavior. The professor, Dr. Horus Oleander, also gave us an essay Rory had completed for the class. Frankly, I use the term *essay* loosely. It read more like a manifesto. In it, he discusses his theories about how our understanding of relativity is flawed and that he has discovered the ability to communicate with "intelligences far beyond our own" in "dimensions incomprehensible to the human mind" by inscribing "sigils of power" beneath the wallpaper of his dorm room. He indicated that he would soon be able to open a portal to visit those dimensions and ends his essay by repeating the phrase "he is coming" about fifty times.

Naturally, Dr. Oleander assumed that this was some kind of joke or performance art piece, but when confronted and given the opportunity to rewrite, Rory became extremely agitated and ran out of the meeting. Dr. Oleander reached out to Robin Colburn, Rory's advisor, to alert her that Rory was in danger of failing the class if he did not re-write his essay. Robin called him in and got a repeat performance of the one Rory had given Dr. Oleander. Following that meeting, both Robin and Dr. Oleander contacted my office to express their concern. As this is the third outreach regarding Rory's troubling behavior, my staff will call him in this afternoon to do an evaluation. I have already alerted Campus Safety at Howard Hall, and when he swipes into the building, they'll get a ping and escort him over.

In the meantime, we should not be discussing Rory's mental health with the Bauers as it would be an obvious violation of HIPAA, so Greg, please do just let them know that someone from administration will speak to Rory and leave it vague.

All best,
Sophie

Sophie LaMonte
Vice President for Health and Wellness

SUBJECT: Re: Re: Re: Re: Fwd: ROOMMATE PROBLEM, PLEASE HELP
FROM: gregory.priven@mu.edu
TO: evangeline.ambrose@mu.edu

CC: sophie.lamonte@mu.edu, francis.mcgill@mu.edu
DATE: Wednesday, February 6, 2019 at 1:28 PM

Roger that—thanks for weighing in, Sophie.

SUBJECT: Re: Re: Re: Fwd: PETITION TO CHANGE THE NAME OF HOWARD HALL
TO: president@mu.edu, gregory.priven@mu.edu, francis.mcgill@mu.edu, pippa.montez@mu.edu, walter.desoto@mu.edu kiara.holyoke@mu.edu, chairman@mu.edu
FROM: gladys.channing@mu.edu
DATE: Wednesday, February 6, 2019 at 1:46 PM

Pippa,

Your thoughts are appreciated. I am going to ignore you though and urge Franklin to do the same.

Franklin,

Please respond and e-introduce me to the group.

Gladys

Gladys Tolbert Channing
MU BA '67

SUBJECT: Fwd: Re: Re: Re: Fwd: PETITION TO CHANGE THE NAME OF HOWARD HALL
FROM: kiara.holyoke@mu.edu
TO: evangeline.ambrose@mu.edu
DATE: Wednesday, February 6, 2019 at 1:50 PM

Jesus Christ. Remind me never to get on Gladys's bad side.

SUBJECT: Re: Fwd: Re: Re: Re: Fwd: PETITION TO CHANGE THE NAME OF HOWARD HALL
FROM: evangeline.ambrose@mu.edu
TO: kiara.holyoke@mu.edu
DATE: Wednesday, February 6, 2019 at 1:55 PM

I assume she's still salty over the way Pippa handled that divestment group's petition to the board. Which, to be honest, was pretty terrible.

SUBJECT: Re: POST DOCTORAL APPLICATION
FROM: algernon.wayland@mu.edu
TO: aiz9@princeton.edu
CC: fiona.landry@mu.edu
BCC: evangeline.ambrose@mu.edu
DATE: Wednesday, February 6, 2019 at 2:10 PM

Dear Dr. Zabarsky,

Thank you very much for reaching out. I would be very happy to meet with you and discuss the possibility of your joining my lab group. I am copying in Dr. Landry, the senior member of my team, who will reach out and set up a time to speak via Skype.

Cordially yours,
Dr. Wayland
President, Miskatonic University

SUBJECT: Fwd: Re: POST DOCTORAL APPLICATION
FROM: algernon.wayland@mu.edu
TO: fiona.landry@mu.edu, evangeline.ambrose@mu.edu
CC: timothy.bryce@mu.edu

DATE: Wednesday, February 6, 2019 at 2:15 PM

Fiona, would you please work with Tim to get this on my calendar?
Eva, please send Fiona Dr. Zabarsky's CV and dissertation?

Thanks - AW

SUBJECT: Re: Re: Re: Re: Fwd: PETITION TO CHANGE THE NAME OF HOWARD HALL
FROM: kiara.holyoke@mu.edu
TO: president@mu.edu, gladys.channing@mu.edu, gregory.priven@mu.edu, francis.mcgill@mu.edu, pippa.montez@mu.edu, walter.desoto@mu.edu
DATE: Wednesday, February 6, 2019 at 2:27 PM

Thank you all for weighing in. Gladys, Franklin will be composing a response to them shortly and will introduce you to the group. Thank you for taking point on this.

Kiara Holyoke

SUBJECT: Re: Re: Re: Re: Re: Fwd: PETITION TO CHANGE THE NAME OF HOWARD HALL
FROM: gladys.channing@mu.edu
TO: president@mu.edu, gregory.priven@mu.edu, francis.mcgill@mu.edu, phillipa.montez@mu.edu, walter.desoto@mu.edu kiara.holyoke@mu.edu, chairman@mu.edu
DATE: Wednesday, February 6, 2019 at 2:43 PM

It is my pleasure. I fought determinedly to get this proposal on the agenda, and it is high time that the student body sees that the board is not some monolithic beast defending the Old Ways but that it is comprised of human beings, some of whom have goals and aspirations not unlike that of the students themselves.

And for what it's worth, I graduated in the 60s, and I can out-protest any of these kids any day of the week. Petitions are cute. If they had real passion, they'd be chaining themselves to that statue and singing "We Shall Overcome."

Gladys

SUBJECT: Re: Re: Fwd: URGENT STUDENT FINANCIAL AID ISSUE
FROM: jessica.kurtz@mu.edu
TO: evangeline.ambrose@mu.edu, michael.martinez@mu.edu
DATE: Wednesday, February 6, 2019 at 3:30 PM

Mickey, Eva:

Thank you for passing along Jeyesh's application—it is truly compelling, particularly his personal essay, which demonstrates an almost preternatural understanding of our collection. His detailed description of the Armitage Wing and his theoretical recategorization of it were actually quite arresting and speak to the great volume of research he must have done to write this. I have to say, I'm quite impressed. Although his GPA is one point below what has traditionally been our minimum threshold for this scholarship, I would be very pleased to grant it to a scholar as dedicated as Jeyesh. Please write to him, and let him know he's been accepted, Mickey.

All the best,
Jessica

Jessica Kurtz
Dean of Libraries

SUBJECT: Re: Re: Re: Fwd: URGENT STUDENT FINANCIAL AID ISSUE
FROM: evangeline.ambrose@mu.edu
TO: michael.martinez@mu.edu, jessica.kurtz@mu.edu
DATE: Wednesday, February 6, 2019 at 3:34 PM

All's well that ends well! Thanks, Jessica. Mickey, enjoy writing Jeyesh with good news!

SUBJECT: Re: Re: Re: Re: Re: Fwd: ROOMMATE PROBLEM, PLEASE HELP
FROM: sophie.lamonte@mu.edu
TO: evangeline.ambrose@mu.edu
CC: gregory.priven@mu.edu, francis.mcgill@mu.edu
DATE: Wednesday, February 6, 2019 at 4:04 PM

Dear All,

An update: Rory McBride has just been taken to St. Mary's after attempting self-harm during a standard consult at the wellness center. He was brought in for evaluation and met with Counselor Yvonne Pellegro. Early into the conversation, he became extremely agitated, shouting things to the effect of, "Don't you see? He's coming! I must prepare the way!" After about five minutes of failing to calm Rory down, Yvonne stepped into the hall to call for a campus safety officer. During those moments, Rory smashed a vase on Yvonne's desk and attempted to slash his own throat but was wrestled down by the officer. He was transported to St. Mary's and was involuntarily admitted. He is on suicide watch. We have spoken to his parents, and he will go on medical leave this semester. Someone from my team will contact Jeremy in advance of Rory's parents clearing out his room. Please do not contact the Bauers if you have not already done so.

My best,
Sophie

SUBJECT: UPDATE: MISSING STUDENT (CODE ORANGE)
FROM: paul.belafonte@mu.edu
TO: president@mu.edu, algernon.wayland@mu.edu, nora.moreno@mu.edu, sophie.lamonte@mu.edu
CC: evangeline.ambrose@mu.edu, gregory.priven@mu.edu, piers.sandersen@mu.edu
DATE: Wednesday, February 6, 2019 at 5:15 PM

This is an update regarding an investigation currently in progress.

On February 1, 2018, at approximately 4:45 p.m., missing sophomore Hannah Jameson (MU 17365227) was found alive but unconscious in the courtyard of the library, outside the Armitage Wing, by graduate student Desire Xavier (MU 16030045). Jameson was naked, covered in an unidentifiable red liquid, and her limbs and torso had several patterns of circular markings 1" in diameter, consistent with petechial hemorrhaging. She was severely dehydrated, suffering from hypothermia and malnutrition, and exhibited symptoms of exposure more severe than anticipated given the time elapsed between her disappearance and her discovery. She was taken to St. Mary's Emergency Center for treatment where she is still unconscious but in stable condition and expected to recover. Her parents have been called. Additional information will be provided as it becomes available.

Paul Belafonte

SUBJECT: Re: UPDATE: MISSING STUDENT (CODE ORANGE)
FROM: algernon.wayland@mu.edu
TO: paul.belafonte@mu.edu, nora.moreno@mu.edu, sophie.lamonte@mu.edu
CC: evangeline.ambrose@mu.edu, gregory.priven@mu.edu, piers.sandersen@mu.edu, timothy.bryce@mu.edu
DATE: Wednesday, February 6, 2019 at 5:25 PM

Paul, well done to you and your team on this. Please keep us all apprised on updates as they develop. We should all sit down and discuss next steps;

I am particularly troubled to hear how similar this case has been to the '86 disappearance of Anges Kennedy, and we should convene to see what can be done for Hannah and the Jameson family should the ultimate outcome be the same. Tim will reach out and get you all on the schedule for tomorrow.

Algey

SUBJECT: Re: Re: URGENT STUDENT FINANCIAL AID ISSUE
FROM: jeyesh99@gmail.com
TO: president@mu.edu, jessica.kurtz@mu.edu
DATE: Wednesday, February 6, 2019 at 6:42 PM

Hello Mr. President and Dean Kurtz,

I have just received the most wonderful news from Mr. Martinez in the Financial Aid Office that I have been granted a scholarship in Library Studies and that I am now able to fulfill my dreams of coming to Miskatonic University. Thank you, Mr. President and Dean Kurtz, for all you have done to allow me to answer the call of the books. Today I can say with great joy that I am happy to accept a place in the class of 2021. Miskatonic University, I am coming!

With humblest gratitude,
Jeyesh Agarwal

§

Gina Marie Guadagnino's debut novel, *The Parting Glass*, released from Atria Books in Spring 2019. Her previously published work includes short stories in *The Morris-Jumel Mansion Anthology of Fantasy and Paranormal Fiction* and *Mixed Up: Cocktail Recipes (and Flash Fiction) for the Discerning Drinker (and Reader)* as well as an essay in *Being New York, Being Irish*. Gina holds a BA in English from NYU and MFA in Creative Writing from the New School and is currently an MA candidate in NYU's Irish Studies program. When not writing fiction or studying, Gina practices the dark art of university administration in the Office of the President at NYU where she spends most of her time writing emails. Lots and lots of emails.

Beyond the Surface

Joseph S. Pulver, Sr.

Two things you do with a broom in New England, and I already have a vehicle, an old FORD pickup (it was once a crisp, midnight-blue metal flake), and I'm more the popcorn, action movie kind than part of the bell, book, and candle crowd.

I push a broom (or a mop or a buffer), clean the halls, offices, lecture halls, and restrooms at MU, Miskatonic University. Clean a lot of windows too. I see things; students these days don't hide anything, and most days, I'd bet heavy on they don't have any shame about what they say and where they say it. It's not 15 minutes of fame these days; it's 2 minutes center stage. I hear about things too. They love to tell their buddies and their girlfriends and anyone who will buy into their "I've got the news" what they've discovered on some blog or on Facebook and Twitter. Not that they've checked into the details and facts of the story—why? 140 characters and chopped headlines tell it all. And if you've missed a dispatch, your pal (or his pal from Know It All 101) will fill you in over pizza and a beer later, or they'll PM you the link to the screen capture.

Yeah, I see and hear things: lot of it normal, day-to-day uneventful but a lot that's not right. Crazy, strange, fucked up, you pick the word, just add spooky or eerie.

I was never a busybody; my business is mine, yours belongs to you unless the authorities think otherwise. I read the paper in the morning, caught the nightly news most nights, maybe *60 Minutes* on Sundays. Live and let live; be polite . . . unless you can't; applies to where you place your fist too. But when I got here, Arkham . . . *things* turned my head. They turn everyone's head in this neck of the dark wood; well, maybe not the stupid. Started looking at the masks and the behavior behind them.

Corn fed. She's from Iowa, trailer park side of the road. *Mean* mean streak. Different kind of gold digger. Sold her soul to get power. Body like that, was easy to get what she was after.

He's local. Family has money—High Society New England money. Fuck everyone below his station

Hip (so he thinks and will tell anyone) and dumb; was in a band that almost had a major record deal. Group's guitar player/lead singer/songwriter OD'd 3 minutes into minor fame. New Yorker, not the good kind. Fuck everybody that he thinks ain't cool.

Hungry. Odd little bug, all elbows, thick glasses, ton of IQ. Wants knowledge and will do just about anything for it. Didn't bank on the dark nest being the best place to rake it in but didn't complain much once he got there.

Loves furry-furry animals (and her menagerie of plushies too) and Mom (who it happens, gave her her first spellbook and happens to head a coven) and magnificent rainy days (best when they stack up two or three in a row) where one, feet up (in her favorite rag socks) and dreaming, does nothing at all or stays inside to frolic (while Lazy Jack, her 2 year old St. Bernard, dozes and drools at her feet). Fucked and tossed out for the gold digger. Goth turned witch turned student of the unnatural forces here at MU. Wants to be a nice girl, kind to the poor and sick and other nice people, but fuck you if you screw her. Also happy to put it to any bully that crosses her path.

He wears a Mets baseball cap. Watches everybody like a hawk or an investigator informed by hatred. His face is a landscape of plans, crazy enough to make you feel bad for his prey. But it's all intent, plot, and fantasy, he has no power and no balls.

Masks and what's behind them. You want to breathe, you mind your surroundings.

These days. Here. I do.

Sometimes, I do more than watch and listen.

19. Land of Sand, doing my tour with the US ARMY. Saw action and some nasty ass, foul shit, turn your stomach, saddle you with a triple helping of shame.

Came to Arkham for Peggy. Cousin of Ken Tremain, corporal in my platoon. Made the best damn brownies I ever tasted. Peggy sent him homemade, scratch brownies in a care package, and I sent her a Thank You letter. That how we started. I sent Peggy the gushing thank yous, she sent a You're Welcome back. More brownies, sent to me this time. More letters. We traded pics for pics; she was pretty, kind of pretty I dreamed about. Peggy didn't currently have a boyfriend. I didn't have a sweetheart—sure as hell wanted one to dream about. Six months later, we had a thing.

Love. Desire. Promises.

Her father knew a guy could get me in the railroad. Arkham and Peggy, here I come. Up. 5 a.m. Every morning. Punch in. The yard. The tracks. Sweat. Do the hard work. We got married, hand-in-hand joyous. She got killed 4 months later, T-boned in a car accident on her way home from work. I drank. My railroad job fell through. Cut backs. Hard times biting everyone on the ass. I got my hands on this broom. Kept me in beans.

I did my thing, kept things clean.

Heard things. Whispers of the unnatural, shit a guy like me doesn't believe. Started watching and really listening. Heard worse. And stranger. Shit that couldn't be true. But it was.

I'm invisible. They see the broom or my mop or buffer, don't see me. I'm no one, nuthin'. You stand there with a squeegee and a bottle of glass cleaner, you're no different than the glass in the window frame.

Stephanie Neznansky should be riding around Arkham on a broom or, better yet, shot. If shot kills a witch? That's what she is. Not just a mean-spirited, stone-cold, distant bitch, but yes, she's that too, but a real witch, practices black magic. Hides it pretty well.

Look quick, you won't see it. Double or long take, all you see is the I-want-you smile, the just-a-touch-slutty clothes, the way they fit her luxuriant curves, the long, million-dollar legs. Listen to the hound dogs on campus, majority of the male students and some of the profs alike, and you'll hear, "That ass that could start a revolution" and "I'd kill to be smothered by that cleavage." That's what she displays: hot, sexy, kinda trampy. Plays like she gives it away too.

Undergrad, has access to the Special Collections, uses them. Smart, enough brains for three overly intelligent people, you hear it in her speech, the parts that don't sound rehearsed. Had the background, the grades, and endless list of qualifications and recommendations, to get in the program. Also helped she was banging the assistant dean of the department, the dean that was fired last year under a morals clause when he got busted for DUI (his second in 16 months) and manslaughter (MU board couldn't ignore the death of a child and the mother's 90-day coma and loss of use of her left arm after he struck the car or the fact he ran a red light). Should have noted this is MU, eyes and ears on everything here and for damn good reason, it's not called "witch-haunted Arkham" to amuse the tourists. People's ears perk up about daunting and frightening things; smart folk call it survival instinct.

Stephanie Neznansky went after a member of the Labyrinth Society, one of MU's oldest fraternities, a very private and secretive one the whisperstream claims has its roots and paws in the occult, the malevolent side of the occult. She got nowhere. Elliot Charles Whitlock was still in love with his wife, at least her old New England family/high society/social status and old-world money, and wasn't having any hot young stuff or taking any chances the purse strings would get cut. Last thing a fat cat like him wants is to lose his money and his connections and have to get a fucking job. I guess no yacht and no hand servants is hell for some folks.

Hell, maybe Whitlock is like Prince Charles and only likes his hot and feral-as-a-wildcat behind the bedroom door and legal?

Spurned.

That didn't put fiery redhead's dream to bed or even turn it. Desire for power and control hooks you, you stay hooked. She turned her attentions to his wife.

Whitlock and his wife, Georgie, are alumni and capitol B-I-G donors. You see them around campus and in the local papers all the time: a sizeable to huge check here, moral support there. Another check with lots of zeros, their influence behind a new project or endowment, they were literally everywhere.

Take out the wife and console the hubbie. Hold his hand, let him cry on your shoulder, wind up in his bed married to his secrets and power.

So how do I know this? I'd seen Stephanie and her witchcraft at work. First time, I was out back, replacing a part and cleaning one of the buffers, and she was behind the bushes in the overgrown lot behind the maintenance department. Spit on a picture of Georgie cut from the newspaper and hissed, "You'll be dead . . . and he'll be mine. All he has will be mine." Lit a small fire in a coffee can and was ready to burn the picture. She'd cut her thumb, smeared blood on the newspaper photo, and in a warped, horror-film voice, was muttering some kind of *tongues* over it, sounded truer that than the shit you hear Jimmy Swaggart and his cult of stupidity utter. Most of the words, looped sounds, organized jammed together, were gobbledygook to my ears, but some were bona fide, you'd find them in any dictionary, *I offer, troubles, the Harms Tremendous, nightmares, pain, make her blood boil, lies in her grave, diet for your grey worms.* The longer she hissed, the less improvisational it all sounded. In fact, it began to sound to me that a decision had been made to strip away all costumes and engage with something as pure and as old as the stars themselves.

Girl might be nuts, but her hate was real. And the anger painted on it was not something you'd want to be close to.

After she was done with her rite, she grinned. Air temperature should have dropped twenty degrees—it didn't—but I shivered anyway.

Fell. Slipped on the basement stairs in the semi-dark. Stupid, went into the basement to check on the fuse to my apartment and missed the step/dropped the flashlight/hit my head on the wooden stairway—awareness crashed into a wobbly dumbness distortion, disconnected, saw shapes that didn't belong in this environment, sensation didn't seem to remember reality. Lights out.

Woke facing an old man sitting on a hardback chair, staring at me. Didn't look like the devil—not quiet, didn't smell of sulfur and bargains. Wore an old, brown felt hat and an old tan raincoat, no shoes. His thick mane of brown hair hung down to his belly, and he had a long full beard; different clothes, could have been a Viking or a rock and roll star.

He pulled a hardpack of smokes and a book of paper matches from his pocket and tossed them to me. "Sorry, I seemed to have forgotten to bring anything to wet your whistle." Grinned. "So here we are in this cold dark place, and you are wondering what and how and how badly you may have banged your head. We'll get to all that."

I sat up and looked at the pack of cigarettes I hadn't caught.

"Now about that drink."

I was blinking and coming around, but that had nothing to do with what he did next. A bottle of scotch and a glass were in his hands. He poured me a triple.

"Drink. And listen."

"Stephanie Neznansky caught your eye. She's a seeker, she wants power.

Should she acquire enough, she'll try to open the gates—to summon up that which should not be released. She believes she will gain power when the Harms Tremendous arrive. She needs to be dealt with. Men are not equipped to defeat Those Imprisoned Outside, but men, or a man, could stop the seekers before they cause harms that cannot be undone. She is still human, still a mere student of the Elizabethan magus . . . a bullet will stop her investigations and put her in the cold ground where she belongs. You've heard of these things. From Curtis."

"Yes, of the monsters outside. From Curtis. And others too," I said.

"Curtis knows. He's chosen not to be hapless."

"Why don't you enlist him to assist you in ending her obsession?" I asked.

"Men grow old and their vigors falter, diminish, and Curtis Hayes had a minor heart attack two years ago. He's sixty-six, willing, but not a candidate. He has spoken of you. I've watched you, you could be our new shield."

"Let's back up here. You want me to kill her? Who the hell are you?"

"I am part of a large work." He pulled up the sleeves of his threadbare, tan raincoat. Each forearm was coiled with forked briars of broken tattoos. "These sigils are the creed of Those Who Stand Against the Outsiders, of those imprisoned in the abyss."

"Abyss? You're trying to tell me there's a hell, a pit somewhere, and it's full of living, breathing evil, like real monsters? Do you know how fucked up that sounds? Crazy shit."

"Poorly worded but yes."

"I'm an ex-soldier, grunt with an M16. I was trained for war, not by academia. Unseen metapsychical bullshit from some invisible hell is not my forte. Anyone watches for five minutes, they might notice I traded my weapon for a broom." I can feel my head pounding and my shoulder hurts like hell from the fall, and he wants me to be a man-eating tiger. Not likely.

"You require proof, yes?"

"You got one of these monsters in your pocket? Maybe you can give me a PowerPoint demonstration: this thing is called a gobbledygook, and . . . it eats souls, human souls. It serves the evil that spawned and controls all forms of iniquity and foul and vile, fucked-up shit. Christian witchhunters called it a demon, but it's not. That about it?"

No grin. No smile. "Talk to Curtis Hayes. After, we'll meet again. And remember, 'We often meet our destiny on the road we take to avoid it.'"

No longer solid, pale, and filthy, he was blue-grey, thin, wispy, smoke . . .

vaporish. His left arm began coiling. His fingers swirled, drifted upward. Strands of his hair and beard separated, became wisps, began to fade, to drift apart. I could see through his dissipating torso. There was a hole where his right eye had been.

His right foot was gone.

"The fuck."

Gone. All of him.

No flashing lights.

No abracadabra.

Not fucking there.

Hit my head, true. It hurt. I'd had a few—three?—beers, fell down the goddamn stairs, true. Imagined the unimaginable, fuck, maybe?

Hallucination?

Basement light was on. Not by my hand.

The pack of cigarettes and the book of paper matches were still there. The glass and the bottle of scotch too.

Scotch sat on my kitchen table, the smokes and matches next to it. I lumbered up the stairs; elderly woman with a bad hip and a walker could have climbed them faster. Brought them up with me.

Glenlivet. 15 year old. One liter. Ninety-bucks-a-bottle range, too steep for my after-taxes take home. Club Filters zigaretten. German tax seal. 5.60 Euros. Rauchen verursacht Herzanfälle.

Wasn't hallucinating and did not buy them.

Heartbeat faster. "Shit."

Hand trembling.

Acid test. Poured two fingers. Was real scotch, good scotch.

Lit a smoke. Took a drag.

Smoked it.

Drank the scotch.

"Fuck."

Was not imagining.

Walked over and got my weapon, a Sig Sauer P226 COMBAT 9mm, from the sock drawer of my dresser. Removed the trigger lock. Checked the mag, loaded. Safety off. Wasn't going back down there without being strapped.

Basement.

Sig Sauer, two-handed, combing the room.

Flashlight exploring the Sig's sightline.

Reeks of salty sea air. Never has before.

Damp too. Never was before.

The old, hardback, wooden kitchen chair that the old man, or whatever he was, sat on, the chair that has hung from a hook in the rafter since the day I moved it, is still on the floor where he put it.

Bump on my head is small. Very small. No blood.

Not drunk. Not even tipsy.

I can see the imprint of his bare feet on the dusty floor.

I did not imagine him.

"Jesus fuck."

Back in my kitchen. Poured from the bottle.

He'd said, talk to Curtis Hayes.

Curtis was a tick or so over six foot. Weighed about 210 lb. Could have been Clint Eastwood if Eastwood was affable and a sixty-five-year-old black man. Curtis had most of his hair, wore it short. Lived alone, no dog or cat. Lived in a cute, little brick bungalow on a small flowered lot over on Washington St. east of East St. His wife Laurinda had died from breast cancer twenty years ago; they had no children. Two years ago, he had a minor heart attack. Curtis cleaned the Special Collections rooms at MU, had for decades. He didn't go to Loyola, didn't attend Rutgers; 18, went to Nam—Danang—on the *Uncle Sam Wants You* plan. Over a beer here and there, over the years, between the war anecdotes and the "deep-in-the-shit" stories, we became friendly. In the late 60s he served two tours in The Nam. "Heavy combat; beehive rounds, bayonets, Cobras, RPGs . . . The VC . . . a resolute, lethal enemy. I heard assholes call them slow-eyes gooks—*wrong*. They were smart, patient . . . Sniper fire . . . Dead before his boots touched the goddamned LZ . . . *Blood was spilled* . . . The unwavering heat and mud and bustin' caps . . . Corpses . . . The limits of a man; his life, his soul . . . Came back to the world . . . *different*." Curtis told me a tale or six about Arkham. Mostly scary-ass weird shit, kind that you can't unhear, the kind that gives you frightmares.

I had another drink and wondered what else Curtis had to tell me.

Clock on the wall silently said, 7:34.

Grabbed the keys to my pickup.

I've got questions for Curtis. Clarifications that won't wait.

Pulled up to the curb in front of Curtis's place. Rang the bell. He let me in, look on his face said he knew why I was there; I said I was invisible behind my broom, didn't say I have a poker face.

Curtis said, "Sorry, it's you. *Was* . . . me. Didn't want it to be. I tried to resist. Did he tell you, 'We often meet our destiny on the road we take to avoid it'? Keep telling yourself no, but he'll win you."

I followed him into the kitchen. He handed me a beer. He had coffee from a pot that was still warm.

"Sit."

I did.

Lit a smoke. Waited.

"Shit happens; you've been there, more than once. You recover. Think you have. Then more shit hits you. While you're drawing breath, that's it, a little sunshine, a few laughs, and shit. Don't come in three's like they say. Comes in waves. Some are high, they drown you. I think it's time you ask your questions. You're going to need to be ready," Curtis said.

"The old man? He's real," I asked.

"Yes, he is."

"You worked for him?"

"I performed tasks," Curtis said.

I could see him, grunt in The Nam, adrenaline, the chaos of the fire fight, discharging his weapon, the target going down—fuck *one shot one kill*, mow everything down. He'd left more than one man dead in the paddies. Knew he'd left more than one dead here.

"And this evil he spoke of . . . it's *real*?"

"The day in the morgue they pulled back the sheet and you saw Peggy lying there; nodded, yes, that's her. It's that real," Curtis said.

"Fuck, Curtis. War's over. I want to sit on my back porch and watch the sun set or, better yet, have a Wachusett and Fenway frank at a Sox game. *Mustard*, could never understand ketchup on a dog."

Took a sip of my beer. "I'm not looking to get back in the shit. Did my tour."

"You took the oath—"

"To support and defend *the Constitution of the United States*," I said.

"Against all enemies, foreign and domestic. *All* means *all*, just like *no* only has one meaning. I was born and raised here; Arkham is part of the United States. Peggy was too. She'd want you to protect what she loved," Curtis said.

"I'm out of that."

"You ain't ever out, son. You weren't a draftee, you enlisted. You chose to serve. You don't get to say, game over I'm going home. The enemy is at the gates, and it's time for you to step up again."

"Jesus, did that weird old bastard sign you up to be his recruiter too?" I asked.

"The mission's not over. Doubt it will ever be. Dead or got too old, old soldiers leave the battlefield and the FNGs show up. No need to squawk, you've had your cherry popped before."

"And the once was sure-as-shit plenty for me," I said. Looked around his kitchen. Spartan counter tops; hell, they were virtually empty. Basic microwave and coffee maker were the main features. No tablecloth. Nothing on the refrigerator door. Roll of paper towels, not napkins. Thought it could have used a woman's take—mine too, for that matter. Did have to give him point for clean though. Lit a smoke. "Been in an FOB, and your kitchen doesn't remind me of it, and mine doesn't have the room or the view. When I pulled up to the curb, I didn't see a ring of barbed wire around a fortified entry control point."

I remember nights in my last ECP. They came by night. They brought hell.

Curtis poured his cold coffee in the sink and went into the living room. Came back with a small pile of books. "You'll need to do some research. These will get you started. After you read them, we'll talk again." He put the books into a plastic grocery bag.

He was done talking, and I'd heard enough.

Went home.

Saturday night.

I was off for the weekend.

I sat.

I drank.

I looked at the bag of books.

10:37 p.m.

I took the books out of the bag.

Poured another cup of coffee.

On the table before me: coffee at 3 o'clock. My Sig at 4. Ashtray to the right of it. Pile of Curtis's books at 10. Pack of smokes and book of paper matches at 8.

Lit a smoke and began to read.

"and its eyes were glowing coals . . .

"Upon these leaves are to be found accounts of living creatures beyond the higher spheres, of lost cities and other places forgotten by the memory of mankind . . .

"*Las Reglas de Ruina* was written sometime in the early 1500s by the Spanish friar Philip of Navarre, *ILLEGIBLE SECTION* a recounting of various legends surrounding an obscure and ancient deity, sister and bride to a chthonic god, who awaited release from her prison in the stars to wreak unspeakable, apocalyptic perversions upon mankind.

". . . they are the shadows between the stars.

"Iro'l ixx Tliat stt stt Obïaa! Aitg'n Vmsse, Shub-Niggurath!

Othaag G'gn Cl'rloomn tte Vnstaa—L'vch! L'vch! Pnuir mnpo!

"Thusa—TZA-KA! Okkokoku—TZA-KO! Aulaniis—TZA-KI!"

Tremendous storm coming. Civilization was going to collapse. Ancient, celestial monsters were coming back. Even nukes couldn't kill some of these monsters.

The occult behind the crystal ball. Conversing with belief systems (conspiracy theorists, whackos, and manipulators) beyond belief. Names I could not pronounce. Felt like I was reading the novelization of a horror movie, one where everyone was dead at the end. Some of these things were coming to farm—*us*, we were their food. Some were, or looked like, half-bug/half-lizard with wings or plant/fish hybrids. Others had ten pyramid-shaped eyes and the wings of bizarre birds. Nightmare worms, bizarre fishmen, shit right out of the horror movies kids love these days. They came in different sizes too: no larger than a tortoise, 6 feet tall, 15 feet, 10 times the height of a tall tall man, right up to Godzilla's brother tall. Egyptians knew about them, the Elizabethan mages too. They could infect and influence human dreams and travel interdimensional pathways. They were buried in the earth and lived in stars in unfathomable galaxies. They walked on the wind and swam in the oceans.

And over and over, the books, *The Book of the Dominion of Mysteries* and *The Wisdom and Sacred Magic of Xylac the Mage*, *The Book of Ceremonies*, *The Dust Transcriptions*, *The Scrolls of the Grey Worm*, *A Tomb of Mysteries*, and *Las Reglas de Ruina*, said they were unstoppable.

There were charts and diagrams, lists and images, maps and sigils. Every entry was there to inform and underscore the fact these things were coming back.

Lunatic *fucking* fringe.

Inbred, assbag relatives of Alex Jones.

Crazies in nuthouses shit.

Had to be.

1:44 a.m.

I'd thought I'd lost my innocence on the battlefield—hadn't. The books showed me, if they were to be believed, another larger, deadlier hell waits.

Went back to work on Monday.

Kept my broom movin'.

Avoided Curtis.

Saw Stephanie Neznansky three times that week. I knew she was monster, wanted to be the queen of evil, but under the slutty trappings, she was pretty and young. One thing to kill a man, an enemy ready to end you on the battlefield, but women and children, that was not part of any mission plan I'd signed up for. Not then, and sure as goddamn-shit, not now.

Maybe she'd grow out of it. I did. I was a warrior and now I'm not.

Yeah, she'd mature, meet someone—a Jeff, or Mike, tall, quiet. A good guy. Good job. Came from a nice family. They'd move into a nice house and have babies. Stephanie soccer mom. She'd do volunteer work for the handicapped and donate blood to the Red Cross. She'd teach her kids to swim in the backyard pool and take them on vacations to Disney World. Maybe she'd join a gym to stay in shape? Maybe she'd take up scrapbooking? Hell, she might write the great American novel.

Or maybe she'd become a brilliant surgeon? Maybe move to Boulder, change her name to Starry Wizdom Moonwitch, and open a shop around the corner from the Metaphysical Toad Magickal Shoppe, a shop dedicated to the healing vibrations of crystals and custom spellwork?

It's a terrible thing to cut off the paths a life might take. "People can change."

TV in my living room snapped on. I was bolt upright. Turned around, facing it. Unbelieving. Looked like high-tech surveillance footage. Stephanie, hair worn in loose curls, drop diamond earrings, black, beaded evening bag, black cocktail dress, black suede stilettos, uncomplicated, chic, fitting in. At an Arkham Historical Society function for the Arkham Initiative. Cocktails and friendly chatter. Elliot Charles Whitlock, his wife Georgie, a large check. Stephanie monitoring from the wings. Patience of a sniper, her eyes never moved from Georgie.

When I turned again, the filthy old man sat at my kitchen table. No shirt. No shoes. Still looked homeless and filthy. Smelled worse than he looked, reeked of rotting vegetation and sea water. He was drinking from my coffee mug. "You're certainly no connoisseur of the bean. Is this the cheapest instant the market stocks? I'm partial to Starbucks Columbia Supremo, whole bean, the darker roast. Nice bold flavor, and it's nutty. You should try it." Grinned. "4. 3. 2. 1."

"Fuck."

"Right on cue, thank you. That will prove helpful as we progress. You recognize the process. The tiger, silent, on the prowl, when the opportunity presents itself, he takes his prey down. You have the training," he said.

"I was not trained to kill women. Fuck the other side of that line. After that, what, you can tell that kid will grow up to be Hitler or something, and I'm to terminate a child?"

I lit a smoke. Glanced at my weapon on the table.

"Are you this Nyarlathotep I read about?" I asked.

"No. I was his bag man, one of them. Stopped on a large planet once, I do not recall why. It was soft . . . and pretty. Lush, colorful forests and fertile plains, sparkling oceans. The warm sunshine and the air were crisp and clean. It was peaceful. I liked it. Nyarlathotep and I had a discussion about pleasant after that and we disagreed. I do my own thing now."

"And *your thing* is to keep these god-monsters away?"

"Precisely. Your thing will to be to stop the summoners from executing their plans to release the Endless Hunger," he said.

"Assassin."

"Sentinel," he said.

"*Beyond the limits of what the eye reveals is another reality where all possibilities are open, a reality without end, beyond ravenous time, outside the borders of physicality, a reality where the Endless Hunger waits. Guard the gates well.*" How many times had I read versions of that assertion in the books Curtis gave me?

"If your thing is to keep them away from here, why don't you kill her? Should be easy for you, the way you come and go, no one would know," I said.

"The . . . let's call them the Rules of Engagement, they *prohibit* me from direct participation."

He took a mug out of the cabinet and was holding the glass pot of my coffee maker. He didn't say a word or do anything I could see, but the pot was suddenly full. He poured himself a cup. Took a sip. "This is the real shit. You should try it."

"Come again?"

"Starbucks. I made coffee. I enjoy a simple pleasure here and there. We can at least act like we are in a normal kitchen in a first world country."

"Not that. Your participation?"

He carried the pot over and poured me a cup. "There are laws, rules in this aberrant chess game. Like a pawn or a knight, I can only move a certain way. Should I defy the regulations, the Harms Tremendous could do things they are currently unable to."

"Monster alien gods walk the fucking line. That's . . . fucked-up strange. Jesus, I don't know what the fuck it is."

"You need to decide. Stephanie Neznansky will poison Georgie Whitlock very soon. She needs to be terminated now."

Georgie Whitlock did a lot of good in and around Arkham. Had for decades. Whispered in people's ears, herded money and handed it out. Mostly for kids and the handicapped, they needed an access ramp, or someone who regularly had dinner with two of the state's supreme court justices or could talk a vote in the state legislature into falling the right way; she was their friend, one with juice. And when it came to eliminating poverty and the destructive indignations and burdens of racial injustice, Georgie Whitlock's Great Society ideals had not diminished. Her death would injure and impair others, people who could not help themselves.

I looked at the cup of coffee he'd poured me. Looked at my weapon. Picked it up. Pointed it.

"If it will answer your question, pull the trigger."

I did.

Or he made me. (With his strange left eye full of stars and sigils, apparitions and immortality, slowly churning.)

Bullet stopped before it struck its target, the eye. Hung mid-air. Hung in the fucking air; if it had been lit properly with the right music steering you, something released from a room of foreign unnaturalness, something that sounds like a primordial utterance from impossibility, it could have been a David Copperfield illusion. Hung there. Can't say how long. No spin. No vibration. Just stopped. Inert. Slowly drifted down on to the table.

"It's that easy," he said.

The shadows under the maples outside Whitlock Hall were sharp, deep, deserts of consequence. The Old Man sat casually, back pressed to a trunk in the center of the stand of trees. He didn't smile. Didn't wave. Not one goddamn word. Watched me; watched me as if I were a landscape with a door that was about to open. Pressed. What he radiated made me dizzy.

I knew what he wanted. I knew what Curtis wanted.

There were aches in my head, in my soul. I knew the books Curtis had given me had taken up residence; I could feel their drafts pushing.

I spent every night in the goddamn books—Toslovnit and Charles Peter Langer, in their lengthy commentaries, were lost in Loftus's terrors. The assault infected me. Tortured me with philosophical questions of chance and necessity, challenged me with arguments on the framework of a man's moral and spiritual development.

"Loftus, quite clearly states, in his *The Fecundation of the Soul*, that Kamm's *A Tomb of Mysteries* expansively illuminates all the evidence a sane and honorable mind requires to prove 'the deadly bloom of darker philosophies,' 'the mysterious algebras of other worlds beyond our own', 'the abundance of celestial dangers dwelling between the stars.'

"Why does Loftus always use the ninth chapter of his books to reveal the terrifying details of his investigation? Why never the eleventh chapter? And why does the eleventh chapter of every single one of his books begin, 'Tell me, reader, what does a responsible person do when they start to suspect a truth they do not wish to know?'"

It's all there under the surface of my skin, scraping, nudging, prodding, a trigger waiting for a finger. "What does a responsible person do?"

Curtis handed me a beer. "We work in two-man teams. One member is the primary research analyst, the stalker. The other, the sword. Rebecca Lancaster is the brains on my team. You'll take my slot, you'll be the weapon. Two to the back of the head. Leave the target where it falls, walk away. Kingsport, Innsmouth, Dunwich, here in Arkham, that was my turf; think of them as power hubs, attracts them like bugs to a buglight on a humid July night. There are other teams, other power hubs; New York, Tromsø, one works out of a papetier on Rue de l'Ancienne Comédie. Hong Kong. LA. Moose Creek, Alaska. Dozens."

I didn't ask how many he had terminated.

"You'll meet Rebecca soon. She's tough, ex-Marine, major. Military Police. She has connections to Interpol and agencies in the Mideast and Eastern Europe. She takes some getting used to."

I'd seen her. Late 40s, early 50s? Six two, six three. Buck ninety maybe? Attractive, but she tried to make herself look plain. Rebecca Lancaster moved like a panther, effortlessly, self-assured. Rebecca Lancaster was the head of MU security.

I picked up Curtis at 8:30 on Saturday morning. We drove into the countryside for forty minutes. Pulled into 2,300 acres of wild owned by a former Marine, Chris Kalley. He walked over on an aluminum, below-the-knee prosthesis. His wingmen, pair of trained rotties—big boys—watched.

I was in his house. Kalley looked me over; drill sergeant assessing motivated and mentally fit. Been through showdown inspections any sane mind would call a bitch, this one was a mutha. Felt like I was in a purebred kennel show, waiting for the judge to see if I had balls.

Must have passed. Chris Kalley stuck out a big hand. "Call me Gunny. And don't mind Hammer and Claw, they won't start the apocalypse until I give them their marching orders."

Kalley had USMC and five tour bars tattooed on his forearm.

"Gunny is our weapons master. He acquires everything: gun shows in the South and from street dealers in Boston and New York. He has a private target range here too," Curtis said.

We went into Kalley's barn. I was impressed.

"Every piece is a throwaway. You use it; it comes back here for disposal. Brass and unused cartridges too. Can't trace what you don't leave, and when I'm done, there's nothing to trace. Play it smart, soldier, you'll be a ghost. C'mon, I'll show you the arsenal," Gunny said.

He did.

He also showed me six gray and tan cars, used, no frills late-model, dented, dinged. "You don't take anything belongs to you on a mission. These are disposable too. They come back here."

Vehicles, weapons, ammo, silencers, knives, I didn't ask where funding for the arsenal came from.

"I can get trank guns and poison too. You guys care for a cup of java?"

Can't take one of these alien monsters out, not if one showed up, but their servants, they can be put down.

Did it.

Mouth full of heat. No debate—precision. Walked up behind the target and put two 9mm cartridges in the back of her head. Left Stephanie Neznansky on the ground.

Blown away.

No dramatics.

No Scream.

Blood.

Art is not a mirror. Art is a hammer. A fucked-up thing to think, don't know why it came to me, but it did as I looked at the blood, not an epiphany not surprising, and bullet holes.

Whatever she was going to be, firm, complex, unblessed, chained to debt, forgotten, candy on the arm of a three-piece, that was over.

No elegy.

I came back to America. I'll worry about *this readjustment* later.

Was a warm night. The insects would start on her before the cops arrived.

I walked two blocks, saw my car. Took the keys out of the pocket of my black jeans. Got in.

Shivered.

Jesus.

Fuck.

Drove the car back to Gunny's.

Hammer looked me over.

Claw looked me over.

Gunny looked me over. "Everything go down all right?"

"No. I just shot a woman." I handed him the car keys, my spent brass, and the weapon.

Went home and sat at my kitchen table. Drank.

Jesus.

"Fuck."

Shit here ain't bad enough. Word came today, Curtis Hayes died; massive heart attack while raking his yard last night. Curtis was a good man and a friend.

HR manager called me to her office. Told me I'd be replacing Curtis, told me my new pay grade would put another 3,120 bucks on my bottom line. Sign here and report to Rebecca Lancaster for a new security evaluation. She'd be instructing me about my new duties.

Wanted to say, I knew that. Didn't.

I push my broom.

I watch every Blavatsky, Dick, and Harry. Probe. Judge. Report.

Damek Sarka transferred to MU from Prague last April, five months ago. Sarka's a creepy-ass bastard, tall, dark, unusually slender; he'd be perfect for a role as a sinister weasel in an early Hitchcock film. Twenty-eight years old, Sarka wears ill-fitting black suits and black bow ties that are always tilted to one side or the other. His baggy suits scream another age, one gone by, say, hundred years ago.

Interacts only when there's no way to avoid it. No friends. Never once saw him stare at a hot co-ed, or a man, for that matter. Damn odd for a kid on this campus; hell, look around here some days and you'd think the *M* in MU stands for *Make out.*

Lives alone, rents a 3rd-story studio apartment above the Gilrein Warehouse on River Street. Owns no vehicle. Doesn't hold a job, and seems to never have had one. No family money, he's an orphan; his funds, not large sums but not insignificant for a student, come from European wire transfers. Sarka lives off takeout; never eats or drinks in public. Doesn't buy books or magazines or CDs, never bought beer or liquor. Never been the movies or a club. Doesn't own a laptop, tablet, TV, or a cell phone. Goddamn strange for a student under thirty on this campus.

When he can't get-out-of-the-way, he's overly polite; depending on your mood, makes you want to puke or kick his teeth out. Cold as fuck-all. Tone of his controlled voice is a hiss of poison. I did see *The Silence of the Lambs* movie; Hannibal Lecter sounded friendlier.

His eyes leave fingermarks on you.

Sarka's been missing classes since Day One; lives in the library, digging through Wu Ch'eng Ling's *Dust Transcriptions*. Spends all his time reading, reading the same book, Ling's. And the book is only 168 pages; that's slim for a book in the Special Collection section of the MU library.

Rebecca informed me, Sarka's an adept, spent years in Belgrade and Budapest, where he scrutinized the works of John Dee and others driven "to see beyond the surface and harness the powers hidden there." Yesterday, she said, "Go see, Kalley. Get what you need and take Sarka out."

(Creedence Clearwater Revival "Fortunate Son"; Red Rider "Lunatic Fringe"; Weather Report "Unknown Soldier"; Billy Joel "Goodnight Saigon"; Kronos Quartet "Black Angels Thirteen Images from the Dark Land", "Doom. A Sigh"; John Denver "Readjustment Blues"; Current 93 "Baalstorm! Baalstorm!"; John Zorn "Spillane")

Joseph S. Pulver, Sr. has released four mixed-genre collections, a collection of King in Yellow tales, and two novels and has edited *A Season in Carcosa*, the Shirley Jackson Award-winning *The Grimscribe's Puppets*, and *Cassilda's Song*. His fiction and poetry has appeared in many notable anthologies, including *Autumn Cthulhu*, *The Children of Old Leech*, Ellen Datlow's *The Year's Best Horror*, *The Book of Cthulhu*, *A Mountain Walked*, and *Best Weird Fiction of the Year*.

Like Candles in a Passing Breeze

Marcus Chan

Each morning, I wake to the sight of tangled limbs in the mirror, hanging above our bed. In the brief seconds before sleep and wakefulness, I smile because I see the three of us together, a world in our bed. Every morning before Tanya wakes, I lie still and look and pretend things are as they were.

Tanya stirs. She—for simplicity's sake, I call her *she*, she calls me *he*—she moves an arm and breaks the illusion. Now, in the mirror, we are as a jigsaw puzzle come apart.

My name is Miguel, hers Tanya. No matter who wakes up, that is who we are.

Tanya brushes a hand across my brown thigh, so today I am Tanya and she is Werner. We bid each other good morning, good morning, and she offers me first go at the bathroom. I roll off the bed.

I brush my teeth in the shower. Tanya has lovely teeth; when she smiles, it's like pulling back a curtain to let in the sun. I spit, watching toothpaste froth mix with shampoo and drain away.

Towel wrapped around my curls, I stare at the mirror. For a good minute, I look into Tanya's eyes. Then Tanya knocks on the door, and embarrassed, I blush and turn away.

She steps back to let me pass. Standing, my eyes are level with Werner's shoulders. She stoops when stepping through the bathroom door so as to not crack his head against the frame.

I make breakfast. Back home, I used to go down to the baker's each morning for pastries, but here they are sold stale and hard, so I think it better to bake my own. But cakes take time, so today it will have to be eggs and coffee, toast and tea.

As I stir the eggs, I hear Tanya singing in the shower. Werner has a deep voice. Humming along, I slide the toast onto platters for serving. Werner rarely used to sing.

When she comes out of the bathroom, we carry Miguel between us and sit him under the water. He hasn't been awake for the past three days. Tanya tells me not to worry. "Tomorrow," she says. "Tomorrow, one of us will wake as Miguel for sure." I try to believe her.

We clean Miguel and dress him and lie him down on the bed. I have only set the table for two. Even if we lift the spoon to his lips, he won't eat. When we dribble water, he swallows.

Tanya and I start on our eggs and toast. She eats like a starving man, without slowing down to chew. Without thinking, I reach out and flick away a spot of egg on Werner's cheek. She curves his lips in a slow smile and nibbles on my finger.

Tanya pulls me forward onto Werner's lap, and I snake my arms around his head. His lips are warm with the taste of coffee. My left hand slips down to wander inside his buttoned-up shirt.

Reluctant as I am to do so, I draw my fingers back. If we linger over breakfast, Werner will be late for class. Being late isn't something we can afford. Tanya and I have our three schedules printed out in laminate and taped to the wall: Tanya has Engineering Ethics at noon; Werner a lecture (Introduction to Metaphysics) and Practical Philosophy. Miguel will not be attending class.

It's thanks to Tanya that we still have any classes at all. Fingers flying over the keyboard, she composed medical slips and letters of exemption excusing our absent days. Her careful forgeries keep our names from being struck off the university rolls. Tanya used to joke that where gardeners had a green thumb, she had a thumb drive. Werner and I had pummelled her with pillows until she shrieked.

These days Tanya jokes far less, though she tries. No matter who she wakes as, she tries; it is brave of her to try. Tears blur in my eyes, and I lean forward to kiss Werner and hold her tight.

"We will get through this," I say, and she says, "Of course we will." And then I let her go.

I wash the dishes. My fingers feel rough against the slippery soap. The apartment is quiet without Tanya. I wonder if she feels alone as I do when left with whoever hasn't woken up that day. Some days when I return late from class, I find her talking to "Werner." Though I don't agree, I leave her be. Solace comes to us in different shapes.

Miguel lies on his side in the exact same position we set him down. His chest rises and falls, in the manner of a person deep in sleep.

I flip my laptop open and hunt for a movie to watch. Before it plays, I turn the volume up to chase away the quiet. The wi-fi in our apartment stutters; the movie plays in fits and starts. Buffer, play, buffer. I turn it off in disgust.

With something close to relief, I leave for class. From home to campus is a five-minute walk in the sun. Arkham's summer is mild, and I enjoy the warmth it leaves on my skin.

I reach class five minutes early. With so many absences under Tanya's name, the least I can do is be on time. The professor arrives and takes names for attendance; in passing by, she accepts my exemption slip without comment. I think she might have despaired of us.

When the lecture starts, I do my best to listen. One hand holds up my phone with the recorder on, to share the lesson with Tanya this evening. We do this for all our classes; it's the only way for us to catch up.

At lunch, I eat with Tanya's friends Renee and Peter. I like them and would like to know them, but it is hard when I don't know if the day before Tanya made the same joke as I did just now or what they think is the reason for me not to remember yesterday's gossip.

Even so, they forgive Tanya for my lapses.

"How are the boys?" Peter asks. Across the table, Renee shoots me an impish grin.

"Well,' I answer, taking a bite of my sandwich. Then as a joke, "Exhausting."

Renee hoots, and Peter turns a bright red. Smiling, I reach for the pitcher of juice. My smile slips a little when Renee asks, "Why don't you all come over this Friday?"

I stammer out an excuse. Her face falls, and the guilt grows in my heart. "Oh," she says and, "Are you sure?"

"I'll check with the boys," I say at last, fingers crossed. "No promises," I add too late; by Renee's expression, I know she's already written us down as guests. Peter flags the waiter over for our bill.

I am so glad to go home.

"It terrifies me," Tanya says, "the things we get used to." Miguel sits at the kitchen table, flipping over pages of a notebook. She looks up from the book at me. "Don't you think so, Miguel?"

I know what she means. Today I am Werner, but I feel as much Tanya, as much Miguel, as I do him. We share everything, Tanya and I. No secrets exist between us when each day you could wake as the other. Sometimes when my mind drifts, I find it difficult to tell the two of us apart.

The semester nears its end; finals are upon us. I'm thankful that this semester has been short; only two exams coincide for Werner and Tanya. With luck, we won't have to miss either of them.

Miskatonic University grants its students a week's study leave, so together, Tanya and I pore over all the subjects we take. Werner's classes are the hardest. Without him to consult over missing classes, all we can do is refer to the texts and hope for the best.

In the past, Tanya scored all As, but now we can barely muster Cs. Though she tells me not to worry, I feel badly, as though I've let her down.

Papers and books lie scattered on every spare surface. Perched on one arm of our couch, I peer at my notebook. No matter who we wake up as, our handwriting remains distinct, and Tanya's is very much a scrawl. When I ask her what this word or that reads, she grows waspish as a cat rubbed the wrong way.

I stare at the notes, and all I can think of is other things to do. The sheets on our bed are rumpled and mussed and in need of tucking in; the kitchen floor wants sweeping. Like buzzards, distractions circle in my head. Whenever I pause in reading, they dart in and harass my will to focus on paper and word.

The room stifles. Sweat drips from my brow and trickles down my chin. I clamber to my feet and tug back a window to air out the apartment. A gust of wind leaps into the room. Papers scatter. Tanya stands up and snaps at me. "Get yourself together, Miguel," she scolds. "Get a grip."

I do not want to get a grip on my studies. What I want is to go outside and sit in the sunshine and forget my books. What I do is sigh and nod and pick up the papers from the floor.

Practical Philosophy: *Ursula's second principle shows that for each uncertainty there must be an equally immutable truth.* Modern Materials: *To build a Stadtkrone, one must first assess the grounds for intrinsic faults and affinities.*

My head feels stuffed and full of bees.

Tanya is the better student, so for the past few days, I have been confined to the apartment to practice and memorize. She leaves the house to buy us breakfast, lunch, and dinner, while I ponder worked examples. To cheer me up, she buys me paella and chicharrón, to which I answer with a wan smile. I am sick to the bone of studying.

More days creep by, and I find myself in lament of Arkham. If I'd stayed back home, I wouldn't have met Tanya and Werner, but would that have been so bad? The ease with which I dismiss them startles and shames me. I banish the thought from my mind.

To Tanya I say, "I'm going crazy stuck inside."

I suggest we go out for dinner, and to my surprise, she agrees. Perhaps she isn't as sanguine about having spent so much time cooped up in the apartment as I'd thought.

We shower, we shave.

Our apartment sits on the fifth floor. After the elevator doors close, I press up against Tanya who stiffens. Underneath the vanilla cologne, I sniff something wilder, like mustard spice. My fingers tighten on his biceps. She turns his head and leans into me, hard.

"Later," Tanya says, and the heat in his eyes delights me. I feel myself growing warm. As we step out into the lobby, I am glad of the autumn wind chasing at our heels.

Possi's Parlour is one of the few establishments beloved by faculty and students alike. Even before the sun has set, a line snakes out the front door. As we join the queue, I recognize one of Werner's classmates. I catch his eye and wave.

Tanya places an order for stuffed red and green peppers; I have the curried prawns. Soon the waiter arrives with the real prize and the reason so many of us frequent Possi's—their excellent mulled wine. He tilts the pitcher and pours us each a full mug.

Over dinner, we talk of trivial things. Werner's classmate comes over with a greeting, and I introduce Miguel. Tanya makes him laugh with a tale of her childhood in Kansas, of crows and everlasting ears of corn. I see the classmate charmed and place a casual hand over Miguel's. With an easy grin, he winks and backs off.

When we return to their apartment, neither of us have eyes for books. Tanya shoves me onto the bed and straddles me. I reach up and start unbuttoning his coat.

Tanya is up before dawn, and in waking, she wakes me. I blink at her, eyes heavy with sleep. Dreams of polymers and processes slip from my mind as I gather the blankets about me. Tanya (Tanya today) will sit for Modern Materials in her own stead. I yawn and roll off the bed, tucking the blankets around Werner before I head into the kitchen.

We'd been lucky so far with only one paper missed. Practical Philosophy offered enough class participation merits that we would still score a C– without sitting for the exam.

Tanya darts from one end of the apartment to the other, gathering papers and books. As part of her study ritual, she carries them all the way to campus and sits just outside the exam hall to read. I'd gone with her once to sate my curiosity and watched her study curled up underneath the building lights. As the sun climbed above the horizon, she'd pored over scribbled notes in the margins of past assignments.

For whatever reason, it works. Before, I'd never known Tanya to get anything less than an A–.

Because it's the last paper, today I feel obliged to follow her. Tanya uses me as a sounding board to drill the information into her head.

"How much alabaster is needed to properly insulate against higher energies? What is al-Farida's ratio, and how is it applicable for the design of safe houses?"

Every question I throw at her Tanya answers with a calm, quiet ease.

Eventually, the sun settles into the sky. Peter shows up and joins us on the bench.

"Brought along emotional support, eh?" he says, nudging me. Tanya pretends to give him a shove, and he laughs. The two of them exchange a volley of questions and answers.

When I reply to one of the questions, Peter glances at me with a surprised look. "You should have signed up for this class with us, Miguel," he says.

I flush, having answered without thinking. Renee's appearance gives me the opportunity to make my excuses. I wish them good luck and leave the trio to their studies before the exam hall opens to entrants.

Without exams or classes hanging over my head, I decide to explore the university. What I'd seen in the past ten months wouldn't come close to scratching the surface of everything MU had to offer. For a while, I divert myself peeking into classrooms and laboratories, watching others bent double over microscopes or stacks of yellowed paper.

Even while exploring, I steer clear of the dorms—three squat buildings ringing a courtyard of cobblestone. In the middle of the courtyard stands a strangely proportioned fountain that draws the eye. The last time I'd been there was alongside Werner and Tanya.

The memory comes unwanted and unbidden.

An invitation to a party, freshmen welcome. But also something more: an offer to join a house, as Tanya explained. To become members of a society. At Tanya's urging, Werner and I had agreed to accompany her.

Fragments are all I remember of the party. I cannot recall the names of our hosts or the exact place where it was held. Only the main event held any sort of clarity in my mind—a drinking game they called the Rite of Mnemosyne.

The game started like this: an amphora, called the vessel, was passed around the room. When the vessel reached your hands, you had ten seconds to fill it as you will; in my case, half a bottle of cider. Once brimming, the pot exchanged hands a second time. This time, you drank.

Somewhere along the way, the mixture had started to fizz. Tanya wiped her mouth and passed me the vessel. Inside, liquid hissed. Someone jostled me, and I raised the vessel to my lips. Fire trickled down my throat. Coughing, I tried to hand the vessel to Werner. He declined.

"Just a taste, man," someone said. "Come on."

The room grew quiet, as though someone had turned a dial. For the first time, I noticed a strangeness about the crowd—a striking resemblance between strangers. Here and there, one student wore the same expression, stood in the same stance as another across the room. Tanya's fingers brush my hand.

"No, thank you," Werner said.

A strained silence followed his refusal. Then someone shrugged one shoulder and broke the spell. "Suit yourself," they said. "Whatever."

No one made further overtures at us that night—no mentions of houses or otherwise. We lingered awhile and then left. Nobody stopped us. Werner complained of a headache and took straight to bed.

Later, when Tanya and I thought to look up the university lists, the name of the house was nowhere to be found.

I shake myself out of reverie. It is too pleasant a day to dwell on the past. I put away the memories of that night and the frantic morning after; what matters is the now. To put my mind on other things, I buy a snow cone from one of the food trucks and let the ice melt down my throat.

An hour later, I pick up Tanya from the exam hall. She waves me over to where she stands with Peter and Renee. Before we part ways, we make plans for the evening to celebrate the end of finals. The first thing we do when we reach the apartment is to throw all our books into a corner of the room.

Humming, Tanya goes online to pull up a movie for us to watch. I rummage about the kitchen for popcorn. With the lights dimmed, we sit Werner between us with a blanket over our laps. I drowse halfway through the movie, lulled into cosy sleep.

When I wake, Tanya throws a clean shirt at me. "We're going to be late, slowpoke," she smirks. "Get your ass in the shower." A glance at the clock tells me she's right, and I jump from the couch.

All cleaned up, we go across the river to find Renee and Peter for dinner. After eating, we wander about the town, stumbling into jazz clubs and dusty bookstores. More often than not, at least one of us holds a drink in hand. Mild intoxication leaves a pleasant tingling sensation across my skin. Renee gets thrown out of a pub for smoking indoors, and we three chase after her, laughing all the while.

On a park bench, we stare at the stars. Renee lights up another cigarette. I make a half-hearted swipe for the lighter and miss. Leaning back, I watch the curls of smoke drifting into the sky. Tonight is as peaceful and still as a reflection on clear water. Tanya curls up beside me, her head resting on my arm.

"I'm going to pass out," Peter says. "Walk me home, Renee?" The girl rolls her eyes at us but follows him down the path. I linger on the bench a while longer before moving my arm and waking Tanya. She yawns.

We head back home.

The apartment door is ajar. Turned into a twisted piece of scrap, the broken lock lies discarded on the floor.

Before I can stop her, Tanya ducks inside. She screams. Heart pounding, I follow only to collide into her. She stands rooted, both hands clapped to her mouth.

Slumped on the floor, Werner stares at the ceiling with empty eyes. I can't hear Tanya over the blood roaring in my ears. A wet, gaping line across where his throat used to be—I fight the need to gag.

Gradually, hearing returns. "Oh my god," Tanya is saying, over and over. "Oh my god."

One step forward and I wobble on my feet. With one hand on the wall, I steady myself and blink away stars. All the drinking I did this evening—a great relief washes over me. If I touched Werner, the nightmare would disappear. Just one touch . . .

Tanya's hand arrests mine as I reach out. "Don't," she says in a hollow voice. "The police will be here soon."

I close my eyes.

Arkham's homicide squad is brusque with us. Werner they take away in a bag.

"To the morgue," the officer tells us. Only when she asks do I notice the things missing from our apartment. She has me look around and make a list: the television set, our three laptops. The microwave. The printer.

Later she says, "You can't stay here." I look at her, not understanding. "We have to sweep the place for evidence. You can't stay here," she repeats impatiently.

Tanya phones Renee and Peter. Peter can't be reached, but Renee rushes to the scene. When she wraps us in a hug, I break down in tears. "Hush now," she says to us. "Come on. Let's find you a place to stay."

Renee calls for a cab while the two of us stand numb on the pavement. After shepherding us into the back, she climbs in next to the driver. The cab brings us to a nearby motel. Renee presses cups of hot drinks into our hands before arranging things with the manager.

She's a good friend.

Renee waves away our thanks and leads us to the room she's booked. I see her stifle a yawn and tell her to go home. "Will you be okay?" she asks. "Promise if you need anything you'll call."

Tanya and I make our promises. Renee still looks reluctant to leave us, but

Tanya convinces her to go. "I'll come check on you in the morning," she says.

She closes the door, leaving Tanya and I huddled on the bed. Neither of us wants to be the first to close their eyes. But the day has taken its toll, and sleep takes me with open arms.

★

"Tanya? Are you up?"

Murmuring, I turn in his arms. Miguel's eyes are closed, his chest rising and falling in even sleep. I press both hands to his chest and push gently. "Tanya?" He rolls over to his side without a sound. All the warmth of our bed leaves me. "Tanya!"

She's gone. I'm alone. Hysteria claws at my throat, wild laughter chasing tears. I howl.

Hours after, someone knocks at the door. My cell buzzes on the bedside table. Arms wrapped around my knees, I sit and stare at Miguel's prone form. My eyes are dry and red; I have cried out all my tears.

Only when the door creaks open do I turn my head. Anger fills the hole within me, and I open my mouth to shout: get the hell out of our room, go away and fucking leave us alone! Then Renee's arms wrap around me, and the words die in my mouth.

Renee doesn't say, "It's alright." She doesn't say, "Everything's going to work out." All she does is hold me close.

I let her convince me to change from yesterday's clothes. The police still haven't finished with the apartment, so she brought a set of her own. I tense when she glances at Miguel, but all she does is look.

Peter comes, and the police, and later a doctor. The last has questions that I don't answer, and when she grows red, I crawl under the sheets and close my eyes. She takes Miguel's temperature and prods at his arm.

"There's nothing wrong with him," she declares. "Just the shock—that's all."

My stomach growls. For a moment, I hate myself for my weakness—hunger surpassing grief—but at Peter's urging, I eat. After three bites, I put down the bun that has crumbled into mealy ash inside my mouth. Peter and Renee exchange worried glances they think I don't see.

When the time comes for them to leave, I almost break down and tell them the truth of us. But something in me takes over, and I swallow my tongue before the words spill out. Renee offers me a sad smile before she draws the door closed, leaving me alone with Miguel's unmoving form.

Outside the motel window, cars crawl like beetles down the street. Neon lights from the bar opposite stutter on and off, tracing a woman in red kicking her heels high in the air. The pinprick points of stars appear, and I yank the curtains closed to shut out their prying eyes.

Turning off the lights, I crawl under the sheets beside Miguel. His body comforts me in its familiar presence, warm and solid. I drape his arms around me and match his breath to mine.

I dream of Tanya crying out in the dark.

Then it is no longer a dream, and she thrashes in my arms. Her nails claw furrows into my back. The sharp pain makes me gasp and shove her away. When Tanya lunges, I seize her by the shoulders and keep her at arm's reach.

"Tanya? Stop! Tanya, it's me! It's Miguel! Stop, stop, it's okay. It's over now—"

She bursts into tears. I pull her forward and wrap my arms around her. Head buried in my shoulder, her whole body shakes. I hold her until she grows still, her sobs reduced to silent weeping.

"Tanya," I say quietly, "I'm going to turn on the lights, okay?"

The moment I'm no longer touching her, Tanya shrieks. She hurls herself at me. The animal fear in her voice breaks my heart. I comfort her with one arm around her trembling shoulders as I turn on the lights.

Tanya's face is haggard and drawn. I flinch from the look in her eyes, like the dreadful calm of a wounded creature hearing the hunting hounds. Her chapped lips are gnawed and bleeding.

I grab a bottle of water from the bedside table, glad to have something to do. Water dribbles down her chin when she drinks. She makes no move to wipe it away.

"What happened, Tanya? I need to know." She doesn't respond. "We'll find a way out. Just talk to me. God, just say something—anything! Tanya, please, I need you here with me." My voice cracks as I beg. "I love you, Tanya. I love you."

"I woke up," she says, and to my shame, I turn away from the dread in her eyes. "I didn't know where I was or what was happening. All around me was an empty dark sea—not black but *empty*, Miguel—and little pinpricks of light. I thought they were candles. Candles in the sea! Can you imagine?"

For a moment, I think I see Tanya, whole again, by her wobbling smile. Then it slips away.

"Space, Miguel, I floated in space. I looked down, and there I was too, a speck of light shining in the vastness. All of us, our conscious selves, that was what we were, like stars." She swallows. "We were so beautiful. So beautiful.

"I wasn't wrong when I called it a sea." Her face darkens, light going out of her eyes. "We were in the shallows. And sometimes"—she breaks off, eyes closing—"sometimes things come up to shore. "Werner," she says. Raising a fist to her mouth, Tanya bites down on her knuckles hard enough to draw blood. "Oh my god, Werner."

I grab her hands and hold them in mine. "What happened?" Her eyes fill with fresh tears. "Tanya! Did you see him out in the dark?"

"He's gone," she whispers.

The dull ache of my heart grows. Tanya's eyes are far away, staring at something I cannot see. Then she clutches at me, crying out, "They're coming, Miguel! They're rising from the sea! The waves in their wake—washing over—so many of us gone—never even noticed—oh, God!

"We can't stay here," Tanya says, her voice hoarse and hollow. "But there's nowhere else to go, is there? There's nowhere else on Earth."

"We're candles," she whispers. "Like candles in a passing breeze." She sobs. I rest my chin on her curls and hold her tight, providing what little comfort I can give. And alone inside my head, I dread the coming dark of sleep.

Marcus Chan resides in Kuala Lumpur, ambling haphazardly through his twenties. When not dozing off in class, he's working toward his first bachelor's degree. Marcus drinks tea daily, wants to learn how to cook, and is probably too fond of all things melancholy. At the moment, he's trying (and failing!) to teach himself to write with his left hand. Also, he should probably do something about that hair.

Since he stuck his nose in a book at a tender age, he's never been quite able to pull it back out. So, one day, he decided to have a go at writing stories instead.

This is his first published work of fiction.

A Lost Student's Handbook for Surviving the Abyss

Gwendolyn Kiste

Welcome to college life at Miskatonic University! We're so glad you chose our esteemed school for your studies. This handy guide is specially designed to assist you through some of your initial questions as you adjust to this new and exciting experience!

Your first day on campus will no doubt be strange and disorienting, and you might be tempted to just pack up and go back to where you came from. We, for one, would recommend against that. Because as everybody knows, it doesn't matter how hard you try; you can never go home again.

I'm standing on the quad, my crumpled schedule in one hand and a key for a car I don't remember owning in the other. Laughing students shove past me, the Miskatonic University logo emblazoned across the backs of their hoodies and the seats of their sweatpants.

I glance down at my own clothes. Blue jeans and a plain white tank top. No college swag. I must be new here.

Rows of brick buildings tower over me like ancient demons. Everything here looks the same, and the architectural homogeny is a dizzying sight to behold. I turn in circles, searching for my dorm. Finding where I live—that would be a good start to the day.

Two chattering girls cross the quad near me, and I try to dodge out of their way, but I misjudge and bounce between the both of them instead.

I stumble backward. "Sorry."

The blonde rolls her eyes. "Freshmen," she says as though the word itself is a farce. My cheeks burn, but the other girl isn't so surly. Smiling, she turns back to me.

"Thurston Hall is that way," she says and motions to a bright, copper-roofed building nestled among the sugar maple trees.

That's it, the place I'll be trapped the next four years. I could have been looking for anywhere on campus—a classroom, the library, a quick escape route—but the girl somehow knew precisely where to direct me.

"Thanks," I say, but she's already gone.

Inside, the residence hall stinks of mothballs and last month's meatloaf. I follow faded arrows on the walls, but the hallways turn in on themselves, and I'm lost in under a minute. The building is like a series of nesting dolls: the moment I'm sure I've reached the end of one corridor, it twists again, and I venture yet deeper inside.

In the stairwell, a weeping student rushes the opposite direction, her black mascara dripping down her chin like acid rain. I want to ask her what's wrong, but I think I already know.

On the top floor, I find my room. My bags are already way ahead of me. I didn't bring them here, and I don't remember packing them either. This is my mother's work. I can see her nervous hands stuffing my dresses and slacks and shirts and even a toothbrush inside, zippering up all the compartments. In my mind, her trembling hands clasp around mine as if to say goodbye, but I can't see her face.

My chest constricts, and I wonder, after everything that's happened, if she even has a face anymore.

Your schedule might seem a little arcane at first, but rest assured, these courses will prepare you for a world that isn't always as welcoming as it pretends to be.

My first class, Spontaneous Vanishings, is an overbooked and over-popular elective—"one of the old MU favorites," the professor boasts from his podium—which makes it a struggle just to find a seat. Among the hundreds of students teeming through the auditorium's double doors, it's easy to spot the first-years. Dazed, they shuffle in, their mouths gaping and contracting like beached carp, searching for names and places they can't remember.

I hope I don't look as ridiculous as that. I hope I don't look worse than that.

I find a seat in the back next to a senior boy who tells me he's taken this professor's classes before.

"Don't worry," he says and leans in. "If this is anything like his Interdimensional Voids and How to Evade Them course, the exams will be a breeze."

He smiles at me, and blushing, I smile back. So much for not looking ridiculous.

The two girls from the quad are in the next row, and they turn around in their seats to watch me. I pretend not to notice them or their mock whispers that are plenty loud enough for me to hear.

"She's like us, Annabelle," whispers the one who pointed out my dorm.

"Plenty of people here are like us, May."

"This is different," May says. "She reminds me of someone."

I stare down at the blank page of my fresh notebook. May reminds me of someone too. I wish I could remember who.

After class, the boy who sat next to me walks me across the quad and back to my dorm. He says his name is Owen. It sounds plausible, so I believe him. I tell him my name is Dorey. That sounds plausible too.

"Where are you from?" he asks, smiling.

I hesitate. "Up north," I say at last, and the words feel like the truth when I speak them aloud. Up north by the ocean. That's where I'm from—or where I *was* from. I lived by the sea or on it or *in* it. I can't be sure which it was, but the soles of my feet still ache for the ridges of seashells and the slick of wet sand. And it must have been somewhere close because I drove myself here. My fingers fumble with the key fob, and I wonder where my car is. I press the red panic button and listen for its calls, but it's too far away to hear.

"How about you?" I ask.

He swallows hard. "I'm from up north too," he says but isn't too confident about it. Nobody seems confident about much here. Nobody except those two girls. Annabelle frowns as they pass by, but May just laughs and glances back at me. She smiles, and the air fills with lavender, a familiar scent like childhood and shelter.

My sister. May reminds me of my sister.

I wish I could remember her name.

Just when you think you're getting the hang of the campus layout, something will inevitably come along to ruin your day. But don't worry. This is a normal period of adjustment in student life at Miskatonic University. Keep going, and it will work itself out!

On a Tuesday morning, three weeks after the start of classes, the main entrance of Thurston Hall vanishes. I cross the quad after Spontaneous Vanishings to find the building looks like a face without a mouth.

In place of the door is a neat row of red bricks that matches the rest of the facade. The shift is so seamless that at first I'm sure I'm the one who's wrong. Even the other students passing by act like it's the most normal thing in the world for a residence hall to change its outfit after breakfast.

I pace the front lawn for half an hour, convinced that at any moment the building will realize its mistake and the door will materialize, a little sheepish at its own tardiness. When it makes no effort to self-correct, I creep closer and run my hand across a pale line of mortar. My fingers come away smudged and oily.

"No entrance today?" May stands behind me, a textbook on Roanoke Colony pressed against her chest.

"Apparently not." I wipe the grease from the bricks on the back of my pants.

"Typical," she says and loops an arm through mine. Up close, her lavender scent is crisp and even more familiar. "Don't get too attached to things in this place. They'll never be where you leave them."

She leads me around back, and we slip inside an emergency exit, using her student ID.

"You live here too?" I ask.

She smiles. "Third floor. You should come up and visit sometime. I share a room with Annabelle."

"I'd love to," I say, "but I don't think Annabelle would be very welcoming."

"She's not so bad. I promise." May releases my arm and drifts down the hall. "See you around, Dorey."

Don't go, I want to say, but the words aren't mine. I hear them in my sister's voice. I had a sister, I'm sure of it. But the same as my mother, I can't recall a name or a face. I only remember her voice.

Don't go.

Those were her last words to me, a command I heard but didn't heed.

By the time I look up again, May has already disappeared. The stairwell door swings in her wake.

In the cafeteria, I stand in line for today's afternoon serving of sentient slop. A mound of spaghetti slithers on my plate, and sitting alone at a table in the corner, I'm almost sure I hear it laughing at me.

I scowl and dump the whole plate in the garbage just to spite it. In the Hefty bag, the corpse of noodles wriggles at me as if bidding me good riddance.

Still hungry, I roam the hallways, more lost than before. Though I don't mean to, I end up on the third floor. May lounges in the open doorway of her room.

"Hello again," I say, and my belly groans in refrain.

May raises an eyebrow. "Pasta day, right?" She exhales a marzipan-sweet laugh. "Never eat anything from that cafeteria. Not unless you're hankering for poison."

She motions me inside. A half-empty jar of chunky peanut butter and a loaf of bread wait in her unplugged mini-fridge.

Before she starts lunch, May lights a candle on her desk. "For good luck," she says. "The flame will warn us. If the fire goes cold, we'll know it's here."

I hesitate, all the breath sucked from my lungs. "Is *it* due here soon?"

"I hope not," May says brightly. "Annabelle doesn't like the candle. She claims she'd rather not know it's coming."

I fold my arms over my roiling stomach. "Why do you put up with her?"

"Because," May says as if to herself, "we knew each other. From before."

Before. Back when we had families and homes and memories.

May cuts the mold from the bread and slathers peanut butter on what's left of the thin slices. Her hands are nervous like my mother's, always searching for a purpose. "Annabelle and I are the only ones left from our town."

"And where was that?"

She shrugs. "Somewhere up north."

Her fingers shaking, she tears the crust off the sandwich, and hands me half. We sit cross-legged on the floor and nibble our lunch in silence. This is a ritual, making a lunch like this and sharing it. This is something she remembers. I'm like someone she remembers.

"Who was she?" I ask before I can stop myself.

May watches me for a long moment before shaking her head. "I don't know."

The last of the peanut butter catches in my throat. "A sister maybe?"

"Maybe." She reaches out to entwine her hand with mine.

We offer plenty of great times around campus, but please remember this one rule: absolutely no underage drinking. Alcohol dulls the senses, and you're going to need all the alertness you can muster.

The all-night party in Marblehead Hall brims with a sea of faces I'll never remember. Revelers bounce from one room to another and back again like a handful of dice clasped in a sweaty palm. The most industrious leave on beer runs, and though sometimes they don't come back, nobody ever looks particularly vexed.

I stand in the corner and wish I was someone. I shouldn't be in this place. I hate parties. I'm only here because May told me she'd be coming too. But it's after eleven, and she hasn't arrived.

Owen is the only person I know here, but he's friendly enough. He gets us a couple beers from the nearest keg. I drink three glasses of the stuff, enough to make my tongue go numb.

It's past midnight, and I'm ready to trudge home when May comes in the door, a stumbling Annabelle at her side.

"Sorry I'm late," May says, but it's clear the delay isn't her fault. Annabelle droops over the sofa and drinks half her body weight in tasteless swill.

"Here's to those of us that got away," she slurs, holding up her red cup. "Not that any of us escape it for long."

I don't want to hear this. My skin buzzes, and I bend a little at the waist, convinced I'm about to be sick.

"Am I scaring you, Dorey?" Annabelle exhales a cruel laugh. "Did you think you were safe here? That anybody's ever safe?"

"Leave her alone," May says, but it doesn't help.

Annabelle steps forward, her face scrunched up and red. "When it's ready for you," she says, "you won't be able to stop it. Just like none of us could stop it before."

"Don't listen." May pulls me toward her. "She's just had too much to drink."

"Or not enough." Annabelle guzzles down another glass. When the kegs are empty, the party loses its luster for her, and she staggers for the door. With a sigh, May plods behind. I wave goodbye, but neither of them waves back.

With nearly all the guests departed or unconscious, Owen loiters alone, and I join him as we sip what's left of our flat beer.

"Would you like to see my baby octopus collection?" he asks.

I assume it's a bad pickup line, but at least it's an interesting one, so I shrug and follow downstairs to his second-floor room.

It wasn't a pickup line. A row of tiny, pink blobs rests neatly along a long oak shelf in his dorm room. But they aren't dead things suspended in plasma. The creatures are all alive, lashing at the pint-sized walls of their saltwater prisons, their liquid eyes watching the world blindly.

"I rescued them from the marine biology lab," he says, pride swelling in his voice.

"Why bring them here?" I inch nearer to the shelf. An octopus belly-flops to the bottom of a jar and ogles me like I'm the specimen.

"I want to set them free," he says. "Somewhere far from here where nothing can catch them."

We're suddenly not talking about the things in jars anymore. Owen keeps talking about escape and freedom, and I can't stand the sound of it, so I kiss his lips, his throat, his chest, anything to stop him from saying what I don't want to hear.

Afterward, he's asleep in bed when I slip from the sheets and wander like a ghost to the window. The outline of the campus glows in the moonlight. I move closer to the glass, and my foot crunches on something in the dark. It's a withered map, crumpled in the corner. On the eastern coast is a circle made with a thick-tipped red Sharpie along with the word, *HOME*, written in block letters in the margin.

But nothing's inside the red ring on the map—no big cities or small towns or even gerrymandered county lines. All that remains are the shore and an ocean that extends to eternity.

We pride ourselves on furnishing a wonderful campus for our students, one that's all-inclusive and cozy and not in the least overcome with a profound sense of dread. However, if you're feeling a bit restless mid-semester, then an afternoon field trip to the beach is an absolute must. It will recharge and refresh you and ensure you can face the rest of your classes with renewed eyes.

"Do you have a car?" Owen asks the next morning.

"I think so," I say.

We wander the outskirts of campus, the two of us huddling together to listen as I press the panic button on the key fob. Between us, the cache of baby octopuses sloshes lazily in a faded messenger bag, the jars nestled next to the map from Owen's room.

After an hour of searching, we finally find my parents' old Volvo parked out past the stadium. My father never liked for me to drive the car, but now he's gone, and here I am, so I guess he doesn't get a say in much these days. Which is good because he wouldn't be happy with what he'd see here—sea salt paints the bumper white, and three parking tickets are tucked under the windshield wipers, but this is it. My ride.

I climb into the driver's seat. The wheel is slick with oil. Owen removes the map from his bag. Cradling the hoard of octopus jars in his arms, he directs me up the coastal highway.

By afternoon, we arrive on the beach. I recognize this place. It's where Owen's from, the spot he marked in red on the map. He's taken me home, even though he has no home left to visit.

The shore is coated half an inch thick with the same fluid from the steering wheel and the mortar on Thurston Hall. A residue is all it leaves behind. It devours towns whole, and it can't even be bothered to spit up the bones.

We kneel in the sand and unscrew the lids on the jars. One by one, the octopuses march into the water. Owen beams after them, his bottom lip quivering as though he might cry over their triumphant exodus. He doesn't seem to understand the babies are no safer or happier now. Their bodies malnourished and instincts atrophied from captivity, they probably won't last the day.

But I say nothing. I just sit back with the map unfolded on the sand and examine a line of coastal towns marked with tiny, black dots. All at once, the paper shimmers before me. My chest heaves, and I blink back in the raw sunlight. When my eyes clear, one of the dots is gone.

"That happens sometimes," Owen says, his jaw clenched. "I wish it would wait until we weren't looking. But it doesn't care if we know. It doesn't care about anything."

The tides come in, and I look again at the map. I've forgotten the lost town's name. Apparently, you can't remember what's no longer real.

"Let's never go back," Owen says. "Let's take the highway inland and keep going."

I peer at him. "To where?"

"Does it matter?"

I shake my head, and my sister's last words echo on repeat.

Don't go, she wailed from her bedroom window, and I shouldn't have left without her. But I did. I was afraid, so I did as my mother told me to.

It's too late, she said. *We can't all make it. You run. Quickly now.*

I never asked her how she knew. There wasn't time. The shadows danced across her face, and with my sister still screaming my name, my mother shoved me into the car. I watched as my whole world dissolved in the rearview.

"Are you okay?" Owen studies me, his toes buried in the oily sand.

My breath ragged, I want to ask if that's how it was for him too, if he saw his life evaporate like summer rain on hot asphalt. But it would make no difference whether he said yes or no. All that matters is that everyone we've ever loved is gone.

"I'm fine," I say and take off alone down the shore.

At the end of the beach, the wind whips around me, and I taste the brine of saltwater.

I taste home.

You might observe a few weird occurrences during your time with us, but whatever you do, don't panic. It's very important to conserve your energy for those times when you'll need to run. And we promise: eventually, you will need to run.

After my last midterm, I walk back to Thurston Hall to find that my dorm room no longer exists. Where my door on the top floor should be is another sinuous hallway that never ends.

"Don't follow it," May says and insists I move into her room on the third floor.

"It's not any safer here," Annabelle grumbles.

"Sure it is," May says. "We have to stick together. Once it comes for one of us, it won't be long until it takes the rest of us too."

My bag and all my clothes are gone, so May lets me borrow her sundress with the screen-printed mermaid across the heart.

"Thanks," I say, and she grins at me.

When May is in class, Annabelle pulls out a flask from under her mattress and offers me a sip. On the nearby desk, May's candle burns close to the wick.

"She tries," Annabelle says. "She honestly believes that flame will help us, that sticking together will help us. But you know better, don't you? You know it's hopeless."

"Nothing's hopeless," I say.

That night, while Annabelle's at the bar, I make peanut butter sandwiches for May and me.

"Do you ever think about leaving?" I ask.

She shakes her head. "If it wants us, it'll find us anywhere. And I'd rather be here. Not on the road, not on the run."

I almost ask her if she wishes she hadn't run before, but regret shouldn't be part of this. We're supposed to be the surrogates for our families, each of us an emissary they sent into a future they never got to see. We're supposed to be grateful. But it's hard to be gracious when there's no one left to thank.

"How about you?" May peers at me. "Are you planning to leave?"

"I don't know," I say.

That night, I crawl into Owen's bed and pretend we can forget where we're from.

I pretend we don't want to go home.

In the dark, I close my eyes and remember how my mother used to tell me to go to college and find a nice boy. I think, *I did that, Mother. I did what you told me to do, but it wasn't enough. It will never be enough.*

All night, I dream of waves like lullabies and of my sister, her voice cathedral-bell clear. Our Vanishings professor says once someone's lost, you'll never find them again. And maybe that's true. I'll never find my family.

Nobody ever mentions anything about them finding you.

I awaken drenched in sweat with Owen still lying next to me. We're alone here ever since his roommate went out for lo mein one Thursday night last month and never came back. I hope he at least got his takeout.

"We should leave," Owen says. "Tomorrow. We should get out before it's too late."

I want to say yes. I want to run with him and not look back.

"Not tomorrow," I say, and though we never speak her name between us, he knows why.

"You can't save everyone, Dorey," he whispers.

I turn away. "I don't want to save everyone." I only want to save her, to protect May from whatever's coming, to not run when things get hard.

Don't go, my sister whispers, an echo in my ear that never wanes. Over and over, I hear those words, murmured in her voice even though she has no lips left to speak.

Even on your worst days, be sure to go to class. Regular attendance will ensure you are your best academic self.

There's less than a month left in the semester when the Spontaneous Vanishings classroom vanishes along with its whole building. When we trudge down to the registrar's office, the sour-faced woman says she has no record it ever existed. She also doesn't seem privy to the irony.

Annabelle rolls her eyes. "It didn't stop them from taking our tuition money though, did it?"

The professor and half the students in the class went with the building, so that night, when someone holds an impromptu school's-out-early party, attendance is thin. If you can even call a dozen indolent students and an empty keg a party.

"Give it until next semester," Annabelle says.

I frown. "You mean, they'll come back?"

"No," she says. "They'll be replaced."

More students out and more students in. Stock to the slaughter.

After the party, I don't go home with Owen. I return to May's dorm room instead and curl next to her in bed, the two of us tucked beneath the comforter like kids at a sleepover.

She's already dreaming when the candle on the desk flickers and winks out. My chest tightens, and I can't breathe.

It sees us. Something is here, watching and writhing and siphoning all the warmth out of the room and out of my heart.

"Hello?" In the next bed, Annabelle's voice is slight and strange.

She was right. Being together doesn't make us safer. If it wants us, there's no solace anywhere.

The last of the light washes away and across the room bedsheets flutter, and the door opens.

My lips part, and I try to scream, but no sound comes out.

As the semester wears on, attrition is to be expected. After all, not every student is as dedicated as you are.

I awaken the next morning, surprised I'm still here and still me.

But not all of us are so lucky. Annabelle is gone.

"Maybe she went out," I say. "For coffee or something?"

May quivers and gnaws her bottom lip until it bleeds. "Maybe," she says, not looking at me.

But outside in the hall, a thick polish of grease coats the floor, and we know beyond reason she's not coming back. May and I search the campus for hours anyhow, but nobody's seen her. Soon, nobody will even remember her face.

When there's nowhere left to look, we settle down on a bench in shade, and May takes my hand.

"It won't be long now, Dorey."

I gulp down a heavy breath. "It's not too late," I say.

But she shakes her head and pulls away from me. "It's always been too late."

Like a woman possessed, she stands and walks the long path back home.

"Don't go," I whisper, but she's already vanished through the sugar maple trees. And no matter how fast I run, I'll never catch up with her.

Your first semester with us won't be easy, but whenever you're feeling alone, just remember: friends will come and go, but Miskatonic University is forever.

I'm the only person left on the quad. It feels like I'm the only one left anywhere.

I cross to where Thurston Hall should be, but the building with the copper roof is gone now.

I could search for May and Annabelle one last time—in other dorms and cafeterias and classrooms that haven't vanished—but I already know they won't be there. I wonder if they're anywhere at all. Maybe they're sitting cross-legged on a floor someplace, waiting for me, just as I'm waiting for them, our lives a photonegative of one another's.

But I don't look for them. I go to Marblehead Hall instead.

"We'll leave now." Owen sounds almost relieved about it. May's gone, and now, at last, I'm ready.

With a steady hand, he packs a bag, but I don't move.

"I'll pull up the car," he says and eases the key from my hand as if all I need to tempt me is valet service.

He leaves me in the dorm, but I'm not alone for long. All around me, the room goes cold, and in the hallway, voices murmur.

My gait steady, I follow the sound. Oil blankets the mottled carpet, and the soles of my shoes stick to the floor. I'll never get there like this, so I unknot the laces and go barefoot the rest of the way. The path coils in on itself, the walls and stairs and hallways corkscrewing to infinity, and because it seems a hopeless pursuit, I almost turn back. Then at last, I see it.

The end of the hall.

The end of the world.

A yawning chasm ripples toward me, and I draw nearer. Nothing exists beyond this point—or else everything does. Sometimes, it's impossible to know the difference.

You can never go home, they say.

But that's exactly what I've done. Here they are—my mother and my sister and even my father, waiting for me just beyond. And they're not alone. It's a choir of sweet voices beckoning me. The entire town has come to welcome me back.

Sea foam spills from the walls, the white bubbles bursting over my bare feet. Annabelle's here too. And so is May. Her voice mingles with my sister's, so I can't tell one from the other. Maybe there's no difference between them. Or maybe they're both waiting there. That would be okay too. We have room for a pair of stowaways in the backseat of my parents' car. I'll lead them out, and we'll escape this place.

From somewhere far behind me, Owen calls my name. My heart clutched tight, I want to go to him, but I can't turn away now. I hope he keeps calling out for me, so when I'm finished here, a familiar voice can lead me out of this place. Or maybe it won't matter. Maybe there's no way back.

But I'll worry about that later. For now, the darkness shimmers like polished onyx before me. I step forward and reach into what's beyond. On the other side, something graces me with greasy, twig-thin fingers. Fingers not entirely human.

My throat closes up, and I twist away because I know this isn't right. I should run. I should follow Owen's voice and never look back. But then a soft laugh rings out, and the scents of lavender and saltwater fill my lungs.

Home. I fled from it once before. I won't make that same mistake again.

With my eyes open, I wrap both hands around the slick, flimsy bones and pull.

Whatever's in the darkness tugs back.

Gwendolyn Kiste is a speculative fiction author based in Pennsylvania. Her short stories have appeared in *Nightmare*, *Shimmer*, *Interzone*, *Black Static*, and *Three-Lobed Burning Eye*, among other outlets. Her debut fiction collection, *And Her Smile Will Untether the Universe*, is available now from JournalStone. Her novella *Pretty Marys All in a Row* is available from Broken Eye Books.

A native of Ohio, she currently dwells on an abandoned horse farm outside of Pittsburgh with her husband, two cats, and not nearly enough ghosts. You can find her online at gwendolynkiste.com.

my Miskatonic University

A collection of just a few of the profoundly interesting people you might meet during your visit to

Arkham!

My Miskatonic: A Who's Who of Arkham

Matthew M. Bartlett
(art by Yves Tourigny with introduction by Scott Gable)

ARKHAM.

I mean, you've seen one sleepy New England town, you've seen them all, right? But I expect this one'll surprise you.

Like everything, it starts at the sea. The town straddles the university's namesake Miskatonic River, which quickly empties into the Atlantic just a few miles away in Kingsport. There is a strong sense of connection here to the water, perpetuating a not-insignificant seafaring culture, but over the years, much of that energy has been redirected into supporting local tourism and the university. Every year sees new restaurants and used bookstores and the ever-present curio shops, ghost tours, and pirate ship rides, everything you could expect. But the town hasn't lost that certain special something that makes it stand apart.

There's just a different air here. Though the locals tend to distrust outsiders, they are also extremely accommodating, having long ago developed a mutualistic relationship with the university. With so many new people passing through in temporary permanence, clear personal boundaries make living together easier. There are really two worlds here: the zoom-zoom, ever-questioning, transitory nature of the university that keeps the region in the public eye and the staid, confident, quirky culture of the locals that keeps the "ship" upright. These worlds certainly clash at times, but it's a struggle that neither side would easily relinquish. "Two worlds" is simply how they exist.

And talk about a penchant for stories! The things you hear from folks around these parts . . .

Samantha Avon-Adsley

Often in Arkham, the passing of the poorer citizens has gone unheralded: wakes sparsely (if at all) attended, and the deceased, possessed of little save their names, whisked away to their pauper's plots unheralded and uncelebrated. Samantha Avon-Adsley, possessed of a strong empathy, a way with words, and an unvanquishable entrepreneurial spirit, saw a market and left behind an unremarkable career as a medical receptionist to become a professional moirologist. Using her retirement money and digging into her meager savings, she founded Condolers for Hire LLC and hired some students to do outreach to local funeral homes. Before embarking on her new life, she studied the ancient roots of the practice, sneaking books and periodicals into work and tucking them away under her keyboard for clandestine perusal during lulls. She carried research into her new profession, acquiring information about the person to be mourned as best she could, and when there was no data to be had, she would invent from whole cloth anecdotes imparting to the decedent the virtues of decency, honesty, and even heroism. Thus Thaddeus Wickleworth, a rapscallion and a brute, became a rescuer of kittens. William Greco, an utter unknown who died with a bottle of Olde English under his arm, became a servant of the lord with a talent for dispelling demons with the arching of an eyebrow and a few choice phrases in Old English. And the greyish, unidentifiable, scaly squealing thing found dying under the wheels of a city taxi became an indigent child named Josephine who had been possessed of an angelic singing voice. Thus Samantha brings peace and a sense of comfort to those who would otherwise weep alone.

Jeffry Blackleach

Every town has its discontents. Every day, they swear they will leave—and leave tomorrow, leave behind their friends, their job, slip free of their entanglements and their responsibilities like Houdini from a straightjacket, like a cat from a bag in the hand of some degenerate fledgling serial killer headed to the mighty Miskatonic to do a terrible deed. By train, airplane, or sending a thumb aloft by the side of the Yankee Division Highway and climbing into any big rig heading west. Jeffry Blackleach is such a soul. He hates Arkham, its Freak House churches and prison-like schools and its tiresome descendants from settlers' families with their jarring, ugly accents and their cleaving to the old ways like kids to the Black Goat's cluster of teats. And the girls? Weirdos. All Jeffry wants is some milk-fed cheerleader with a guileless smile and dainty hands, not some would-be witch with creepy tattoos and a habit. He works in the graveyard among the dead, both the long-since and the newly. It is, if anything, peaceful. And what does that say, going to work to escape the annoyances of daily life. So every night at the Red Tavern over countless beers, he bends the ear of all and sundry about how terrible a place Arkham is and how any day now he'll up and leave it behind. And every day, Jeffry Blackleach rises, eats a desultory breakfast, and trudges two blocks up Boundary Street to Hangman's Hill with a bag lunch and a dream that one day the dead will burst from their earthen cells in explosions of worms and black dirt and ash and descend upon the city and destroy it if only to give him a few hours entertainment and an excuse to finally make good on his promise to leave.

Aethylswith Couper

Some children know at a very early age what they want to grow up to be. Aethylswith knew when she was four years old, on the frigid winter day when two figures in white coats came to spirit away her raving, frothing father to the Arkham Sanitarium. Instantly gone were the angry glares and the absurd accusations, the whiskey breath and the recriminations. The people who took Father out of her house? Well, they were angels. And twenty-five years later, she found herself in the role of head psychiatric nurse in that selfsame asylum. Her father had since passed, and she detected no trace of a lingering spirit, happily. She treated her charges with patience and an almost saintly forbearance, instructing them in moral discipline, overseeing deep-brain stimulation for the more "far gone" patients, lowering some poor souls into baths of ice water to slow the blood flowing to their fevered brains. She also tended to the duller tasks, the recordkeeping, the budget, the procurement of equipment and supplies. All this she did dutifully, accurately, and in a timely fashion. The other nurses adored her. The doctors deferred to her. She had no family to speak of, and no one knew where she lived. It seemed she was always there, always awake, counseling lunatic and nurse alike. So it was a terrible shock to everyone when she was discovered perched barefoot and gibbering on the exposed rib cage of a patient who had been admitted for mild neurasthenia, holding a knife in each hand. The patient had been disemboweled and partially dismembered, and Aethylswith was . . . chewing on something. Thus has the head psychiatric nurse become the asylum's most troublesome patient. She fights the nurses, calls them unthinkable names, and accuses them of deeds that make even the guards go crimson.

Mysteria Crocante

Born in the brambles on the brooding bank of the Miskatonic River on an unseasonably warm November morning, Mysteria Crocante, named by the cloaked and masked figure who found her, spent her early childhood years in the hollowed out trunk of a great dead tree. Furnished with discarded chairs and a purloined mattress and supplied with thrift store toys and stuffed animals, the modest space was, to her young mind, a well-appointed abode. A bonfire outside the entrance kept it reasonably warm in winter. A pile of mismatched blankets and quilts warmed her sleep, and a canopy of entwined branches mostly shielded the spot from snow. Her needs nutritional, educational, social, and medical were tended to by the same strangers who kept the fire going, masked men and women with kind voices and tender hands. Sadly, the forces of order and godliness intervened, as they so often do, to the detriment of Ms. Mysteria. Agents of the church in league with operatives of the state, all frowns and frigidity and harsh tones, came for her in the April of her seventh year. They spirited her away to an orphanage in Beverly whose owners and staff were of a savage, cruel bent. Mysteria was renamed Judith. She is credited with the disturbances that ended up with the orphanage being claimed by fire; the entirety of the staff and owners disappeared, orphans spirited away to Arkham, where a certain circle of free-spirited townsfolk, dispensing with the dispiriting entanglements of bureaucracy, found a home for every last child. Mysteria, who immediately reclaimed her given name, was but ten years old. By the age of fifteen, she is a beacon for the lost and the cast away. She introduces them to her early keepers, now unmasked and with names and faces known and highly regarded in town.

Constance DeMurcurio

Each weekday after working eight endless hours at the First Bank of Arkham, Constance DeMurcurio goes home, bathes, and goes to do the work she truly loves: volunteering at the Arkham Home for the Elderly. This is far more fulfilling than teller windows, grey walls, and grimacing managers, more edifying than the filling out of currency transaction reports and the tension of reconciling cash drawers. The bright colors of the senior center are a relief, and even the grumpiest oldster is more fun than the unhappy crowd that stands in line to conduct this or that dull transaction. She accompanies old ladies to the grocery store and plays chess with half-blind old men in bathrobes and pajamas. She reads books to Granfarb Willoughby in his bed, strange and unsettling books she picks up at his request from the Miskatonic University library. As moribund and unsettling as the subject matter is, it seems to awaken something youthful and wicked in the old man; his lips pull back to reveal glistening dentures, his pupils grow small, and he whispers happily to himself before falling into blissful dreams. She accompanies Gladys Wattford on her walks around the grounds and listens to hair-raising stories of her wild days in the Arkham streets, surely tall tales, the product of dementia with devils pouring like smoke through open manholes and the sky warping and cracking to reveal portals to dimensions where worms the size of trains roam and six-armed men wrestle for coins made of gelatin. It is mutually beneficial, and when she falls into dream-filled sleep and wakes exhausted to do it all over again, she thinks of the people and their strange lives and resolves to give her weekends to the wonderful, demanding seniors of Arkham

Rick Dionne

Everyone in Arkham knows Rick Dionne. He's the man who delivers not only packages but also an endless stream of expletive-laced monologues about the state of the world, the destructive greed and crookedness of politicians and billionaires, and the corrosive nature of supervisors who make you work overtime when they know your back went out three months ago and you're still recovering. He zooms in and out of businesses along the main strip, the university mail rooms, and the front porches of Arkham residents, always talking, always laughing, even when carrying a tower of boxes or lugging a heavy hand truck. He's the one who just told an entirely inappropriate joke right in front of your supervisor, spat on the sidewalk in full view of your customers, the one whose wild laugh disrupted your important meeting. Rick fell into the job young, and the pay was just too good, well worth the hassles. Plus, Arkham residents receive such interesting packages: stained food boxes from the Middle East, damp and reeking packages from Innsmouth, extravagantly taped envelopes from Oxrun Station in New Jersey. Sometimes the mystery is too much for him, and crouched in his delivery truck, he wields his utility knife and peers at the contents of the packages. He's seen a strangely shaped skull in packing peanuts; a slimy, vibrating book; a withered human foot; and so much more. Sometimes he keeps his finds, displaying them on shelves in his apartment. It makes him feel like he is part of some bigger secret. One day, he got into his truck to find a large box addressed in a scraggly hand to . . . him. It radiated with evil, ill intent . . . punishment. He'd gone to lift it and found it surprisingly light. He keeps it in his truck to this day—a totem, a reminder, a warning.

Father Jared England

St. Isaac Jogues Church is one of two Catholic churches in Arkham. With its cross-topped tower and its fierce, muscular brass angels affixed to the outer walls, it is a refuge for the stolid Catholics who eke out anxious days in the shadowy city. Two priests remain at the church, four others having moved away. As with old-fashioned barbershops owned by two barbers, one is always generally favored over the other; at St. Isaac Jogues, Father Jared England is more popular than Father David Docker, a morose, defeated man. Father England's sermons are fiery and defiant. Some call them heroic. He derides followers of the fallen angel Lucifer as cowards, their lives just long, miserable hurtles into hell. His uncompromising rhetoric and lectern-slamming fists bring in the donations in piles and even draw people (and their dollars) from the surrounding towns. What does it matter, Jared wonders, if he should take a little of that money for himself. Wasn't even a priest, a man of the Lord, entitled to his secrets? So he meets with traders and nefarious characters at the warehouses in Innsmouth where he gambles and trades relics for unseemly books and forbidden recordings on microcassette. So he's a secret artist who paints strange alien vistas and creatures of impossible aspects and stores them behind the rectory walls. So he lingers in the confessional with the more attractive parishioners. So what? What does it matter as long as he forms a human barrier between his people and the temptations that would lead them to a fiery eternity? He is certain . . . well, fairly certain . . . that when his deeds are tallied on Judgement Day, he has done more good than bad. Especially if you leave out the Cthulhu worship. Which he did. That was a long time ago after all.

Nicolas Flaque

Flaque's was once Arkham's upscale restaurant. Near the university, it was where the Athletics Division would woo potential recruits with confits and risottos, truffles and mousses, artful plates for the discerning gourmet. The more wealthy locals dined there as well naturally. When business slowed two summers in a row, the Flaques had a small addition built with a window out of which would be sold ice cream and milkshakes. They put Nicolas, their only child, in charge. Combined with Doris Flaque's idea of adding to the menu a few more-affordable, run-of-the-mill entrées, this tactic paid off. Lines were long, and Nicolas pulled in a great deal of money for a young man, and each night he fell to bed exhausted, his wrist sore from the scooping. He importuned his parents to let him close the shop at the same time as the restaurant since business falls off sharply after 9 p.m., but they refused. For those last two hours, he imagined shadows moving stealthily through the trees that bordered the river, figures on the bicycle path bridge gesturing oddly in the starlight. He tried to distract himself by reading but was always drawn back to the window. Some nights, odd, hooded figures stepped from behind lampposts and boldly stared in his direction, causing him to duck down in terror. One night, two frightfully pale young boys, twins, rang the bell and requested pennies in cracked voices. When he put them in their palms to appease them in the hopes they would go away, the pennies crumbled to ash. Upon the death of his parents in a tragic case of carbon monoxide poisoning, he has taken over the restaurant and turned it into a burger palace. The ice cream shack is shuttered for good.

Devon Haberlin

Devon's Book Repair and Restoration occupies a closet-sized space between Best Buy and Tutti Frutti Frozen Yogurt on the second floor of the Arkham Square Mall. Devon always knew he'd somehow make books his life's work. He was a reader from a very early age, devouring Encyclopedia Brown, the Hardy Boys, and on to the poets and philosophers and thinkers and scribes of esoteric tomes ancient and modern. He's fixed the spine of a very rare copy of *De Vermis Mysteriis*, assisted a very strange young man in artificially aging a reproduction of the collected Pnakotic Manuscripts, and even restored four smoke-stained pages of the *Necronomicon*. Some of his work required extreme delicacy; his customers frequently issued ultimatums, forceful demands, and even thinly veiled threats. When he botched a restoration of *Unaussprechlichen Kulten* several years ago, his apartment and all its contents disappeared from the tenement building in which he lived. That is, the two tenants who lived on either side of him suddenly lived next door to one another. After some very confusing arguments with said tenants, he moved into the shop with a cot and a mini-fridge and lived a threadbare existence. He'd considered restricting his practice to more common books, but the allure of the esoteric was too delicious to pass up. He sold the shop two Decembers ago and disappeared with several extraordinarily valuable tomes. Those who are looking for him know one thing for certain: he is still in Arkham, for a spell was cast that he may not pass through its borders. His house and the mall are under constant surveillance as are the alleys, cemeteries, pedestrian tunnels, and strange interconnected basements that spread like a virus under the dark Arkham streets.

Rokka Kahn

Claiming to have descended from an unsavory lineage, including the notoriously mad pirate Squid-Eye Billy and Adelard Fullecoppe, a 13th-century priest accused, with some merit, of a dark litany of unspeakable cruelties, Rokka Kahn's family moved him from Innsmouth to Arkham in part due to a distaste for the "low-tide" smell that seemed to permeate the crumbling town, even in frozen winter, and to extract the teenager from the coterie of petty thieves and knifefighters who dubbed themselves the Throw-'Em-Backs. Once in Arkham, he fell in with an even motlier crowd and transitioned from thievery to thuggery, from mischief to murder. He was wily though and managed to elude capture. In recent years, he's left off his dissolute, wayward life to become "muscle" for a dark mage whose cruel and debilitating spells manage to irritate the local arm of a notably violent Massachusetts crime concern. Whatever battles can't be won with black magic, he fights with knives, clubs, and guns. The risks to his life are worth the rewards granted him by the mage, which are considerable. He lives in luxurious comfort in the fortified tower of a church abandoned by its priests and their flock. There are lovers and the stamina and energy to take them on. An armored car. The finest clothing. A watch that costs more than the house in which his doddering parents wander, abandoned by their son. But the nights are torture. A haunted man, sleep is rare and fitful. While in the company of others, he is stoic, implacable, nigh inhuman. But at night, oh at night, he watches the woods from his windows, fearing shadows, or sweats in his too-large bed, stark staring away, contemplating death or incapacitation or of becoming a victim of violence or of the capricious magic of his fickle and unknowable master.

Karen Lake

The life of a parking officer involves as much walking as that of a postman but with the added element of dealing with disgruntled drivers who attempt to cajole or threaten their way out of a citation. Karen Lake kept with her a canister of mace and a shrill whistle, along with a stoic nature. She would wait quietly while the angry person raged and protested, inform them of their right to challenge the citation in court, and be on her way. Large events at the university provided a lot of challenges; many visiting professors and academics had a sense of entitlement combined with a disregard for the rules that surely was the result of either absentmindedness or arrogance. Strolling the campus in the winter cold and early darkness, she often heard strange sounds in the woods, not the random and erratic sounds of animals but what sounded like great processions or drumming. Stalwart, she would continue her work. She sometimes felt like the most disliked soul in the city, and confrontations only exacerbated her sense of loneliness. Finally, one night after being berated, insulted, and nearly physically attacked, she dropped her mace and her whistle and her ticket book and marched into the woods to find the source of that somehow alluring noise. She did not return to work the next day, nor thereafter, and finally the contents of her apartment were boxed up and put into storage. Whispers around the college have it that she has joined a strange cult and become their leader. Other quieter whispers say she has been a sacrifice to Great Cthulhu and that the endowments and grants bestowed upon the university shortly afterward were not by happenstance but a direct result of what has befallen her.

Agnes LaVoisin

Many of Arkham's trees are older than the city itself. Agnes LaVoisin, Arkham's certified arborist, makes their health and vitality her life's work. A keen science major, she also holds expertise in phytopathology and parasite identification and eradication. She cleared the Harberson's horse farm of black locust, rid burning bush from the woods backing the Dotterson household, and fought to save the city's venerable elm trees from chestnut blight. She talks to the trees, people say, earning her the nickname "The Tree Whisperer," only occasionally applied with sarcasm. She cares for trees as though she is one of them and might be seen standing by a tree, arms outstretched, face pointed up into its canopy like a sapling looking hopefully at its parent. It was she who, with the aid of a small crew, took down a great dead ash tree whose brittle arms stretched over the intersection of Crane and West Streets, only to find a cache of human finger bones in the base of the trunk. It was she who, it is said, pulled a fifty-foot-long worm of unknown origin from an ancient, ailing old quaking aspen on the Reinhart property. As with any prominent figure, there are rumors too. She'd chastised a teenager for carving his name into a birch tree; when that teenager was soon after spotted in the waiting room of a dermatologist's office and subsequently withdrew from school, it was whispered that his skin was slowly turning to bark. When her grandson, up for a visit with his parents, disappeared, it was claimed that she sacrificed him to a black larch tree behind the Baptist church. She laughed off those rumors. It is fact, though, that she sleeps in the treetops; for that there are sufficient witnesses to corroborate.

Michael McAffee

In the Jonathan R. Knickerbocker Intermodal Transit Center in Arkham, where he spends a not-insignificant amount of time commuting each day to his graduate studies, Michael McAffee witnesses a fascinating cross section of visitors, travelers, hobos—what he considers to be the real throbbing heart of Arkham, coming, going, hiding behind newspapers, sleeping rough. He's seen figures with faces obscured by the shadows of the brims of their hats, carting huge oblong crates; worried-looking souls, boarding westward trains with only a crammed-full laundry sack, peering out the windows, tapping their fingers nervously on the glass; bookish types, standing to greet hunched women in shawls and veils; the half-dead curled on benches, a bottle-shaped paper bag in their clutches; blood of unknown provenance on restroom floors; curiously pale and hairless spiders the size of hands; scurrying sounds above the rust-stained tiles. Every day is a dark adventure. On one occasion, after an especially late night on campus and in an especially vacant station, down a train tunnel with only a fluttering bulb for light, he saw a thing so tall it had to bend its neck, wrapped in a slew of sewn-together coats, loping along in the middle distance, two limp human beings flopping around in its makeshift pockets. It turned toward him, and he bolted, ran like he'd never run before. He was discovered the next morning, to his relief, sitting at a cafeteria table, a cup of coffee clutched in his hands, a white streak in his hair. Ever diligent and stalwart, he still makes the same daily trek. He hasn't seen that tall figure again, not even on his latest nights . . . though he is certain he hears it whispering.

Cotton Palsgrave

Of all the sagging gambrel roofs that comprise the warped Arkham skyline, surely the Palsgrave home would win the Saggiest Roof Award were there such a prize. Curling shingles, leaf-choked gutters, grime-smeared windows—an unassuming edifice, to utilize a bit of understatement. The interior proves just as disordered with strewn clothing, mold-stiffened outerwear, yolk-caked plates, and coffee-stained mugs. Mouse droppings pepper the bare floors. Cobwebs gild the trim, and the stove and surrounding walls and floors bear great brown splotches. In the summer, ants hold sway. One might be surprised then to learn of its storied inhabitant. Cotton, the last scion of the deteriorating Palsgrave family, has a head as orderly and well tended as his domicile is not. He holds the decades-unchallenged office of unofficial town historian, his brain a veritable card catalog of dates, facts, little known lore. Town trivia is his forte, his mission, his raison d'être. Agoraphobic and photophobic, he has never once crossed the threshold of the Arkham Historical Society (to his great regret). But his library of copies of the *Arkham Advertiser* and its predecessor, the *Gazette*, puts theirs to shame. Would you like to know the details of the typhoid outbreak in 1905? The disturbances in the sanitarium that shook the city in the early twenties? The scandal at the university that resulted in the early ouster of its president in 1935? Well . . . too bad, for Cotton Palsgrave isn't telling. All that knowledge sits unutilized in his head, a shuttered university, a library at the wrong end of a washed-away bridge.

He is also, one hastens to add, always extremely well dressed.

Lucas Parzych

After a hardscrabble early life on the streets of Arkham where he collected coins in a Maxwell House can and took his meals outside the backs of restaurants with milk crates as both chair and table, Lucas Parzych found himself as an adult in a field he never would have predicted for himself: a feng shui consultant. His services are in high demand from many of Arkham's secretive religious figures and leaders of secretive sects. He knows the best placement for materials on altars, the methods for placing wall hangings and sigils on walls so as not to interfere with their magical properties. With his unerring eye for color and light placement and his wealth of esoteric knowledge, he is responsible for the look and the efficacy of storefront churches and home worship-rooms. Though frequent attempts have been made to inveigle him into converting, he is a tough customer and is not shy about strongly declaring his agnosticism and his unwillingness to allow his individuality to be subsumed. Yet he is discreet and nonjudgmental, and word has gotten around. He is trusted with the contents of the most treasured reliquaries, and he handles grimoire and blood-smeared cloth and homunculus and ancient necklace alike. He never steals, does not smoke while working, and does not demand extra pay for working in dangerous conditions nor with unstable people. It is often remarked upon that his own home is a shambles; through his windows one can see ill-placed furnishings and thumbtacked posters on the walls. Such, it is said, is the dissolute life of the faithless. But professionally, his reputation is the stuff of legend; from hierophant to shaman, no one dares construct their own place of worship without consulting him. As a benefit, he is protected from the darker forces that stroll the Arkham night, both human and otherwise.

Konstantin Pichler

Drawn by mysterious tales of a place darker and more alluring than his charming, mountain hemmed hometown of Bad Aussee, Austria, with its teeming tourists and brine bathers, Konstantin emigrated with alacrity to Arkham, Massachusetts. In his mid-thirties, he drifted aimlessly from job to job, lover to lover, so he'd thought, why not drift to another continent? He landed in a shamble of a boarding house with neighbors blessedly silent if a bit elusive and strange, just misshapen silhouettes darting to the stairwells or ducking into doorways at his passage. The main difficulty was the heat, which tenants were not allowed to control. It was a damned furnace in the place. Konstantin spent his nights on a bare mattress, surrounded by box fans like a god surrounded by hissing hierophants. One night, unable to sleep, he forced open the stuck drawer of the night stand adjacent to his bed and found a pile of photocopied pages. Coffee-stained and reeking of tobacco, the pages bore illustrations, maps, and incantations, which led indirectly over a course of months to a foray into the dark (and blessedly temperate) Arkham woods where he stood within a circle of black-hooded figures, waving a censer vomiting pinkish smoke, and pledged his eternal soul to great Cthulhu. The figures doffed their robes and danced nude in the leaf-bestrewn moonlight, slender men and sinuous women, pale as cream. He does not miss the silent mountains of Austria, the salt baths, the strange fossils in the Kammerhofmuseum, the silent and soothing lakes of the Salzkammergut. Konstantin is home.

Elias Prower

A wanderer who often found himself very lost indeed, Elias Prower often woke in this or that New England town, working a job for which he held no qualifications whatsoever, faking it without ever making it. Due mainly to the fact that his superiors were similarly unqualified and faking it as well, his fears of being caught out as a fraud never seemed to materialize. But the fear would be so profound, so debilitating, that he would relieve himself of his responsibilities simply by not showing up one day and never going back. When he arrived by train at Arkham, the place grabbed something inside him . . . and twisted. The town, dark and secret-strewn, was a puzzle to be solved, a new world to be explored. The shadows fell oddly, the townsfolk seemed to him furtive, enigmatic in their dress and their ways. He was intrigued. He has found work as a clerk in the general store, selling lottery tickets, candy bars, tobacco, and weak coffee. Also on offer are a proliferation of odd trinkets and jewelry in curious shapes that could not possibly fit any human appendage. These the proprietor, a stolid, stoic hedgehog of a man called Myer, keeps locked in a glass case at the counter. Prower is the sort to try to initiate conversation, to learn about the customers, but they simply look at him askew, scatter coins across the counter, and lope out into the dark alleys. A lesser man would be put off, feel unwanted, and move on. Prower is not such a man. Prower is a man in love.

Archibald Robey

In legend-shadowed Arkham, searchers after a late-night bite sometimes find themselves wandering down the starlit path between Peabody Avenue and Powder Mill Street where the glow of red and blue neon shining on the uneven surface of the flagstones announces that Archibald's, whose hours are catch-as-catch-can, is open. The sharp-eared know in advance because as twilight falls they can hear Archibald Robey's knife sliding down the sharpening steel like some otherworldly bird with a strange, rasping call. Archibald, a master chef and lone wolf, having returned to Arkham in middle age after a triumphant stint at a famed Bavarian bistro, works with a skeleton crew of troubled youths who tend to customers, brew coffee, bus tables, and wash dishes. He is considered by those in the know to sling the best hash in the commonwealth and always cooks eggs, steaks, and hamburgers to order with an almost eerie accuracy. *Witchcraft* and *alchemy* are words often whispered when the topic of his pies arises. His clientele consists largely of academics and students from the university, drunks, opium addicts, and third-shift, rough-handed men who glower under curved, worn ball caps. There is no music, little conviviality nor conversation to be had, only the clinks of silverware on ceramic, the smacking of lips, and the grunts and mutters of the food-sated. Archibald labors through the night at the griddle, visible through the pass-through in a dramatic cloud of steam and smoke, burners shining blue behind him like mystical glowing rings, brow furrowed under a black kerchief, mustache moving like a caterpillar as he murmurs to himself incantations of old, gesturing and turning this way and that like some kind of mad conductor leading a hissing orchestra of a decidedly Satanic bent.

Susan Tripp

The Walker is the sobriquet applied to Susan Tripp. Her unceasing perambulations through Arkham rouse whispers in all corners. Is she looking for something? For someone? Or is she perhaps an amateur cartographer, mapping out in her mind some mathematical formulae involving the angles of the streets to one another or to the leaning walls of the small-windowed houses? The questions do not stop her; wicked, rock-throwing children do not deter her; construction cones cannot redirect her route. She was born in Arkham and had led a reasonably normal life, untouched, it seems, by the shadows of the city and the seldom-seen things that scurry there. Until one day, she donned brand-new walking shoes and a sweat suit and took to her feet. You might at some point spot her in a high window of the barred and boarded mill; balancing like a tight-rope walker on the low wall bordering the reservoir; standing, curiously dry, on the shore of the small, uninhabited island on the river, looking skyward. Her face might pass your window in the shaded alley between your house and that of your neighbor, and then you might hear something like footsteps in your blocked-off attic. More than once, officers have caught her peering into car windows, lurking in the kitchens of closed restaurants, traversing bridges, trespassing behind closed university gates. She is sometimes spotted by more than one person in separate locations across town at the same time, leading to rumors of cloning, of conjured doppelgangers, of things more sinister. Broken windows are blamed on her as are missing items and people. No charges stick. She has not been seen to sleep. Her house is but a byway on her wandering; she stops in there as frequently as she does anywhere within Arkham.

Catura del Vetro

Catura del Vetro was the elusive and mysterious matriarch of the Hangman's Brook Seven—an unstable and dangerous coven whose meetings, held every fourth month in the attic of a Second Empire house on the south side of Washington Street, often began with great conviviality and efficacy before dissolving into bickering, typically over minutiae, and then into strife, and finally violence. Catura led the coven, whose membership was, to say the very least, fluid, and also provided cocktails of her own making. She was a keen and inventive mixologist; one might, at one of the meetings, find oneself drinking a concoction of absinthe, soda water, and bat blood; gin, virgin tears, and tonic; perhaps even just the standard whiskey sour. Each evening's tipple was without variation frightfully strong, and often even they of the stoutest and hardiest constitution found themself greatly compromised after just two modest glasses. One notable evening, she summoned a spirit who ravished the members of the coven in a graven and hideous orgy, absorbing their drunkenness in the process, and left the house a terrible shambles. The cleanup put the coven out of commission for two months. After, Catura disappeared. The members of the coven, past and present, searched the nearby woods and found her laughing merrily in a treetop: mad, one of the searchers said, as the maddest-conceivable hatter. She was committed to Arkham Asylum. Bereft of her creative outlets, she went madder and madder still. Confined to solitary in some forgotten, barred cubicle in the deepest depths of the cellar, she cackles away her days. Guards who bring her bread and water swear that the aroma of strong liquor permeates her cell, and they often hear the whispering of more than one voice when approaching but always find her alone and unexpectedly cheerful.

BROKEN EYE BOOKS

NOVELLAS

Izanami's Choice, by Adam Heine

Never Now Always, by Desirina Boskovich

Pretty Marys All in a Row, by Gwendolyn Kiste

NOVELS

The Hole Behind Midnight, by Clinton J. Boomer

Crooked, by Richard Pett

Scourge of the Realm, by Erik Scott de Bie

Queen of No Tomorrows, by Matt Maxwell

COLLECTIONS

Royden Poole's Field Guide to the 25th Hour, by Clinton J. Boomer

ANTHOLOGIES

(edited by Scott Gable & C. Dombrowski)

By Faerie Light: Tales of the Fair Folk

Ghost in the Cogs: Steam-Powered Ghost Stories

Tomorrow's Cthulhu: Stories at the Dawn of Posthumanity

Ride the Star Wind: Cthulhu, Space Opera, and the Cosmic Weird

Welcome to Miskatonic University: Fantastically Weird Tales of Campus Life

Stay weird.

Read books.

Repeat.

brokeneyebooks.com

twitter.com/brokeneyebooks

facebook.com/brokeneyebooks

CPSIA information can be obtained
at www.ICGtesting.com
Printed in the USA
FSHW020117240219
55895FS

9 781940 372235